3-27-80

JOHN
1220 SPANGLER N.E.
CANTON, OHIO 44714

Glitter & Ash

Dennis Smith

Glitter & Ash

E. P. Dutton • New York

Library of Congress Cataloging in Publication Data
Smith, Dennis, 1940-
Glitter and ash.
I. Title.
PZ4.S6448Gl   1980   [PS3569.M52]   813'.5'4   79-20279
ISBN: 0-525-11420-3
Published simultaneously in Canada by
Clarke, Irwin & Company Limited, Toronto and Vancouver

Designed by Nancy Etheredge

10   9   8   7   6   5   4   3   2   1

First Edition

Contents

WEEK ONE

The tall man in the dramatic black cape hid under the trees at the edge of Central Park, only his breath visible in the wintry night air. He watched the impeccably dressed men and women step from their limousines at the bright marquee across the street; he was intent on seeing the faces before they disappeared into the city's newest discotheque, in the leased basement of the Astor Hotel.

Downstairs, the Marchesa di Totti Gambelli was receiving her guests as they crossed from the tiled foyer into the ballroom. The opening of her club had been touted by the society columnists for weeks, and all the guests suspected that the private party this evening would be the premiere event of the season. The Marchesa was beaming a proprietary smile. She could feel the excitement in the air: the Sophia—her Sophia—was coming alive.

Nearly two hundred people of her selection were milling in the main room, clustering around the ornately carved pillars that defined the dance area, congregating in corners, table-hopping to greet friends already seated at the round tables set with china and crystal. One woman, dressed in yards of ecru chiffon, was standing on a chair, waving furiously at her escort as he emerged from the checkroom, and managed to spill champagne on the head of the elderly man at the next table. Fortunately, he did not notice and continued devouring the rich hors d'oeuvres piled in profusion on his plate.

Most of the guests peered over shoulders into the semidarkness to see who else had been invited. Phrases like "I think I see the governor" and "Isn't that a Rockefeller?" could be heard around the room. One fashionable young man in an unconstructed black tux and white aviator scarf, his face a map of Fairfield County, attempted to impress a Brooke Shields look-alike fresh from Indiana by pointing out all the famous people he knew, starting with board chairmen and corporation presidents, investment bankers and commercial realtors, publishers and politicians. She started staring only when he began to point out the stage and screen directors, producers, and actors, designers and models, artists and writers.

The bar, on the opposite side of the brilliantly colored mosaic dance floor, was packed six deep with people eagerly reaching for bottles of champagne. The quadraphonic system was playing nondescript European disco sounds at background-music level to discourage dancing before dinner. It was barely audible over the chatter, but one couple, apparently moving to music of their own, glided around, oblivious to the crowd around them, his hand inside his partner's blouse, hers down the back of his trousers.

The Marchesa's guests felt aggressively free to do as they liked, since there were no cameras present. She had

4 0

asked the press photographers to attend the special photo session and reception a few days after the opening so that her guests wouldn't be disturbed. As usual, her natural graciousness and charm had done the trick, and not even the uninvited gossip columnists could really fault the proprietor of the Sophia for wanting the privacy of her guests to be respected. An "official" photographer, hired for the opening, knelt at the Marchesa's feet, getting flattering shots of the elite as they kissed their hostess.

Giovanna, Marchesa di Totti Gambelli was the center of all attention. Though not a great beauty, "Totti," at fifty, had the aristocratic bearing and expensive pampered look which frequently earned her the label of "handsome." She was wearing a low-cut Givenchy gown in deep red velvet, with a large emerald-cut ruby nestled in her ample cleavage. The effect was opulent, the Italian Renaissance as seen by Cecil B. DeMille. The entrance door at the foot of the stairs was left open for the arriving guests, and the Marchesa shivered slightly with each downdraft of freezing air. Yet her smile was constant: nothing could cool her happiness at this occasion.

An aristocratic-looking couple approached the Marchesa. "My dears!" she gushed. "Ciao, Babe, ciao, Tony! You flew in from Dublin for me! So, you like it, yes?" She gestured expansively, enveloping the red-brocade walls, "Byzantine" mosaics, plush carpeting, and the lush furnishings in one swoop of her arm.

Babe Hennessey hugged her and said, "It's so vibrant, so vital! It's 'you.'"

"Rather inelegantly expressed, my dear," her husband jokingly scolded, "but it is beautiful. You've done it again, Totti."

"Grazie to you both. You are such darlings. Grazie, grazie."

The Hennesseys then posed their centuries of

Anglo-Irish breeding for the camera, while the newly married governor and his oft-married bride moved up to the Marchesa.

"Governor, caro, Anne, darling, I am so pleased to see you both," the hostess said to the couple. She and the First Lady did not smile at each other. They were loyal to their friends, two of whom were feuding.

"And I am so pleased that your first American club is here in New York, Totti," the veteran politician responded.

"Thank you, Governor," the Marchesa said, "grazie. I am glad that you could come. The mayor, it is too bad, could not come. He has a speech to make in Harlem."

The governor smiled. "I've made a bridegroom's promise to forget politics for this evening. It's good for the city that the mayor is unmarried. In any case, I don't think this is his milieu!" he said, and winked broadly.

The Marchesa laughed and winked back. Another couple came right on the heels of the governor. They exchanged polite greetings with Totti, and the man asked about someone. "No, Jenks," she told him, "Rodney has not yet arrived."

The Marchesa beamed as Tony Hennessey moved beside her with a glass of champagne. "I'm sure all of New York has turned up," he said. "You have the governor, and I think I see Philip Steuben—isn't he the president of one of the networks now?—there in the corner."

"Sì," the Marchesa said, happily accepting the drink, "and if you can look all the way back to the right of the kitchen door, you will see the marvelous Mrs. Staravakos."

"Goodness, Totti," Babe said. "That is a coup. She's the stamp of supreme approval in New York, isn't she?"

The Marchesa spontaneously gave Babe Hennessey a small hug. "Sì, veramente. I am so pleased. And if you look you will see many others. There is Gaetano Compazzi with his latest skinny girlfriend. He comes always to my openings, and always he is naughty and dances before the dinner." She laughed. "It's his drugs," she whispered.

Just then, New York's deputy mayor for economic development, Rodney Lettington, swooped down upon the Marchesa and began kissing her. "Totti, Totti," he said when he released her, "this is marvelous. What a contribution to our great city."

"Oh, Rodney, dear," she exclaimed, "this opening should be dedicated to you." Holding Lettington by the arm and nodding slightly to his silent wife, the Marchesa turned to the Hennesseys. "I could not have opened tonight without this young man. These inspectors that come around, they did not want to give me the certifying of occupying, or however you say that."

"Certificate of occupancy, Totti," Lettington said with an indulgent chuckle. "Grazie," she said, kissing his cheek. "It was such a big problem, because they wanted me to knock down a wall to make two exits when there is already the exit in the kitchen, and the one here to the street. Two, no? But they would not give the approval until Rodney"—here she stopped to kiss him again—"got for me the various."

"Variance, Totti," he added, laughing.

"It does not matter, the name. We are here, and only because of your importance."

"Not at all, Totti," Lettington said. "It is simply that sometimes the bureaucrats need prodding for special things, special people."

"Grazie, darling, grazie. Is that your wife? She is lovely. Jenks Monroe was looking for you. Take her now to find Jenks and have fun. Go!"

Her face lit up at the sight of the young couple, both girl and boy very pretty, blond, and stoned. "Jeremy," she cried, "you are here too, how wonderful! I adored your *last album. You must do some of it for me later, my pet. There is a so lovely old piano from Italy for you to play— do say yes,* caro!"

"Of course, Totti, whatever turns you on. And the three of us should have a dance together, carissima," *he said, grinning from ear to ear. He kissed the Marchesa on both cheeks.*

"Grazie. Now you and the lovely lady go and enjoy, enjoy," *she said.*

"You know such entertaining people, Totti," Tony Hennessey *noted as the couple walked into the discotheque.*

"Jeremy is divine. To be androgyne is so chic, n'est-ce pas? He is my beautiful little friend." *She paused to sip her champagne.* "They are all my friends, my family, my raison d'être. *The creators of business and culture, the makers of the news, they will all come to my Sophia because they love me and I love them. Look at them all laughing and drinking and enjoying each other, the darlings. That is why the Sophia is here and why I am here." She sighed and waved to two more entering couples before she turned once again to the Hennesseys.* "Believe me, building this has been so great effort. Below the street makes such grief. The damp, you know, and no ventilation. The frescoes on the ceiling would not dry,* madonna mia, *and so we could not complete them. At the last minute I had them cover the ceiling with silk, but I am not certain. Do you like the color?"

Babe Hennessey took another look around and said, "I think the gold is absolutely perfect, Totti. I'd have thought it had been designed that way." *And* Tony Hennessey *added,* "The ceiling is glorious, Totti, like clouds in sunset."

The Marchesa was especially pleased to receive such compliments from these people, who carried with them the refinement of centuries of wealth, and she respected their opinions.

"Do let us have a drink together after you have finished greeting your guests," Babe Hennessey said, taking her husband's arm to enter the party.

"Certo," the Marchesa said, "I look forward to it, my darling." Those were the last words the Marchesa di Totti Gambelli ever spoke.

It seemed to come in slow motion, unnaturally, like a bright, graceful shooting star crossing the sky, until it crashed against the terra-cotta tiles of the foyer floor. There was the sound of a million wind chimes, then a heavy thunderous roar as flames exploded before her. The Marchesa's hand jerked to her cheek as a fragment of glass shot into her, just a split second before the erupting wall of energy lifted her from her feet and carried her into the inner room of the Sophia. She did not scream. There was no time to scream. The tidal wave of flame billowed over her, over the Hennesseys, up into the clouds of silk on the ceiling. Some of the guests were immediately aware of what was happening, but many of those toward the rear did not at first see it or hear it over the music and talk and laughter. Just as the silk started disintegrating, a waiter held the swinging kitchen door open for two other waiters carrying trays of hors d'oeuvres. The open door created a shift in the movement of the air within the room, setting up a convection current that sucked the night air from the street above, through the discotheque, the kitchen, and out the open service door to the alley beyond. The fire then began to ride the current, in undulating blankets of destruction.

Within seconds, as if a giant wind machine had pushed the tidal wave of fire into the room, it was too late for most of the stunned partygoers to escape the sudden heat, the strange, choking smell of smoke, the crackling sound of burning wood, the odor of burnt flesh. The mood was instantly transformed as people began running, screaming, and pushing, racing the billowing flames to the clear air that lay past the kitchen doors.

There was no other way out, the entrance was now an impassable wall of fire. The kitchen and the small lighted exit sign above the swinging doors had become their only hope.

Rodney Lettington was one of the first to reach the kitchen. He thought of himself as a survivor. It was an instinct. In his desperate haste he knocked down the woman in front of him, who was assisting an elderly gentleman to the exit. The woman fell and the old man began to topple with her, but she quickly got to her feet and steadied her escort. It was pandemonium. The terror of the fire became contagious as screaming men and women rushed to jam through the swinging doors. Both doors were open, it was the only way to go. There were no windows, no stairs, no hallway. As they struggled toward the rear, their sobbing and screaming grew in intensity. One man stopped suddenly, not five feet from the kitchen door, and turned to look for his wife. The crowd behind him slowed and then surged, sending him to his knees. Others tripped over him, being forced forward by those behind. Then one of the swinging doors was forced shut just as a thin, beautiful woman reached it, and the crowd quickly pressed her against the closed door. A man grabbed at her neck for support to pull himself toward the other, open door. She collapsed to the floor, and he stepped on her legs as he lunged through the door. Another man lifted a woman and threw her across the heads of the others before him.

On the dance floor, the one couple continued moving, oblivious to the panic and chaos around them. "The people are running, Tano," the woman said vaguely. Her partner didn't open his eyes, he just pressed her frail body closer to his. "You intimidate them, my pet," he said. "With your beauty."

"No, Tano," she suddenly screamed, "there's a fire, a fire."

But it was too late. The flames were now directly

10 o

above, and a large sheet of burning, shredding silk fell from the ceiling and set them ablaze.

The discotheque was now sun-bright, and the snapping of the flames grew louder and angrier. The fire was on the walls, devouring the brocade. It was racing across the ceiling silk, pushing the gray, silky smoke forward. People began to stagger, choking and coughing violently, some vomiting. The crowd at the door now became a wriggling pyramid of fear and pain, blocking the single kitchen door completely, wedged into it like rags into a hole. Others on the perimeter tried to climb over the human mound, but it was hopeless. Men and women who only moments before were kissing and embracing were now tearing at each other's clothing and skin in desperation, hoping to escape the sudden nightmare. There was no order anywhere. Gallantry and manners vanished in the face of death. Men and women stood on the backs of fallen friends. The odor of flesh, the screaming desperation, and the fire, the immense violence of the fire, were too powerful for them. It was beyond human comprehension, beyond human endurance.

The entire room was a fiery apocalypse, a maelstrom of tables, chairs, lights, glasses, bodies. There was a final chorus of shrieks, a coda of agony from the dying. And then only the sound of the fire's fury as it passed over the bodies of its forty-three victims.

The figure in the black cape lingered a moment as he heard the muffled screams drift through the night air. The Astor doorman yelled "Fire!" and the carriage horses at the park's edge shifted nervously. The man smiled, and then he quickly strode away.

Monday

It was the kind of day that made Terry Ahearn wish he were rich. Dark and overcast, the skies were threatening a barrage of ice pellets. It was too cold for snow. If he were rich, he would get on a plane and go to Bermuda.

Terry and Jose were working four-to-twelves this week. This was the second Monday in February. It seemed, the last week or so, that winter had just begun. It would be ages till spring.

He wrapped a red Pierre Cardin tie around his neck and stood before the bureau mirror to tie it. It would go well with the brown cashmere jacket he had bought at Barney's. He took the snub-nosed .38 from the top drawer and fit it into the holster on his belt. He felt for the safety as he snapped the leather strap over the handle.

In the hall of the converted brownstone on West 13th Street, he turned the dead bolt gingerly. He stopped then and listened to music coming from the apartment next door. Melissa always had the stereo or TV on when she was in. Now, there was only the sound of his keys rattling as he slipped them into his pocket. Good, he thought, she must be out. She wouldn't open the door and say, "Why don't you drop in after work tonight?" It wasn't that he did not want to see her, he was afraid it was becoming a habit; he was beginning to feel a little used. Anyway, their lives were worlds apart. Education, money, you name it. She had more of everything, and he couldn't figure her opening up her future to him. Her bed, maybe, but not her future, and he resented that.

He began to walk down the squeaky wooden

steps, but then he stopped and looked back at her apartment door. Should he leave a note? Christ, he thought, chastising himself, there was more to her than he was willing to let go. He could always call later. Maybe I will, he said to himself as he walked into the afternoon shadows.

Eight fire marshals were sitting at assorted shabby desks when Terry signed the time journal. He stepped through the airy, fluorescent-lit room and sat on the edge of the desk across from his partner, Jose. "*Qué pasa*, pal?" he asked.

Jose looked up from a report he was writing. "Not much. Surveillances, a couple of interviews for fire reports, a meeting with Burke in ten minutes." Jose gestured toward the partitioned corner office of the chief fire marshal, Jack Burke.

"I hope it's a quiet night," Terry said.

"It's shitty enough already."

"How come?"

"I hear the mayor's office is trying to sandbag us."

"I heard that months ago."

"Right," Jose said. "I think that's what the meeting's about."

"Yeah. We'll see. Listen, I have to go out to Brooklyn on the meal break. I haven't seen the folks since Christmas. It's a guilt run, you know?"

Jose smiled. "Gotcha," he said. "No problem."

Terry picked up a folder from Jose's desk and began to look through it, filling the time until the meeting. It was a typical case, a factory building in the South Bronx, a failing business, a fire to collect insurance.

Unable to focus his thoughts, Terry dropped the folder on his partner's desk and began to stare at an empty wall. He felt uneasy, as if something destructive were about to happen. It was that kind of day, he thought. Gloomy. A gloomy day when nothing seems quite right.

Maybe it was Melissa. Maybe he should just end it all with her and go on to someone else. In New York, there was always someone else. But there was something about Melissa, her warmth, her directness, her delicate good looks. Something. He didn't want to give that up. Not yet. And then there were his folks. He wished he got along with them better than he did, but it was hard. He and the old man were in different worlds also, they spoke different languages. Jesus, he thought, I wish Burke would get in here and get this meeting over with.

Tall and red-faced, Chief Fire Marshal Jack Burke walked out of his corner cubicle and gave an envelope to a young black clerk, who left the room with it. Burke followed him to the door and locked it. Terry could see that whatever the chief had to say, he didn't want any outsiders in on it.

Burke sat on top of a front desk, and the fire marshals moved toward him. "I just have one thing to say to you, and there's no point in having questions and answers, 'cause I don't have the answers. The commissioner called me into his office this afternoon and told me that the mayor's office figures they can save two million dollars by phasing out the Bureau of Fire Investigation. . . ."

"That's bullshit," a marshal standing behind Terry called out.

Burke looked at him hard, said nothing. Then went on. "The police department evidently has more friends in the mayor's office than the fire department does, 'cause they want to give all fire-related homicides to the P.D.'s Arson and Explosion Squad, and then all arson investigation in Manhattan and the Bronx. The rest will be ours, at least for the time being. . . ."

"What else is there?" someone asked.

"We'll still have arson investigation in Brooklyn, Queens, and Staten Island, but in Manhattan and the Bronx we only get to determine the cause and origin of fire. There's nothing official, but it seems believable that they want to tear this office apart. The commissioner just wanted to make me aware of which way the wind is blowing, and I just want to make you aware of it. Thanks."

The gathered fire marshals were then left to look at each other as the chief grabbed his coat and left the office. "Shit!" They said it almost as a chorus.

O O O

The roar of the departing train mixed for a moment with the screech of an oncoming fire truck as Terry walked down the stairs from the elevated platform of the Smith and 9th Street station. He took the steps in twos; he had only an hour to look in on his folks.

The siren grew louder as he reached the bottom step. Terry stopped, cupped his hands against the graffiti-scrawled side wall of the stairway, and lit a cigarette.

As the ladder truck sped past, he noticed two firemen braced against the wind on the side of the apparatus. It was a cold, overcast night, and they had the flaps of their helmets pulled down over their ears and their boots pulled up to protect their thighs. Terry waved spontaneously, as if they were old friends, but they just looked back vacantly.

His hands stuffed into the pockets of his trench coat, he stepped briskly through the dismal Brooklyn streets. He smiled, the cigarette bobbing from a corner of his mouth; he couldn't expect all ten thousand of New York's firemen to recognize him.

As the truck disappeared into the mist, he wished them a false alarm, anything other than a fire. It was a tough winter night, the kind of night he had always hated, when the cold and the water and the ice came after the fire. Nights like this were one reason he wasn't fighting fires any more.

Not the main reason, though. The cold of winter always passed, like that night of the five-alarm lumberyard fire on 143rd Street. Jesus, I was frozen that night, he thought. I thought my eyes were going to crack like frozen glass. The goddamn metal in my teeth became needles driving into my nerves. But we ended up finally in undershirts in the firehouse kitchen, with sausages and eggs and dirty jokes. They were good times, and warm. The cold always passes.

The memory of being a fireman triggered a sudden anxiety within him, and he stopped as he turned down Court Street and looked into the window of a vacant store. He pulled his collar up and looked at his reflection. It was still the face of a fireman, he thought, still rugged, a small burn at the left temple, the constant reminder of a falling roof. Yet, he wasn't a fireman any more, and suddenly he felt his face pale as he wondered if he could ever be one again. He wondered if the flames could ever come that close again.

He had become something less of a fireman after the Bernstein fire. It stole his confidence, so that afterward every floor and wall seemed about to break away and fall down into the flames. It took him more than a year to realize it, that he had begun to stand back at fires, to pause a little, consciously building courage to move ahead, wondering if he was going to be there when one of the brothers needed him or, worse, when some kid lay choking in the smoke of a back bedroom of a Harlem tenement. The memory of the Bernstein fire had eaten at his stomach and stained his mind until he knew that he couldn't take it any longer, he knew that he had to get out of fighting fires.

He thought of that fall morning when the fire engines pulled up in front of the Bernstein warehouse on 127th Street, a block from the Hudson River. It was an

Greetings from
Myrtle Beach

POST CARD

0   42877 00101

Plastichrome®
PRINTED
IN IRELAND

P335923

EAST COAST MOST BEAUTIFUL BEACH

Myrtle Beach

unattached one-story building, with an unusual half-moon roof, a rain roof they called it. It was unoccupied, filled with old, forgotten trunks and furniture, and smoke was pushing from the eaves into the quiet Sunday morning air. They knew it was an arson job. A quiet morning, an unoccupied building, a large body of fire, it stank of arson.

The chief ordered a first hose line into the building, and then he directed Terry's company to stretch a second to the roof, where two ladder companies were cutting ventilation holes. He was a reputable chief, known to the firemen of his division as a good guy. How was the chief to know, they said after the fire, that the roof was supported only by a series of thin metal bars, twelve inches long, bolted together to form the half-moon truss that gave the rain something to roll from? How was he to know that there was a regular roof below it, covered and unseen, that had burned through?

Terry had the heavy brass nozzle in his hands, waiting for three men to cut through the thick tar of the rain roof, watching two other men with six-foot hooks stab at the openings. They were halfway up the truss, working, doing their jobs, saving a building that was barely worth its taxes. The roof felt spongy, Terry thought, but he said nothing. He knew, everyone knew, that you didn't question a chief's orders. They were there because they were told to be there. Suddenly, the roof fell, the series of metal bars having expanded in the fire below them until the weight of the tar could not be sustained, and the roof went *whoosh* in one split second, leaving an abyss of raging fire where footholds had been. Terry watched the five men ahead of him swimming madly with their arms, disappearing from view down behind the flames, and then in a grotesque flash of anguish he realized that it was the flames level with his eyes that had obscured his vision of the five falling men. He was up to his eyes in fire, and he was falling too. He held his breath instinctively, felt the heat searing the skin of his face as he fell. He hit a burning plank, and the plank cracked and split from the rest of the planks that made up the second roof below. He kept falling until his feet hit a stacking shelf, he bounced from that, continued downward until he hit the hard surface of the warehouse floor. He yelled, but there was no answer, just the noiseless whirl of smoke around him. The planking did not crack and split for the five firemen. He knew they were caught above him in the full fury of the fire, trapped and burning. He had gone through the flames. He was alive. Why? Why was he alive?

He stopped asking the question several weeks after the Bernstein fire, and after the wakes and funerals. The widows were left with fatherless children, and he was left with only a few marks from the burns on his legs and neck and temple, and the searing mark of the memory. He felt less a fireman from that moment on, for he knew that there was no answer to the question. And throughout the following year, he watched the Bernstein warehouse as it was rebuilt with insurance money and quietly put back into operation. The building showed no trace of a fire that took five men from five women and fourteen children. No plaque, no memorial, no reminder that the tragedy of the past might leave a lesson for the future. The building had been saved, the square footage salvaged, its destruction delayed for perhaps another generation. Five lives had been traded for the bricks and mortar. It was a dark symbol for Terry, and each time he saw it, or thought of it, he wondered who or what would protect him the next time. They shouldn't have been there. The chief should've known. Terry could not live with that. It wasn't that he was afraid of dying. It was the fire. The fire had come too close, and it was the next alarm that he couldn't live with.

But that was six years ago, part of the past. The department had understood when he requested a provisional appointment to the Bureau of Fire Investigation. It was an alternative to crawling into the fires. And it was a way to punch back against the arsonists.

He continued to walk toward the Gowanus Canal, feeling the tragic lifelessness of the neighborhood. Even on rainy days, he remembered, this neighborhood once had the movement of people huddled on stoops, kids chasing one another, mothers running to the grocery store. Now it was mostly vacant buildings and garbage-filled lots. He had walked two blocks, passed just two people. He turned down Hamilton Avenue. The few remaining stores had steel curtains drawn down in front of them. Even the corner grocery store which had always stayed open until ten was gated shut now, at eight-thirty.

Up ahead, in the shadow of the overhead Gowanus Parkway, he could see the Hideaway Bar, which used to be called the Thirteen Corners Bar. A neighborhood gin mill, it had changed with the neighborhood over the last ten years.

As he approached the Hideaway he could see his father through the fogged-up window, hunched over a glass of beer at the end of the bar, slapping his companion's arm as he talked. He wondered if the old man was having another of his barroom arguments.

Terry stopped for a moment at the window and watched his father, who was now pounding the end of the bar. The old man was still muscular, even though he was pushing sixty, but his face showed the years clearly enough. It had always been the face of a failed fighter, but now it was caved in at the cheeks, and the veins at the sides of his nose had become thick and red. Terry shook his head slightly as he was reminded of how his father had described himself one night many years before in a barroom argument. "I'm a man of the docks," the old man had said, "and a fuckin' labor socialist who was in the middle of it

19 o

when it mattered. I got my nose broke for organizin' an' I swallowed a tooth one night 'cause a guy was yappin' at the mouth just like you're doin'."

Terry was smiling as he entered the bar. He stood and watched his father's silver head bob up and down in conversation until the old man spotted him and gave him a wave. As Terry reached his side, he put his hand around his son's forearm, saying, "I'll be with ya in a minute, kid. I just gotta give this guy a better pitcher of the world."

He continued talking to the man seated next to him, the only other white Terry could see in the bar. "Ya see," the old man went on, in a harsh, cracked voice, "there wouldn't be no sellout rat pricks among the workers if it wasn't for all their rat wives out in the fuckin' suburbs breakin' their chops about dishwashers and fancy furniture." He kept slapping the man's arm as he talked. "Ya see, Marx never figured on the fuckin' suburbs to brainwash all the rat wives of the workers. He never figured on the exploitation of the quarter acre, ya know. These guys today don't give a fiddler's about shuttin' another man outta work if the overtime is gonna put an ugly fuckin' grandfather clock in his ranch house."

Terry cringed and raised his eyes to the ceiling.

"Yeah, Petey," the man replied, "it ain't like the old days, that's for sure."

The old man slapped the polished bar top and continued. "But the point is, it's not any better; in some ways it's worse."

He stopped and leaned over, out of earshot of the others in the bar, whispering, "Ya see, now it's all the niggers who are shut out, and the time will come soon enough when they'll want a piece of the fuckin' quarter acre. The country will be in trouble then, when they want what the working man has, instead of wanting to be doctors and lawyers and businessmen."

"Oh," the man said, clearly confused.

With that the conversation was ended, and Petey Ahearn turned to his son. "How are ya, kid? What brings ya across the bridge?"

"I just thought I'd pay a visit," Terry said. "I called and Ma told me you'd probably be here. I only have an hour. Ma said she'd give me something to eat."

"Yeah, sure. What time is it now?"

"Eight-thirty, a little after."

"Okay, one drink an' we'll go."

"Yeah, sure, Pop," Terry sighed. "Have you ever left a joint without saying, 'One more an' we'll go'?"

The Ahearns lived on the top floor of a four-story walk-up called the Franklin Roosevelt Housing Project—or the "Noose Deal" housing project, as Petey Ahearn called it.

The old man disappeared into the back bedroom. Rose Ahearn was in the kitchen, stirring a pot of gravy over the stove. She turned and smiled slightly at her son, as if it were only temporary. She always hung back, he thought, reluctant to display her feelings. It was the trait of the quiet, accepting mother and wife, a trait that had emigrated with the hordes from Ireland.

Terry kissed her cheek. "How're things, Ma?"

"I have some chicken left from last night, and some gravy. I'll put it on toast for you."

"Terrific. How're things?"

The frail, gray-haired woman put the gravy spoon on a dish and sat at the Formica table. She folded her hands, gently, as if in prayer. "Your sister is out with her new boyfriend again," she said. She paused then, and Terry noticed the despair in her eyes. "I don't know what we're going to do, Terry," she continued. "Maureen is seeing too much of this boy. Maybe we had her too late in life, God only knows, but she's acting crazy. And I haven't even met him yet. Your father told her not to bring him home 'cause he won't let him in the house. I only know that he's a guitarist, but the kind that plays high-class music on the stage without a band. He's not Irish or even American, and your father told her a couple of weeks ago to bring him home a hard-working kid from the docks, that there'll be no bongo players from South America in this house. He asked her if the boy was a colored, and she went mad as a banshee and stormed out of the house. She hasn't talked to him since, and that was just a day or so after Christmas, just after you were here last. Do you think he might be a colored, Terry?"

"Who knows with Maureen?" Terry answered. "She's pretty independent. She might have just resented the question, but then again, her boyfriend might be as black as Willy Mays."

"Your father loves Willy Mays."

"Yeah, I know."

"There's a picture of Willy Mays on the bedroom wall."

"Yeah, I know."

"Would you talk to her and see what's going on?"

"I'll talk to her, Ma, first chance I get."

"Do you have some time now? To eat, I mean."

"Not much, a half hour or until something breaks. Jose will call me here, but maybe it will be a quiet night."

"Do you have enough bullets?"

Terry laughed. "Yes, Ma, I have enough bullets. You always ask me that, and I always tell you I have enough."

"Well, I had that dream, remember, and you ran out of bullets. It was the worst dream I ever had."

Petey Ahearn came out of the bedroom, opened a can of beer, and sat in an old wing chair in the tiny living room. Terry followed him and sat on the sofa, waiting for his father to speak. Perhaps, he thought, the old man would say something about Maureen. But Petey Ahearn sat silently sipping the beer.

Will it never change, Terry asked himself, this silence between me and the old man? We just sit and stare at each other when anything personal needs to be said. When we do talk it's the same old talk about politics and the working stiffs, just as it's the same old furniture, the same old view of the canal. And Maureen, the same old problem with her too. There was an Italian boyfriend when she was in eighth grade and a Greek when she went to high school, and the old man told each of them to take a walk. A nice harp kid, he said to Maureen, won't ever leave you flat. Christ. He thinks the Irish come with a paid-up Social Security account. He's got Maureen on his mind, but he can't talk about it.

Terry touched a hole in the faded plastic that covered the sculpted-velvet couch. The hole had been there as long as he could remember, like the rug that had been patched in places by his mother after a dog, long since dead, had chewed through it, and like the imitation French provincial coffee table that had been worn at the top by his father's feet. There was never enough money for better furniture. The old man hadn't ever worked consistently enough to save anything or to get credit, and when he had those few jobs that lasted, like operating a fork lift or counting grain bags, most of the extra money went over the bar. He had a lot of friends and so he always found some work at the docks or at the shipyard. He was a worker if he was anything. But he always seemed to find a reason to call a foreman a scab-licking son-of-a-bitch Pinkerton. And, he was always right, he would say, because the workers agreed with him.

"Come to supper, Terry," his mother called. The food was already on the kitchen table, and Terry began spooning the gravy across the open chicken sandwich. The circular fluorescent ceiling light was flickering.

Petey Ahearn also sat at the kitchen table and began picking at a coffee cake.

Looking at her hands, Rose Ahearn said, "I went to Julia Clancy's cousin's wake last night. She was a young woman, not even sixty yet. The funeral's tomorrow. It's a terrible thing to die right after Christmas."

"It's a terrible thing to die any time, Ma," Terry said.

"Yes, I suppose so," she responded. "You know, you'd think her son would have crossed himself. He just knelt there before his mother—he's a college professor or something—and someone told me he doesn't believe in God. Can you imagine? You must promise me, Terry, that you'll cross yourself at my wake."

Terry smiled. "You're never going to die, Ma. You're as fit as a rich man's mistress. Anyway, I believe in God."

"Yes. But sometimes you miss Mass."

"That's okay," the old man interrupted. "Stephen Dedalus went to Mass every Sunday, and he wouldn't even kneel before his mother's coffin. Can you reach me another beer there?"

Rose Ahearn took a can of beer from the refrigerator, saying, "There he goes again, saying things I don't understand. He's always doing that to me. From the first day I met him, in the back of Flaherty's Bar in Flatbush. What was it he said? He kept saying he was a swan, of all things, and I was his Lena, or some Italian name like that."

Terry looked at his father knowingly, and they laughed together. "It was the drink talking, Ma," Terry said.

"The hell it was," the old man said. "That was in the days I thought poetry was something to believe in."

"No more?" Terry asked, cutting into the chicken sandwich.

"Not today. Poetry don't work for people who live in tenements and projects where there ain't any flowers to cream over. Look around. You see any flowers? It's for people who dream of a pure world tryin' to forget the world they're in. It's like takin' dope, unrealistic, tradin' the real thing for dreams. Poetry is bullshit in a world of exploitation. A deception."

"C'mon, Pop," Terry said, lifting a forkful of chicken. "Not everyone's exploited. I don't feel exploited, for instance."

"Jesus," the old man laughed, "that's poetry if I ever heard it. Didn't you learn anything in thirty-three years of knowin' me? The public needs protection from the dregs of the world and they give ya a badge for your pocket and a gun for your belt, and then the politicians pay you less than they pay a competent plumber. And I'm not talkin' about a good plumber, who would earn twice what you make."

"You putting down plumbers, Pop?"

"Naw, even good plumbers are raped by the system, but they don't have to wear guns to protect it." Terry stabbed his fork into the sandwich and put both hands on the tabletop. "I'll tell you this, Pop. If a man likes what he does, if he gets up in the morning and feels good about himself, then he isn't exploited."

"Poetry," the old man shot in. "A gun is always an exploitation."

"Oh, Pop," Terry said impatiently. "I know what I do, the risks I take, and what I earn, and there's nothing wrong with being proud of it. If it wasn't for people like me this society would crumble, and you wouldn't be so smug."

Terry paused a moment, waiting for a reaction. There was none. "I'm a fire marshal," he continued, "and so what? I might not be overpaid, but I put my heart into my job, and it's not because I'm working for the politicians or the editors of the *New York Times*. I work for the people of this city, rich or poor, but mostly poor. The people living in the goddamn tenements and projects are the ones who need the protection. Us. And there's a decent sense of service that goes along with that, you know, a meaningfulness."

The phone rang then, and Petey Ahearn got up without a word to answer it. He handed the phone to Terry.

It was Jose.

Terry turned to his parents. "There's a fire at the Astor Hotel. A discotheque."

Terry put his arms around his mother and said, "I've got to go, Ma, and that shoots the rest of the chicken sandwich. I'm sorry."

"I understand, Terry," she said. "Can I fix you something to take with you?"

"It's okay, Ma." Terry put his arm through the sleeve of his trench coat. "Jose and I will grab a hot dog on Broadway later on."

His father got up and walked with his son through a long dark hall to the apartment door. As Terry shook his hand, the old man said, "Anything the matter? You was awfully quiet sitting in the living room there."

"No," Terry replied, "nothing with me, Pop. I thought maybe there was something on your mind."

"With me? Naw. Nothin.'"

"I gotta go, Pop."

"Yeah. Sure. I'll talk to ya."

"Right," Terry said, beginning to walk down the dimly lit stairs.

The old man called after him. "And don't do no dancin' at that discotheque. That's the problem with the world. People are fuckin' dancin' while Brooklyn is fallin' apart."

Terry smiled as he put his collar up to the cold street air, thinking of a reply to his father. "It's *one* of the problems, anyway," he said to himself.

O O O

Terry thought over the old man's speech as he looked absently at the faces about him on the subway. The old man is wrong, he thought, solidly wrong. A cop might be exploited in suppressing a riot in Harlem that was caused by the indifference of politicians, but fire marshals are different. They come after the fact, after the fire, to get to the root of it, to zero in on an arsonist if the fire was made. There's substance to that, importance. The goddamn gun is not central to the job, just a part of it. It's not an exploitation.

Terry rushed up the stairs of the Brooklyn Bridge station on the east side of City Hall. He saw Jose sitting in the battered Ford sedan, biting the fingernails of one hand and rapping the other against a thick chrome handle on the steering post. Terry thought he might be drumming to a Latin rhythm playing in his mind.

The department radio blasted a static-voiced order just as Terry slid onto the smooth plastic seat of the duty car. Jose put a hand up in a command for silence. He lowered his hand when it became apparent that the message had nothing to do with the fire at the Astor Hotel.

"How're things?" Terry asked.

"Bad," Jose replied, shifting into gear. "A code one came in over the air three minutes ago. Multiple."

"Christ," Terry said, placing a portable mars light on top of the dashboard. "How many?"

The red light began to click on and off as the car sped past the massive government buildings. The siren wailed continuously, and Jose was forced to speak above it. "Don't know, or maybe they don't want to give it out over the radio." He pressed hard on the chrome handle as he braked the car around the turn onto the East River Drive.

Terry could tell that his partner's leg was hurting. He wouldn't press so hard if he weren't in pain.

The chrome handle was at the end of a long shaft chained to the steering post. The bottom end of the shaft had a casing that slipped over the brake pedal, an ingenious device, Terry thought. Jose was proud of it, proud that he had resolved the problem of driving the worn out department cars. They drove like cement trucks, and Jose couldn't trust his right leg for strength enough to brake them.

He had been shot one winter night five years before on the rooftop of a South Bronx tenement.

They were silent as the car wailed up the Drive, weaving in and out of traffic. There was no point in talking about the fire alarm. Anticipation was pointless to fire marshals, just as it was pointless to firemen on the back step of a fire engine: neither can know fully what they've got until they get there.

Terry always felt uncomfortable when Jose's leg was acting up, and he bit his lower lip as he took sidelong glances at his partner. He admired Jose in the same way the old man admired Willy Mays. He had proven himself to be the sharpest guy in the Bureau of Fire Investigation, street wise, tough, the best there was when it came to analyzing the fires, finding the origins, tracing the spreads. He was the best of the team, yet there was a constant, agonizing thought in Terry's mind that his partner had become like a three-legged tiger who was hungry but reluctant to admit that he could not hunt, that the leg was gone.

The leg was a taboo subject. Terry had brought

it up once, a few years back, but Jose cut him off after the first sentence. "Forget it," Jose said. "I do."

The only time Terry ever heard Jose talk about it was in the emergency room of the Bronx-Lebanon Hospital the night of the shooting.

He had paced the floor of the emergency room for more than three hours before a nurse gave him permission to go upstairs to talk to his partner. The fire commissioner had been there, and the chief fire marshal, and the chief of the Bronx borough command, and after they all thanked God Jose wasn't killed, they shook Terry's hand and left him with the assurance they would be back in the morning to visit his partner.

"*Qué pasa?*" Terry said, entering the pearl-gray room.

"Bad luck," Jose returned. His leg was bandaged and tied up to a sling, and glucose dripped into his arm from a plastic bag. His eyes were half closed.

"I should've never left you," Terry said, the apology shaking in his voice.

"Bullshit, we almost nailed him."

"The stairs were gone. Fuckin' abandoned tenements. I had to crawl up the six flights like I was on monkey bars."

"No sweat. It hadda be, I guess." Jose always accepted things as they came. Terry remembered him once saying that surprises were for kids at Christmas.

"How's the leg?"

Jose forced a smile. "The doctor said the bone was split, and he had to put a steel plate in to hold it together. Right in the middle of the thigh. The plate'll bite with the cold, he told me, and sting with the heat, but I told him I'm gonna stay home during the winter and the summer anyway."

29 o

Terry knew that Jose expected him to laugh, to take the edge off.

"Shit," Terry said after a silent pause, "I shouldn't have left you."

"It coulda been worse," Jose replied in a thick, drugged voice. "It coulda been a requiem at the neighborhood church. I think maybe if you came at the wrong time I'd be dead. The white mother . . . the guy was a fuckin' maniac. He was comin' down the stairs when he saw me on the third floor, and he shot back up to the roof. I caught up with him there, and took him down easy enough. . . . I should've placed one through the bridge of his nose when I had the chance. . . . He just looked at me and said, 'Okay, man, I'm yours.' I thought he was wise, you know, that he understood when you play the game, you get caught, you take your lumps, case closed. I had the piece on him, and leaned him against the parapet. I made the mistake then. I holstered the piece and took the cuffs from my belt. I never figured. I forgot that those roofs are arsenals—rocks, bricks, pieces of iron, all kinds of junk to throw at cops and firemen."

"It's okay, Jose. Take it easy."

"The mother grabbed a piece of wood and swung it at me, caught me here." Jose pointed to his temple. "Christ, I got a headache that would kill a stud horse. I fell back a little, dropped the cuffs, and went for my revolver, but he swung around again and caught me on the shoulder so hard that the piece came outta my hand. Jesus, he was fast, like the frames of a movie, and before I knew it my fuckin' revolver was in his hand and he was pointin' it at my face. He had the strangest look on his face I ever saw in my life. A very weird guy with long, curly blond hair, a couple of teeth missin' in the front of his mouth, and he was cockeyed, you know, one eye was looking at me and the other one was lookin' out toward Jersey. Anyway, if you came to the roof then I think he would've just pulled the trigger, 'cause he was very scratchy. He just aims the piece at my face for a minute, smilin' all the time like his arms were wrapped in Creedmoor, and then he just lowers the barrel and gets me through the thigh. The white mother . . ."

The sedan swung off the East River Drive at the 61st Street exit, and Terry noticed Jose's round, dark face again spread with pain as he brought his foot up to the brake pedal, just as it looked that night in the hospital five years before when he had tried to move the leg out of the traction sling that hung down from a bar above his head, when he had said, "I'll tell you this, Terry, the white mother will be there some day, 'cause this city ain't big enough for him not to be, and then I'm gonna trade this leg for that ugly fuckin' grin he gave me."

Terry knew the memory of the face of that "white mother" kept coming back to Jose, like a bad dream. But he also knew it wouldn't get in the way of the job. Because Jose was too much of a pro. Because he loved his work too much. Jose should have taken the pension, Terry thought, when it was offered, but too much of his life was tied up in the job to sit at home collecting checks for doing nothing. He was not the kind of guy to bail out with a limp, not Jose, but still Terry wondered if his partner felt a little the way he did after the warehouse job, reluctant, maybe, even scared? How else could you feel after someone puts a gun to your face? After coming that close to tapping out?

They passed the Pierre Hotel, turned down Fifth Avenue, and waited for a moment as a patrolman moved a street barricade to let them through. "This is it," Jose said, stopping the sedan with the chrome handle. "Our stop."

Terry grabbed a clipboard from the back seat, and Jose picked up a small briefcase from the floor. As they were leaving the car, the department radio finally delivered a report of the fire. "Fire located in a basement disco-theque," it squawked. "Astor Hotel. Code one. Fire under control. Multiple fatalities. Area hospital disaster units notified. Dispatcher forty-one. Time: twenty-one fifty-five hours."

It was almost ten o'clock.

"That's the same report they gave me twenty minutes ago," Jose said.

"Not much more to say. I wonder how many?" Terry then paused a moment before he answered his own question. "One is always one too many, huh?"

Jose nodded.

O O O

Terry slammed the sedan door, pinned his gold shield to his lapel, and began to push through the crowd that had backed up to the fountain in the plaza. The small street before him was a circus of flashing red lights, arriving and departing ambulances, police cars, and fire apparatus. Through the still evening sirens wailed and stopped. Some of the onlookers wore elaborate evening clothes, the rest were just dressed for winter. A hotel doorman in red and gold stood among them, tears in his eyes. "I knew them all," he kept saying, to no one in particular.

Still pushing, Terry passed scores of cops and ambulance attendants who stood idly, waiting for instructions. Jose was just a little behind, as always.

An assistant chief of the department stood with his hand on the polished brass railing that separated the hotel entrance from the steps to the basement discotheque. Terry was about to report to him, but then stopped himself. "He looks like he's trying to decide what to tell the fire commissioner when he shows," Terry said.

"Gotcha," Jose replied. "And the mayor. They'll all be here."

Two firefighters lay on the rug-covered steps of the hotel, mask canisters dropped at their feet, sucking noisily for air. Two other men came up the stairs from the Sophia Club carrying a young woman on a stretcher. She seemed to be wearing only glossy underwear above her blackened legs.

"That's the twelfth stretcher," someone said.

"No, it's the fourteenth," another countered.

From the top of the stairs, Terry and Jose could see a group of firefighters sitting on a table below, waiting to pack up their hose. Small wisps of smoke floated up the stairwell. It had a strange smell, curiously sweet. Perfume, Terry thought.

He and Jose passed a police officer on guard duty and went down the stairs to the tiled entry foyer, stepping carefully over the two lengths of two-and-one-half-inch hose that ran into the basement. Terry looked closely at the brocade-covered walls in the foyer and noticed that the black charring started three inches above the gold-plated baseboards. He made a note on his clipboard. Clearly the fire had originated on the floor, two, maybe three feet out from the wall. How it had originated was still a question. Jose would answer that one.

Terry walked into the large inner room and saw brittle shreds of silky fabric hanging like patchwork from the ceiling. He shook his head and made another note. The lighting, protected behind a copper frieze around the side walls, was still working. The fire had crossed the ceiling but had not been sustained long enough to burst the bulbs.

He had to step over two badly burned bodies and cross the charred, soot-stained red carpeting to get to the edge of the dance floor. The carpet was soggy under his shoes, and he was aware of the squishing noise he made as he walked. The sight of the bodies made his stomach turn, he could suddenly taste his mother's chicken sandwich again. His eyes were smarting now from the stench of burnt skin combined with that strange odor, like perfume, but not perfume. He stood at the edge of the oval dance floor. It was a smooth and shellacked mosaic, a scene of a naked Eve feeding an apple to a naked Adam, done in small green and brown and white tiles. The figures, wide-eyed, and expressionless, seemed to be in shock. Lying just above the mosaic scene, at the far end of the dance floor, were two more bodies, joined as if they had died dancing. Their skin was crisp and steaming as the water from the hose evaporated from the heat within them. The woman's shoes were on and she had a small diamond tiara around her darkened forehead. The rest of her clothes had been burned away. The man, too, had his shoes on and the upper part of his tuxedo jacket had not burned completely. His arm was around the woman's neck and they were one now, fused together unalterably.

Six columns placed around the dance floor rose to a vaulted ceiling. It was black, but Terry could see beyond the burnt silky shreds that it was made of plaster with uneven coloring. The capitals of the columns were also made of plaster, carved into small scrolls and intricate foliage. He reached up and with a penknife dug a triangular piece out of one. The charring was less than one-sixteenth of an inch deep into the plaster, more like half that. He made a note and put the piece of plaster into a small bag. He would measure it later.

He could see the rest rooms in a far corner, and he counted four bodies stretched out in front of them. He looked toward the opposite corner and what he saw made him stagger. In front of the swinging kitchen doors was a pile of people, twenty-five at least, all steaming, peeling, horribly disfigured. Terry was transfixed.

Jose had limped up behind him, and his voice startled Terry. "The battalion chief counted forty-three dead."

Terry turned quickly. His face was ashen, and he put his hands up, as if in defense against an attack.

"Hey, man," Jose said, "are you okay?"

Terry turned back again toward the dance floor. "Yeah, I'm all right. It's just the thought that I have to be here, that I can't run up those stairs and out of here forever . . . that's all."

Jose put his hand on Terry's arm. "Me too, partner. But we got work to do."

Two companies of firefighters were in the room, sitting at rest, waiting for a chief to direct them to pull down another piece of the ceiling, or pry up another piece of carpeting, or move another table or chair. The men were not speaking. There was none of the usual small talk that was customary during a cleanup operation. Terry looked into their faces and felt the gloom thick in the air. He let his eyes wander again to the kitchen doors and to the pile of death lying there.

Human beings, he thought. No matter who they were, or what they stood for, it's still a horrible end.

"Terry," Jose called, again interrupting the reverie. "Let's go, pal."

"Yeah," Terry replied, "coming."

As they went back over the soggy rug toward the entrance, Terry noticed the body of a man on the floor in front of the coat-check counter at the front wall. He looked over the counter and saw a woman lying in the rubble, still grasping the remains of a fur coat. The coat-check girl, he thought, shaking his head. God rest her, it had to be a lousy job to begin with.

A battalion chief came over to join them. "Some mess, huh?" he said.

"Awful," Jose replied.

"There are a dozen or so injured, but none of them critical. Those forty-three others didn't have a chance. It was too fast. We told the men not to touch any of the roasts until you guys got here. How long will you be?"

Terry shrugged, thinking, I'll be here a long time. We all will. Even the firemen can't just pack up their hoses and leave a thing like this behind them. He answered the battalion chief, "The department photographers ought to be here soon. When they're finished you can ship the roasts to the morgue."

"I think they're going to set up a temporary morgue in the hotel lobby," the chief said. "The only problem is that we don't have enough body bags."

"I guess you could use blankets from the hotel," Jose said, "and they must have a few rolls of masking tape. That won't be as good as body bags, but they'll stay closed anyway if you wrap the tape tight enough."

"Yeah, that's an idea," the chief said. "Listen, you know how it started yet?"

Terry ignored the question. It was always better to be silent than to offer conjectures. He asked in return, "How many people got out?"

"About a hundred sixty, seventy maybe. All through the kitchen exit," the chief said. "Most of them are up in that bar, the Red Room, or else outside."

"We know that the fire came in through the front," Jose said. "The survivors should be able to tell us more. By the way, what happened to the sprinklers?"

"We're checking on it now," the chief said, "but it's peculiar to begin with. They must have gotten a variance to put a second exit out through the kitchen, though in a place like this in the basement they should never have gotten one. We'll see. The sprinklers are connected, but they were never charged, never tested. The hotel engineer tells me they were worried about the fucking ceiling if a head blew out, because they were painting pictures on it. It's a mess, but whoever owns the place is in trouble, we know that."

"The Bureau of Fire Prevention will do all the legal work on that one," Terry said. "We have our own problems with . . ." He nodded toward the mound of bodies at the kitchen doors.

"Okay," the chief said, "I'll be around. One other thing. How are you going to I.D. the roasts?"

"The police department Homicide Squad will be here," Terry replied. "They have all the equipment. They'll just tag and number them."

The chief walked off, and the two fire marshals stood at the coat-check counter. Jose began to draw a schematic of the room, but he suddenly stopped and looked up. "You know, Terry," he said, "there's a funny smell in here that reminds me of something, the way the smell of shoe polish reminds me of the army. Only, I don't know what this is."

"I smelled it too," Terry replied, walking to the entrance doorframe. "It's more noticeable over here. Not gasoline."

Jose joined him, walking around the two bodies that lay in front of the doorway. "Yeah, it's stronger here," he said. "I'll think of it."

Terry stared down at the bodies, a man and a woman. Most of the man's tuxedo had been burned away, but parts of it seemed to be melted into his skin. He was lying face down. The woman was on her back, the front of her long dress was missing and most of her underwear had been eaten away by the fire. The body of another woman lay to the side of them, farther inside the main room. She had large breasts, and they were hanging to her sides. Her hair seemed to be a coil of burnt wire, brittle and flaking, and her skin was blotched, black and crisp in parts, with splashes that were pink and moist. She was wearing an emerald-cut ruby on a heavy gold chain, but one side of the chain had fallen strangely over a blistered ear, and the ear seemed to be breaking apart with the weight of it.

Terry knelt beside the woman, gently lifted the necklace from her ear, and placed it on the side of her neck. As he drew his hand away, he brushed against the side of her face. His hand was trembling slightly, and he felt the back of it sweep across the crisp, rough skin. The skin crumbled. But then, oddly, he felt a hard, smooth surface. He pulled his hand away quickly, and looked closely at the woman's cheek. It was totally burned, but he saw, embedded in her skin, like a phenocryst in a soft black rock, a small piece of glass, smoothly curved and covered with the black grime of carbon. It was less than an inch wide. Terry picked the glass gingerly from the woman's face and put it into the plastic bag along with the cut of plaster. He squatted again and looked at the woman, at the small patch of skin which had been protected by the glass and which now stood out like a birthmark against the surrounding ash, the only unburned spot on her body.

Jose also squatted down and began staring at the necklace. "A lot of glitter here," he said.

"Yeah," Terry replied. He looked from this body with its heavy ruby necklace to the pile of dead at the kitchen doors, to the ornate capitals rising into the ceiling, to the steaming woman on the dance floor and the diamond tiara embedded in her charred forehead. His eyes swept the room. It was a room of riches, yet all but the stones had become rubble. The room was black now, dank and grotesque, and the stink of death was overwhelming.

Terry inhaled heavily, held his breath a moment. "Yeah," he repeated finally, "glitter. A lot of glitter. And ash."

The stench was heavy, almost viscous, and Terry turned from Jose and wiped the moisture from his eyes. He walked to one group of four firemen sitting on the floor in the far corner of the room, near the rest rooms. He saw by their helmets they were from Engine Company 8, and their faces looked as if they had been wiped with crankcase oil, their hair wet and matted.

"Were you guys first due?" Terry asked.

"No," a lieutenant said, rising to his feet. "Engine Thirty-four was first due, but they were out at a false alarm, and we were first to arrive."

Terry wrote on his clipboard and continued, "You wanna tell me about the fire, everything you remember."

"Jesus Christ, it was awful," the lieutenant said, sitting on the edge of a water-soaked table. "I never seen nothin' like it in thirty years. Maybe if Engine Thirty-four got here a couple minutes before us, they could've got some of them out."

"Yeah," Terry said. "What's your name?"

"Lieutenant Mills, Ed Mills."

"What'd you see, Lieutenant?"

"We came across Fifty-seventh Street, and up Fifth against the traffic. I smelled it soon as we got on Fifth. I told the chauffeur to take the hydrant on Central Park South, and we backstretched a two-and-a-half-inch line. It was an easy stretch, not more than thirty yards, but I remember thinkin' if I had another man I could've stretched a second line. Goddamn city, and their goddamn cutbacks. We put the masks on, and the doorman told us there were a hundred people down there, maybe more, so we got water and went down as fast as we could. Jesus Christ, it was like walkin' into a cellar of fire. You ever walk into a cellar of fire? Walkin' straight down into it?"

Terry knew there was no answer expected, and he nodded as the officer went on.

"It was murderous, the first minute, and I thought the heat was gonna push us back up the goddamn stairs. All of us got burns on the ears and neck."

Terry looked at the man's ears as he spoke and saw the blisters rising up under the grime.

"You notice anything at all peculiar? When you got here, when you were responding?" Terry asked.

"No, nothing. There was just one big fire, no gas cans or anything. Ya gotta wonder, though, how it got so big so fast."

Terry pointed to the burnt and tattered sheets of fabric hanging from the ceiling.

"Yeah," the lieutenant said, "a hanging ceiling of material, that would do it. We couldn't have made it without the masks, but I don't think it would've mattered anyways. They musta all been dead when we got here. We got on our bellies over there at the foyer, right up against the fire, and I was just hoping there wouldn't be a backflash, you know, 'cause I knew there wasn't too much oxygen to feed a body of fire that big. That's all I was thinkin' of, that the fire would jump at the air behind us, but then I felt the first body. We couldn't see anything with the smoke an' all when the water hit the fire, and as we were crawling in, my hand sunk into the body of that woman there at the entrance to the room. I put my light on and saw the skin peelin' back all over her, and I knew there was nothin' we could do for her or anyone caught in that amount of fire. I felt rotten, you know, we all felt rotten when we knocked the fire down and saw what we had, that a fire could do this to so many people. And that was it, didn't take us more than a minute to put the fire out. That's what's sad, you know, that it only took a minute to put the thing out."

The lieutenant got up, blew his nose into his hand, and ran the hand over the wet tabletop. "I feel sick, you know," he said, "just 'cause we couldn't do anything for them."

"Yeah," Terry replied sympathetically, "I know what you mean. This isn't one of those things where it's supposed to be just part of the job."

40 o

Looking up, Terry saw four plainclothes detectives enter the room. He recognized Lieutenant Sirkin among them, the head of the police department's Arson and Explosion Squad.

Ending the interview, Terry said, "Thanks, Lieutenant. The name is Ahearn, and if you think of anything more, you can reach me at the marshal's office."

Terry turned to leave, but Mills called after him, saying, "Hey, Ahearn, why can't we move these bodies out? It seems a goddamn sin against the dead to leave them lying here in all this shit."

Terry forced a smile. "I know," he said. "But they have to be photographed first." He turned and walked toward the police detectives.

Sirkin, a tall, acne-scarred man, saw Terry approaching and turned the other way, talking to one of his men. Terry continued past him, talking to Jose, who was just completing his schematic. "Sirkin pretends he doesn't see me," Terry said.

Jose looked up at the police detectives who were now in the middle of the discotheque. "Fuck 'im," Jose said, a sour look crossing his face. "If he doesn't need us, we don't need him either. Remember Saint Pat's."

Sirkin had shafted them on that one. The front doors of St. Patrick's Cathedral had been bombed six weeks ago, on Christmas night, and though bombings were out of the fire department's jurisdiction, a passerby had automatically involved the fire department by pulling the fire alarm box on Fifth and 51st Street. Jose and Terry had responded as much because it was a slow night as because the department dispatcher had called to inform them of the bombing. When they arrived on the scene, they learned that forty detectives were searching for a note from a radical group that was claiming credit for the blast. Terry and Jose offered their assistance. Sirkin, sounding cool and confident, said he didn't need any help from the fire department.

The two fire marshals were just leaving the cathedral when Terry got a wild idea. He told Jose if a radical group wanted to intimidate the Catholic power structure in the city by bombing the cathedral, they might leave the note at the center of power. So they drove to the chancery offices on the corner of 56th Street and First Avenue, where they found a note from a group of Puerto Rican radicals hanging, like Luther's theses, on the entry doorway.

It wasn't their job, there wasn't any fire, but Terry felt a certain glee in beating the police department. As Sirkin stood before the destroyed cathedral doors, he and Jose approached him from behind. "I've got the note," Terry said to his back.

Coldly, Sirkin refused to turn. He bent down, picked up a piece of debris, studied it for a moment, and then threw it back to the ground. Still without turning, he said, "Well, let's see it."

"Turn and face me," Terry said. Reluctantly, Sirkin turned. "I want you to promise," Terry said, "you'll tell the press that *two fire marshals* found it. I just want to read in the papers tomorrow about *two fire marshals,* okay?"

"C'mon, Ahearn," the detective said. "I'll have you arrested. Give me the goddamn note."

"Well, it's evidence, right? I could lock it in our safe until I get a chance to voucher it in the morning. You know I could do that."

Sirkin looked at Terry's eyes, and the look became a stare, a long stare. Finally he said, "You got it: two fire marshals found the note."

Now, as Terry watched the police department photographer join the group of policemen in the center of the Sophia Club, he sneered as he remembered that Sirkin told the press that two of his own men had found the note, for the cathedral bombing. "Yeah," Terry repeated to Jose, "fuck 'im. He's a rubber."

"What're you doing now?" Jose asked.

"I'm going up to the Red Room and interview the witnesses. See ya in a while."

"Right," Jose replied, going back to his drawing. He added, "There's a load of newspaper and TV people upstairs, I can hear them screamin' to get down here."

Terry knew that was Jose's way of saying that all the rules changed when there were forty-three homicides strewn before them on the floor.

"Yeah," Terry replied. "I'll be careful."

○ ○ ○

The flowered carpeting of the Astor's lobby felt luxuriously soft after the charred, wet rugs of the discotheque below. Terry tried to shake the picture in his mind of the burnt corpses piled before the kitchen doors, but it was too strong, too horrible. The bright lobby chandeliers offered no relief from the dark scene below, and again he could taste that sandwich. He had seen roasts before, too many, and they always became bad memories, but he knew this would be the hardest to live with. It was inexplicable. One bomb, one solitary action, and such utter devastation. A single madman shooting Jose was one thing, a face-to-face confrontation, but that kind of thing happens plenty of times in the street life of the city. This was something else, though, something more ugly and more sinful. One action and forty-three dead. Christ! Who could do something like this? And why?

He passed the makeshift morgue that was being prepared in the open restaurant area of the lobby and entered the Red Room at the end of a wide corridor. A hundred or so men and women mingled about, dressed in evening clothes, sipping nervously at drinks, puffing at cigarettes. They looked harried, tired, disheveled. A fireman, a chief's aide, was standing near the bar, and several police-men stood off to a side of the room. They were biding time. The room was noisy with subdued, anxious conversations.

Terry was studying a young man who was crying openly when a gray-haired police captain approached. He looked closely at Terry's badge, apparently satisfying him-self that he would be talking to another civil servant.

"You know who he is?" the captain said, pointing to the crying man.

"Who is he?" Terry asked in return.

"He's the deputy mayor, for economic develop-ment or something. It's funny, isn't it, we work for the city and we don't know who these guys are. His name is Rodney Lettington, the third, mind you. His wife is one of those people downstairs, God help her."

"Anyone get the names of all these people?" Terry asked.

"Most of them," the captain replied, "but some of them went home, and others went off in ambulances. It's an orderly bunch, given what they've been through, but then this is a rich territory, if you know what I mean, different from us. They might put their pants on the same way, but the pants are better, if you take a close look. The governor was here when it happened, but he got out, and so did the head of the New York Stock Exchange, and others, all big-time people. I suppose the ones downstairs are big-time too. Or were."

"Did your men take any statements?" Terry asked.

"No, I just asked them all to stay until the bomb squad gets here, and also when they set up a morgue maybe some of them can help identify the bodies. Did you see them? I took a look, just once. They didn't look human. It's a cruel way the Lord has with fire, isn't it?"

The captain was Irish, and had the lingering tone of what was once a brogue. Terry thought him flippant. This wasn't an Irish wake where humor and asides are expected or, as his father would say, where friends and relatives get together to help the corpse get in the right attitude for passing into the hereafter. This was horrible. And sick.

But the police captain, Terry surmised, was not involved in the fire; he was just assigned to bring a police presence to the scene. In the morning, he would go about his duties, and the fire would be just another strange memory in a job of strange events.

It was different for Terry, for already he sensed that his life was being caught up in the tangle of cadavers that lay in the discotheque below.

"You know the saying," the captain continued, "that hell can be holy for them that works hard to get there."

Terry moved away from the captain without answering and walked to the deputy mayor. "Excuse me, Mr. Lettington," he said, "I'm with the fire marshal's office."

Lettington, not much older than Terry, his blond hair perfectly in place, his bow tie straight beneath his chin, looked up momentarily, and then returned his face into his cupped hands. His shoulders shook as he sobbed, but Terry thought that his eyes were peculiarly dry.

"I know this is a bad time," Terry said, standing across from him, "but could you tell me something about what happened downstairs?"

Lettington reached for the white silk scarf that hung around his neck and applied an end of it to his eyes. He faced Terry then, and his sobs slowed to heavy, regulated breaths. "I do not wish to talk to you now."

Terry was shaken by this reproach, and he suppressed what would have been his natural reply: "That's tough shit, pal. When there are all these fatalities on my mind I don't make appointments." No, this wasn't a slumlord in the South Bronx, some wormy leech sucking on the backs of the poor. This was a goddamn deputy mayor, and Terry reluctantly rose to his feet. "I'm sorry," he said, "but I thought under the circumstances . . ."

"Look," Lettington interrupted, "I lost my wife down there, and I don't want to talk to anyone at the moment."

"Sure, I understand, Mr. Lettington," Terry said, shifting his weight from one foot to the other, "but you know we have to have an investigation on this, and maybe you could be of some help. If you could just tell me what went on, what you saw."

Lettington again put the silk scarf to his eyes, and he said, "I don't know anything. I simply saw a flash of fire, and I left immediately through the kitchen."

"Did you notice exactly where the fire started, where it came from?" Terry felt uncomfortable, standing above him. It wasn't the right way to conduct an interview. Be at eye level always, he was taught, standing, sitting, or even lying on a beach. Looking down at a person intimidates, and intimidation should always be avoided, unless it has purpose. He did not want to intimidate the deputy mayor. But curiously, the roles had reversed. This time Terry was on the defensive.

"It was by the entrance, at the front of the club," Lettington offered. "People started running, and I was standing near the kitchen, and so I left that way."

"You said, Mr. Lettington, that you believe your wife to be among those who were lost. Do you know what happened to her? I mean, there have been no identifications yet."

Lettington suddenly stared coldly up at him, and his lips tightened as he said, "I don't know where she was at the time. I waited at the alleyway, but she never came out."

"I see," Terry replied. "I'm sorry. Is there anything else you can think of that might mean something, anything at all?"

Lettington looked away and said with quiet arrogance, "If I think of anything I will call the fire commissioner."

"Sure, thanks," Terry said, walking away. Jesus, he thought, as he stopped to light a cigarette, this guy is something.

Then Terry saw Mrs. Christiana Staravakos sitting against the back wood-paneled wall with a short, squat man of about seventy. He had admired her thousands of times on television and in newspaper photos, but now she was just a few yards away, and she was even more beautiful in person. Terry made his way through the crowd.

"Excuse me," he said as he approached her table, "I'm Marshal Ahearn from the Bureau of Fire Investigation."

The old man rose and offered Terry his hand. "Peregrine Westheim." Terry recognized the name of the chairman of the city's largest bank. "And this is Mrs. Staravakos." The woman presented her hand, and Terry held it briefly, filling himself with the moment.

He pulled over a chair from an adjacent table, sat, looked closely at her. Although her white chiffon gown was wrinkled and her careful make-up smudged, she seemed remarkably composed. "What would you like to ask me, Mr. Ahearn?" she said in a clear, whispery voice.

Terry set the clipboard at the edge of the table and folded his hands on top of it. "Would you tell me," he said, "exactly what you saw, what went on downstairs?"

Her eyes were steady as she replied. "I'm sure I won't be of very much help, for I saw little. We purposely looked for a table near the rear of the room, because we were afraid that the media might storm the opening. And we had not been sitting for long when there was a flash, an explosion. Mr. Westheim and I quickly left through the kitchen with many of the other guests."

"Yes," said the older man, "and we were knocked over as we were passing through the doors."

"It is not important, Perry," Mrs. Staravakos said.

"But it is, darling," Westheim said in gentle reprimand. "The fact that we escaped does not diminish the ungentlemanly manner in which young Lettington behaved."

"Rodney Lettington?" Terry asked.

"Yes," Westheim answered. "He left in such haste, and with such unconcern for others, that he pushed us both to the ground. Fortunately, Mrs. Staravakos never loses her composure, and it was she who helped me to my feet."

Mrs. Staravakos smiled at the older man and reached over the table to pat his hand. She turned to Terry. "I think we have told you all that we saw."

Terry stood up and thanked them. Again scanning the room, he saw a woman with her head down on a table. Her dress was torn at the shoulder, and her body was shaking. The man sitting beside her had his hand on her neck, trying to calm her.

Terry walked across the crowded, buzzing room. It was tough to conduct orderly interviews here. And he knew the guest list would be found and each person would be questioned in the days ahead. Yet, while memories were vivid, he wanted to hear what happened during the fire, how it spread, what people did, how they got out, and the woman before him looked as if she had been through more than the others in the room. He approached the table, introduced himself, and sat down.

The woman could not speak. She appeared inconsolable.

"She was pinned by another person," the man said, "and it was all I could do to pull her out. I had her hand and had just passed the kitchen doors when she was yanked down onto a pile of wriggling bodies. It was terrifying."

The man took a handkerchief from the breast pocket of his tuxedo and blew his nose. "I'm sorry," he said.

"It's all right," Terry said. "Please."

"Oh God . . . God . . ." The man began to breathe heavily, trying to hold back the tears. Finally, his body began to jerk, and the tears fell in broad wet strokes down his cheeks.

Terry waited silently for a few moments and watched as the man rubbed at his eyes with the handkerchief. The woman then lifted her head from the table and pressed it into her husband's shoulder and they cried together.

"I know it's difficult for you," Terry said, "but could you tell me what happened from the beginning?"

Holding his wife tightly against his shoulder, the man spoke quietly, just above the surrounding murmur of the room. "We were sitting toward the front of the room," he began, "watching Totti greet her guests. . . ."

Terry began scratching single words and phrases on the note pad: "explosion . . . foyer . . . not loud but voluminous . . . flames jumping . . . panic . . . ceiling on fire . . . kitchen doors . . . screaming . . . door blocked . . . wife caught, wedged . . . . thick smoke . . . agony . . . pulled wife . . . fire everywhere."

When he had finished, the man leaned over and kissed the top of his wife's head, and then he closed his eyes. "Even I ran and screamed," he whispered. "Calm is not possible in a fire like that."

He's wrong about calm, Terry thought. It *is* possible to be calm in a fire. What is not possible is to think of anything but survival. Maybe only a fireman could know that, and maybe only a fireman who had fallen through a burning roof and into a smoke-filled warehouse.

Lieutenant Sirkin entered the room and stood on a chair. In the background, Terry could see the blanket-wrapped bodies being carried through the lobby and into the temporary morgue. People were turning their heads away.

"Can I have your attention," Sirkin said. But few people stopped their nervous chattering, and Sirkin became visibly annoyed. He put two fingers into his mouth and whistled. Crude, Terry thought. Crude and unprofessional.

Terry stood at the bar, leaning on an elbow as he listened to the commander of the police department's bomb squad.

Sirkin had a scratchy voice. When he spoke it sounded as if air was being forced past a growth in the larynx. "Thanks for stickin' around," he began. The men and women, some still weeping, looked at him expectantly. "We hafta keep you here just a little while longer," he continued. "In a couple of minutes we will have a set-up in the lobby, and maybe some of you can help us to identify the deceased. It won't be easy, but we need your help, and I suggest that some of you men who knew most of the people here take a look for us. It's not a pretty sight, but it's got to be done. And, in the meantime, my men will be going around taking statements from those of you who feel up to talking. If not, we have your names and addresses, and we can arrange interviews some time in the future."

Terry walked to the end of the polished bar. He stood there a moment and watched as Sirkin stepped down from the chair and talked with two plainclothesmen. Soft, anxious murmurs again passed through the room.

Sirkin turned, and his eyes met Terry's briefly, but the police detective made no sign of acknowledgment or recognition, and he turned again with his back toward the fire marshal.

Terry walked out of the room, passed the row of bodies in the lobby of the Astor, walked out onto the street. Screw Sirkin, he was thinking, all he's good for is identifying bodies. He doesn't know the right time when it comes to finding the cause and origin of the fire. No one knows that like the fire marshals, no one really gives a shit either. Except the fire marshals.

The winter night felt cool against Terry's face. Inside the Plaza he'd been sweating. It could have been the temperature; it could have been the corpses, wrapped in blankets and tape like so many bags on a pier.

He noticed patrolmen walking through the crowd behind the barricade, asking questions, taking names. If there was an eyewitness, Terry thought, they would have found out about it by now. This wasn't Harlem, where the cops fought a neighborhood silence.

He walked to the brass railing fronting the Sophia Club and stood a moment. He wanted to clear his head before he went back down to Jose. And to the charred residue of . . . what had been the event of the season.

He was beginning to feel tired, as if the blood wasn't moving freely through his veins. He wanted to lie down for a few minutes, close his eyes. Maybe with Melissa, he thought. Yes, to press his nose into her neck and smell her hair, to move into her, to feel her life. Like last night. He had been braced up on his arms, looking down at her. Her hair was matted, and she was laughing, sighing and laughing and out of breath. He adored her for that, for the way she responded when they made love, and he wished she were next to him now so he could tell her so.

He turned and walked down the colorful tile steps. Jose was talking to a deputy chief as Terry reentered the burnt-out Sophia Club. "You think sprinklers would've saved them?" Jose asked, as Terry approached them.

"Might have, hard to say," the deputy chief answered. "There were no sprinklers at the Beverly Hills club in Kentucky or the Coconut Grove in Boston either. It would depend on how fast the fire spread, how fast the heat built up to set off the sprinkler heads. Certainly some of them would have gotten out if the sprinklers worked, but I think panic would have killed some of them anyway, by the looks of the way the bodies were piled at the exit. Christmas, you think we would have learned a lesson from fires like that one in Kentucky. Only God knows how they ever got a certificate of occupancy to open this club here."

"Well, it won't be too long before we know, too," Jose replied.

The chief fire marshal walked into the room, and the two fire marshals saluted him. Jack Burke did not return the salutes. He nodded at the deputy chief and gestured the two fire marshals toward the corner of the room.

The smoke had completely cleared. Only the stink of fire and death remained. Burke stopped before one of the few bodies that had not yet been wrapped and removed. He looked down at it, shook his head from side to side, and reached for a handkerchief. He blew his nose forcefully as he stepped around the body.

"How many?" he asked Jose.

"Forty-three," Jose replied.

"Shit," Burke said. "What the fuck is goin' on?"

Burke did not look much like a lawyer in his plum-colored double-knit suit, Terry thought, but he sounded even less like one when he spoke. It was his style to sound like a street cop who just happened to be an attorney.

"It's arson two," Jose said. "A bottle probably. There were a couple of people cut up at the door. We have to sift for glass shards yet. You can see the line of fire very clearly, beginning at the door. It looks like it traveled across a layer of silk tacked to the ceiling. The wind was being pushed in. You can still feel it at the doorway."

"Gasoline?" Burke asked.

"Undetermined," Jose answered, limping slowly toward the foyer. "Take a smell over here. It's not as strong as when we first got here, but it's still lingering."

Again they walked around the body that lay charred on the floor. Burke looked away as two firemen began to wrap a blanket around it.

At the foyer, the chief fire marshal inhaled deeply, as if he were judging a wine. He inhaled again, this time even more deeply, and then he snapped his fingers several times. "Geez," he said, finally, "it's been a long time, but it smells like a popper."

And Terry could see the lights go off in Jose's brain, and the rays shine through his eyes, and the smile come to his face.

"Popper?" he said to Burke, grinning, "where in hell did an old Irishman like you learn about poppers?"

"At college, wise guy, and yeah, even old Irishmen get to college. I happened to go to Columbia—on a scholarship—and a buddy of mine in medical school gave them to me. Snap one in half, whiff it, and, bang, you're awake for another two hours—even if the subject is math. Amyl nitrite is the proper name, for your information, although everybody says 'nitrate' these days."

Now Terry saw Jose smiling and nodding. "The Macedonian Bathhouse," he said, and then he said it again. He looked to Terry. "The fag fire—you remember . . . what'd they call that stuff we found? Uh, yeah . . . Jac-me. Sure, that's it, Jac-me." Jose sniffed. "Smelled just like what we're smelling now. It was *butyl* nitrite—got to be a first cousin to amyl, I betcha."

"Might be," Burke said. "I remember you sent a bottle of that stuff to me for analysis, but the chief of the department sent it back because there wasn't enough of it in the city to care about."

"Not enough, hell," Jose said. "There's a bottle of Jac-me in every gay closet in the city, I'll bet. This stuff's amyl or butyl—gotta be one."

"Christ," Burke said. "It's amazing what you can retain."

"It's like 'Name That Tune,'" Jose said. "The first couple of notes brings the whole song back, you know? I've been pulling a lot of specimens from everything around here, and the police lab will tell us how close we are to amyl or butyl. It's one big head start, anyway."

53 o

Burke thought a moment, his eyes closed, his thumb and forefinger wrapped across his nose. "No, listen," he said, looking up, "don't take anything to the police lab. Take it all to the FBI lab, and ask them to do it for you. If they can't, tell them to send it down to Washington. And don't say a fucking thing about butyl or amyl or anything to anyone, you understand. We have the biggest fucking case here any of us have seen, and if the cops want to storm our walls, we'll fucking well let them, you got me?"

"Gotcha," Jose said. Terry said nothing. It wasn't news that it was an important case, and it was for that reason he was unsure if the fire marshals could make an end run around the police department. He just nodded and let the chief fire marshal continue.

"As of this moment," Burke said, "I'm assigning you two to this investigation. You're off the chart, and you make your own hours, but I want an accounting of every hour spent, see? I'll give you all the support from the office you need, and even manpower when we got it. And I want you guys to remember that the case is ours, and ours alone. Just do your job, and let the cops do theirs."

"Lieutenant Sirkin and the bomb squad are upstairs now, interviewing," Terry said.

"They have jurisdiction," Burke shot out, "so do we."

"I wouldn't want to impede them," Terry said, "not on something as big as this. Jesus, forty-three homicides."

"I'm sure they won't want to impede you either," Burke replied sarcastically. "The bottom line is to arrest the prick who did this, and if you think the jurisdiction isn't properly yours, then your ass should be back on the tail end of a fire engine. This is an arson, an arson two, the setting of a fire in an occupied building. You're an arson investigator, don't forget, and it's your testimony that's gonna send this prick north when we get him. That's all that's gonna be in your mind, understand?"

Burke lowered his voice. "Look, Ahearn, this isn't interagency bickering, or rivalry, or jealousy. They want our jobs, it's as simple as that. And as long as the authority's still ours, we're gonna use it. But we'll do it our way, you know? This is an extraordinary tragedy, and no one is better trained or motivated to see justice out here than us. None of us will be able to sleep nights if we let this prick get by us. This case might get fucked up, but we're not gonna fuck it up, okay?"

O O O

It was a little after two when Terry went back to his apartment on 13th Street. As he walked, he felt the night's labor in his calf muscles, a constant discomforting pain that was beginning to move up to his knees.

He walked the one flight of steps quickly, undecided if he should knock on Melissa's door. He needed sleep, yet he also wanted to be defused, to be diverted, to clear his mind of the discotheque fire. And to forget Sirkin. It was a shitty thing to do, Terry thought, the way Sirkin moved about the fire scene collecting charred specimens like he knew what he was doing, ordering his men around, even interviewing firemen, and all the time pretending we weren't there, avoiding us completely or looking through us. He wasn't hiding the fact that he wants to box the fire marshals out of this one, that was as clear as piss on snow. Not even a touch of courtesy from him. Burke is right. We have to protect ourselves from that guy.

Melissa's stereo was on. She was probably waiting

up for him. With his own apartment key in his hand, Terry paused a moment, and then knocked on her door. As his knuckles felt the hard wood, he began to wonder what she would be wearing.

Melissa Reid opened her door. She was smiling, her teeth as white, as straight, and as perfect as brushing and orthodontia could make them; her skin clear and as silky as the silk of her dressing gown.

"Well, hello," she said. Her long blond hair fell over her right shoulder in even waves, as if she had just been brushing it. Her blue eyes gleamed even in the dim hallway light, enhanced by the blue of the dressing gown. The robe was untied, and as she turned against the wall to let him pass, it opened briefly. She closed it matter-of-factly and tied it, but not before he noticed her nakedness beneath.

Terry threw his trench coat over a side chair and sat on the delicate tan sofa, which he would always contrast with the hard, plastic-covered couch in his parents' apartment. He shrugged off the thought, and put his head back.

Melissa sat next to him, the robe falling away from her long legs, which were still tanned from New Year's in the Bahamas. "I wish you wouldn't leave your door unlocked," he said.

"Oh hell," she said, "if they can pick the downstairs lock, they can pick mine. What's the use? I may as well be prepared to surrender my TV set and my body. But I'd rather give them the set and you the body." Quickly, lightly, she kissed his neck.

"That's not funny. You don't understand," he scolded. "You're inviting trouble. This is not one of your Park Avenue and Seventy-second Street co-ops, with doormen and elevator men and closed-circuit TV."

But, Terry supposed, he was the one who didn't understand: What she was doing with him, what she was doing on West 13th Street at all? Sure, she said she wanted to be near the New School, but hell, she could come down in a cab if she wanted. And he didn't understand what he was doing with a beautiful girl from the WASP upper caste who had a Chagall print on her wall. Not a poster, but a goddamn print—she'd shown him the little number, 25/75, which indicated it was a print, and he'd been embarrassed.

"Well, you're not saying anything. Would you prefer the TV set to the body?" She kissed him again, this time on the ear. When he stayed silent, she asked, "Will you have a drink? A cup of coffee?"

"No. Thanks. I just want to relax a bit."

"I heard about it on the news."

"Yeah."

"Let's go to bed," she said softly, running her tongue down the side of his earlobe.

Terry braced. "Just like that," he said, his voice cracked with sarcasm. " 'I heard about it on the news' and 'let's go to bed.' Christ, Melissa, I don't know where you're coming from sometimes."

She shifted her body away so that she was now facing him on the couch. He looked at her. As she moved, he could see her stiffen. "Don't be angry," he said, knowing that he had reacted a little too strongly. "I just come from another planet. We're light-years apart."

"No we're not," she said fiercely. "We're sitting right here, together, and you've been through a hell of a lot—God, it must have been horrible—and I want to get you to think of someone else. I know it's your job, but you're not on the job when you're sitting here with me, on my sofa. There's only so much of yourself you can give to your job."

Now it was his turn to stiffen with anger. "You see, we *are* light-years apart. I *am* my job, it defines me. What the hell else can I say of myself?"

"That you're a man who likes certain kinds of books, music, food, plays. That you care for a certain kind of woman—a certain woman. The woman sitting here. Me."

"The more you talk," he replied, "the more the

gap widens. You were brought up to ride, and collect paintings, and go to the Bahamas on your holidays, and teach at the New School two nights a week and go to concerts and the ballet and movies—sorry, *films*—and theater and live this rich life. I was brought up to get a job and keep it. And find a woman and keep her."

"That is what I . . ."

Terry interrupted her. "Let's change the subject." He reached for her hand.

"Let's go to bed," she said. "The subject will change considerably."

Terry forced a low laugh and shook his head in consent. Maybe she's right, he thought. There was no point bringing the job here. Why did he knock on her door anyway if not to get away from the job?

They stood, Terry held her, cheek against cheek, for a long while before he pressed his lips hard on hers. Their mouths stretched open, and he began to suck gently on her tongue, letting his hands fall to her buttocks, pinching her, pulling her forcefully to him. He waited then to feel himself harden against her, but strangely, even as his hips moved slowly from side to side, he remained limp.

As they lay in bed, Terry closed his eyes and determined to concentrate on the breath that flowed against the inside of his thigh, and on the small wet chill that came each time Melissa moved her head.

But he felt no passion, no movement within himself. The concentration was not focused enough, he knew. If only he could lose the images that were filtering into his mind. The woman's hair, like burnt straw. The strange fragment stuck into her cheek and the moist pink skin beneath it leaping out like a birthmark. He felt Melissa and wanted her. He opened his eyes and watched her. Her eyes were closed, and her hand wandered over his stomach. He saw her breast move, heavy and firm, pressing against his leg. Concentrate, he told himself. God, she is a beautiful woman, more beautiful than I've ever known. Concentrate. Watch her. But it was useless. He was useless. He could not shake the pictures of the fire.

Melissa raised her eyes to him. She smiled gently, saying, "You're soft."

Terry put both arms around her. "I'm sorry, sweetheart," he said, "my mind is in another neighborhood."

"Don't be sorry," she said.

Terry reached up and turned off the lamp and they lay in the dark for a few minutes. Terry watched the light from the street seep into the room through the blind. Finally, he turned away from her, closed his eyes, and tried to sleep.

Tuesday

Terry and Jose sat at adjoining desks on the sixth floor of the department's Church Street headquarters. Both had telephones caught between their shoulders and cocked heads. It was near noon.

As he talked to an official of the American Association of Bottle Manufacturers, Terry fingered the shard of glass he had taken from the cheek of the Marchesa di Totti Gambelli. "All I can tell you," he said, "is that the raised letter could be an M, an N, or a W, and from the curvature it looks like it came from the side of a bottle at the base. In the meantime, could you send me the bottlemark identification booklet? . . . Great, thanks a lot."

He replaced the phone on its cradle, suddenly thought of his sister, Maureen. He had forgotten all about her and the conversation he had had with his mother yesterday. He would have to call her, maybe take her out to lunch some day soon, talk to her, see what was on her mind.

What the hell do college students know about life, anyway?

Terry was about to write himself a reminder when he was distracted by his partner's voice. He looked over and saw the bottle of Jac-me on Jose's desk and heard him talking to the president of the Hyfloat Chemical Company in Houston, Texas. "Look," Jose said, "there's no point talking to your lawyer about this now. I can subpoena all your records through the Texas courts if I want, but all I'm asking for is a list of your distributors here in the New York area. . . . Yeah. . . . Yeah . . . I realize there's nothing illegal about your product, but that isn't my interest here anyway. In fact, I couldn't care less. . . . Yeah. . . . Just one distributor, huh? . . . Who's that again? . . . Yeah. . . . Stamford, Connecticut, terrific, thanks, you did the right thing. . . . I know there are other manufacturers of butyl nitrite, I'm getting the same information from all of them. Thanks again."

"How ya doin'?" Terry asked, drinking from a cup of cold coffee.

Jose sat back and scatched his head. "The guy's worried about litigation, but he came around. I'll have a list of every store that sells butyl nitrite by the end of the day."

"Did the FBI say how long it will take to analyze the specimens we took?"

"It won't take too much time, as long as they know what they're looking for. If it's not butyl nitrite, they'll have to send the stuff to their Washington lab. Later today. Maybe tomorrow."

Terry carefully placed the glass shard on the desktop. "I'm learning just about all anyone needs to know about the manufacture of bottles, and going nowhere," he said. "Glass is glass is glass, at least when it comes to bottles, and the only way you can track a bottle down is by the bottle-mark that tells what company made it. It doesn't matter if it's vinegar, ketchup, pancake syrup, liquor, wine—it's all the same. Jars, too. Every bottle maker has a mark. They call it a punt mark. The punt marks are registered like cattle brands, little symbols or raised letters, usually at the bottom or base of the bottle. Sometimes a series of letters. Our problem here is we have part of just one letter, and we don't know what kind of bottle the letter comes from, or even the exact letter."

"So," Jose asked, "is it dead or is it alive?"

"Alive," Terry said, "but just barely. They're sending me a catalogue of American bottlemarks. Something might click. In the meantime, I'm going to start on the invitation list." He leaned back in his chair, shook his head, and sighed heavily. "God almighty, the idea of forty-three people dead. It's hard to accept. So many people dying so needlessly, so quickly. It's gotta be a fluke, some mad fluke. Some poor, demented prick who read about the opening in the papers and decided that rich people were responsible for his troubles. Maybe. Or radicals doing a number on the capitalists. But they would have demanded credit for it, and we have nothing but silence. It's gotta be a single madman. Christ, I hope something turns up so that we can bring this guy down".

"Well," Jose replied, again picking up the telephone, "it won't turn up unless we begin to turn over the stones, huh? It might be one maniac, but who knows? The restaurant business in New York is not so clean, and maybe this marchessa—"

"It's mar-*kay*-sa, I think," Terry said.

"Well, anyway, maybe the lady stepped on someone's toes. Not a crime family, though. If it was simply business, they would wait until the place was empty to burn it out. It could be an employee with a vendetta against one of the guests. Just take a look at the list of deceased, they're all heads of companies, big shots, and you can bet they all generated enough hate in one day's business to blow a computer fuse. It could be a jilted lover. We'll get through all the possibilities before this is over." Jose put the phone to his ear.

Terry began to search through the directory for the numbers of the guests on the invitation list. He had his hand on the telephone when it rang. It was Melissa. "How are you, Terry?"

"Fine, sweetheart. Busy."

"You were so exhausted last night."

"Yeah. I know."

"Father called me this morning, even before I read the newspapers. It's just horrible, Terry. A good friend of ours was killed in the fire last night. Father is so upset by it. But there's more than that. Mother and Father were on the invitation list, too! In fact they accepted, and decided at the last moment not to go! When he told me that this morning I almost fainted. So close, Terry, so close!"

"Thank God, sweetheart, thank God." And he meant it. But the next instant his mind was on the friend. He had a new link to the fire. "Your friend. Who was he?"

"She, Terry. Lucy Hartfield. You might know that name, she inherited the Hartfield Pharmaceutical Company."

"Yes, I've heard it. I'm sorry for her. But I'm glad for you."

"She was a wonderful woman. Oh, Terry, I hope you catch whoever did this."

"You and the rest of us here, sweetheart."

"Shall we have dinner tonight?"

"Sure. Late though, maybe nine o'clock."

The day passed quickly for Terry and Jose. They had the mandate of a special assignment and were unaffected by the routine of the Bureau of Fire Investigation. There would be no more long and tiresome fifteen-hour or twenty-four-hour tours for them for a while, as long as this thing lasted, or as long as they protected their jurisdiction from the likes of Sirkin. They'd be working straight days now, like gentlemen.

They ate lunch at their desks, dialing repeatedly, talking, making long and numbered notes, keeping a control sheet with corresponding numbers annotating each person interviewed. At five o'clock they had not learned anything significant. At five-thirty an FBI technician phoned. Terry took the call.

"I found evidence of butyl nitrite in specimen C," the technician said.

Terry shuffled papers across his desk until he found the specimen list. He brought his finger down past specimen A, which was labeled SILK AT ENTRY CEILING, and past B, CHARRED FRAME OF INTERIOR ENTRYWAY. At C was written LEATHER, LEFT SHOE, BODY NUMBER 3.

He again moved papers across his desk until he came to the body list. It had been made as the bodies were found, numbered clockwise from the club's entry and around the room. Body number 3 was listed as the Marchesa di Totti Gambelli. Bodies number 1 and 2 were Mr. and Mrs. Anthony Hennessey.

"Thanks," Terry said. He slammed the phone down and said to Jose, "Things might begin to go our way now. At least we know we're not shufflin' our time with butyl nitrite."

O   O   O

It was nearly nine o'clock, and Terry was shaving when he suddenly remembered that he hadn't called his sister. He was furious with himself. One simple family duty, he thought, and I blew it. He raced to the phone, one side of his face still covered with shaving cream, and called his parents' apartment.

"I ain't seen her," Petey Ahearn said. "I guess she must be out with the Aztec. If she don't stop all the bullshit soon she's gonna find herself out on her ass."

"Relax, Pop," Terry said.

"What relax?" his father shouted. "When my daughter is runnin' around with a guy who isn't the same color she is? What the hell is the world comin' to when I gotta put up with this in my own home? I only have her interest at heart, ya know. It's embarrassing to think of people turnin' their heads, starin' at her and this gaucho on the street or in the subway."

"Take it easy . . ." Terry tried to stop him.

"No," Petey shouted, "it's not normal, it's not like it's supposed to be. I don't want my kid martyring herself for a cause that's goin' nowhere."

"Jesus, Pop, what do you expect, when she's been listening to you talking about politics and social justice all her life?"

"Listen, kid," the old man said, "I'm not talkin' about anything social here. I'm talkin' about my family, my own goddamn daughter. It's her attitude toward me and what's good for her that I'm worried about."

"I gotta go now, Pop." It's crazy, Terry thought. *He's* crazy. Drink isn't the curse of the Irish. Family is.

Terry finished shaving, dressed, and went to knock on Melissa's door. The gloom he had been feeling for the last twenty-four hours since the Sophia fire was beginning to lift. The sight of the charred bodies lingered at the back of his mind—you didn't forget that at will. But here he was, clean and well turned out, eager to fill more of his life with this woman who had been only two months before presented to him magically as his neighbor. She was a gift, there was no doubt about that.

He kissed her cheek lightly when she opened the

door. They both went to the sofa. As Melissa sat, one side of her long, black, slitted skirt fell open. Terry playfully covered her leg with her skirt.

"Too sexy for you?" she asked, cocking her head in mock questioning.

He didn't answer. There was nothing to say. He felt a swell of desire but, strangely, it was not sexual. He just wanted to be near her, to look into her eyes, to hold her face, bring it slowly close to his and kiss it gently, again and again, to say with each kiss, "I've never known this before, and I don't want to lose it."

Yet something, he didn't know quite what, was wedged between them, keeping him from sharing his feelings with her.

The sex part of it was all right. Except for last night it was terrific. But that seemed to be all that was terrific, and sometimes it seemed to be all that she cared about. He wasn't sure, really. Sometimes when she winked at him in a restaurant or squeezed his hand in a movie he felt the obstacles removed, the distance closed. But he couldn't sustain that feeling. And he wanted to. He wanted to make it last. Yet he was so unsure.

They stared at each other briefly, uncomfortably. Melissa then stood and grabbed his hand to pull him to his feet.

"Where should we go for dinner?" he asked, more to break the silence than anything else.

Melissa came in close to him, turning her head slightly so that her mouth would press fully against his. Then she pulled her face back, smiled, and said, "Somewhere nearby."

Later, after midnight, perspiration on their bodies, they lay beside each other looking at the ceiling. With one hand Terry stroked her stomach and with the other he held a cigarette.

"Not like last night," she said, "thank goodness."

Until she said that, he'd begun to feel calm and relaxed. At first he said nothing, got up on one elbow, stubbed out the cigarette. Then he said, "You know, Melissa, sometimes I get the feeling that most of what I mean to you, I mean to you in bed. It's not a good feeling."

"That's not *true*. Why do you say it?"

"You talk about sex as if it were the most important thing between us. As if I were some sort of prize bull."

She turned angrily onto her side and stared at him. "First of all, aren't you the one who said a little while ago, 'Let's make love'? God knows I wanted to, too, but you said it, naturally, happily, just the way it should be when you're not . . . you'll hate me for this Terry, but I'll say it anyway . . . not being an Irish-Catholic prude. When I decided to sleep with you a couple of months ago, I wanted it to be part of an honest, open, equal relationship. *Part* of that is sex! Sometimes I'm not sure whether you'd rather take me to bed or put me on a pedestal. Pedestals are *out*, Terry. Bed is *in*."

To his own surprise, he didn't get angry, maybe because he knew the Irish-Catholic prude *was* part of him. "I like sex, Melissa, and when I say this maybe it's what the woman usually says, but I think it's true: it's just that sex is not enough. Maybe I'm afraid we're not sharing enough, that I'm not a big enough part of your life."

"Oh, Terry," she said, putting her hand on his cheek, "we've been seeing each other almost every day. Enjoying each other. What else is there? Should we plan a vacation together? Should you sit in on my classes at school? Go to the library and the dentist with me?" She withdrew her hand and lay back on the bed. "You tell *me*, Terry," she continued, sounding more hurt than angry. "I don't know what you want."

He looked at her, at the soft blond pubic hair, at the flare of her hips and the dramatic curve into her waist, and at her full breasts, which threw a delicate shadow at her sides. He did not know what he wanted, except that he wanted her. He put his hand on her waist, and ran it slowly up to her shoulder. "Well," he said, "you hardly ever talk to me about your family."

"There's not much to say." He noticed the tension in her voice. "There's the obligatory twice-a-week phone call, in which we politely discuss what they're doing and what I'm doing. You've been here when they've called."

"I've never heard you mention me," he said.

"They know about you, Terry. They're happy that I'm happy. And I *am* happy."

Terry felt a bit better; he did not want to be anybody's secret. He leaned over and kissed her cheek.

"Would you like to meet them, Terry?"

"Sure."

"Father first, I think," she said. "Mother is not so good about first meetings, but Father will soften her up. He'll like you, I know."

He clenched his teeth. The idea of having to soften up her mother made him feel rotten, like he was a scar across her daughter's face that might take some getting used to. But then, he thought, maybe that's just the way they do things. Maybe Melissa's mother would have to be softened up even if he were the Prince of Wales. He smiled as he remembered the words of a song his father used to sing around the house:

> *If I were the Prince of Wales, yoo hoo,*
> *I'll tell you what I would do,*
> *I'd strangle me ma*
> *And garrote me da*
> *And paddle the king's canoe.*

"Of course," Melissa continued, "Mother will like you too, she's really a loving woman, but it takes time with her."

Terry turned over on his stomach and pressed his nose against her shoulder. He closed his eyes.

After a minute or so, Melissa's whisper broke the silence. "What about *your* parents, Terry?" she asked. "Do I get to go out to Brooklyn?"

"Any time," Terry replied in a sleepy voice, brushing his lips against her skin as he spoke. "But approving *you* won't be the problem. They'll probably wonder what you see in a guy like me. Good night, sweetheart."

Terry kissed her shoulder as Melissa raised her arm to shut off the lamp. Awake, they lay for a long while in the darkness.

He was nearly asleep when she spoke. "You know what? We didn't talk at all tonight about the fire."

"Yeah, I know."

"The funeral is tomorrow. Lucy Hartfield's funeral."

Her face was close to his in the darkness. "Terry, it will be so sad. How could anyone have done such a thing?"

He slipped his arm around her waist, lay his forehead against her cheek, and fell asleep.

Wednesday

Terry and Jose sat in the chief fire marshal's office watching snowflakes melt on the window sill. The storm that had been predicted to move in from the Great Lakes had dissipated somewhere west of the Hudson, and only small, gentle reminders of winter were falling from the sky.

The two fire marshals were waiting for the chief to get off the phone. He was talking to the fire commissioner, and the most Terry and Jose could extract from his end of the conversation was that the commissioner was dominating it, leaving occasional slight pauses, time enough for the chief fire marshal to say, "Yes, sir."

Finally Burke put the phone down gently, then slammed his hand on the desk. From his desk, he grabbed a handful of letters.

"Fifty of 'em. At least. And the commissioner says he's got another batch at his office. But they'll be here soon enough, don't worry about that. Listen to this!" He dropped the letters to his desk, picked the top one. " 'Dear Commissioner, I know who set the discotheque fire. There's this crazy on our block plays forties big band music all the time, freaks out when he hears disco, says it's destroying society. He's always flicking his cigarette lighter on and off. . . .' "

Burke threw the letter to the desk. "So we got a Glenn Miller avenger with a lighter." He reached for another. " 'Dear Commissioner, it is painfully obvious the gays are trying to take over the discotheque business in this city just as they have taken over . . .' " He dropped it.

"So it's a fag plot. I've got another one here somewhere claims it's a straight plot against the fags. Another says it was all aimed at the president of a network who was at the opening. About ten more that do likewise about other stars who were there. Then we got a couple telling us about plans to kill celebs who *weren't* there. We got political letters, we got sexual letters, musical letters, disgruntled-employee letters. Name 'em, we got 'em. It's fuckin' ridiculous."

Burke laughed. "And does anybody seriously expect us to pay attention to this shit?" Then his face turned hard. "Yeah. The commissioner does. I do. *Every single letter*. Because the public will demand it. Because our jobs and our asses are on the line. Because somewhere in this shit, a pearl *may* be buried. And it may not. But you never

69 o

know unless you wade through it. So put on your hip boots, guys. Every single one has got to be followed up. And a report written. I get tired of tellin' you, and . . . I know . . . you get tired of doin' it. Go on." Burke kind of waved to them, looking discouraged.

Terry and Jose stood up, gathered the letters, started to go, when Burke added, "By the way, what are you two doin' tonight?"

"Checkin' out letters." Jose tried it, but he knew it wouldn't work.

"Can't check out letters at night," Burke replied wearily, as if he hated to do it to them.

Both men knew what was coming. "Ahh, c'mon, Chief," Jose said, "I'm supposed to take my daughters roller skating."

"I'm going out to see my folks," Terry added.

"Listen," Burke said, "I'm sorry. Callahan is out sick, and Victrioni had court time coming to him, and I have no one to cover the Manhattan car tonight. It's ordered. Do a six-to-two tour and you can work on your own stuff here in the office. I just need the manpower."

"This fuckin' city," Jose said.

Terry just shrugged. He knew Burke had no choice. Seven fire marshals had retired since the economic crunch began, and not one man had been hired to replace them. And the city was burning down.

He tried to keep his mouth shut, but on the way out he had to turn and say something. "Can you tell me what this goddamn city thinks is important? Tell me, will you?"

Burke just waved a hand at him, as if to say, Don't waste your breath.

On their way to the elevator, Terry said to his partner, "Over a hundred lousy freak-show letters. My God!"

"And more coming in every day," Jose replied. "And maybe over two hundred names on the invitation list. And dozens and dozens more names that the people on the list—those that are willing to go slumming and talk to us—will give us as friends, or enemies, of the guests. And maybe a couple of dozen places in the city that sell the fag's best friend, Jac-me. And we gotta check them all."

Terry laughed. "Why can't we have a fire that gets us five letters and three names on the guest list and two places that sell Jac-me? Why can't we get lucky?"

"C'mon, pal," Jose said, "don't be a pessimist. You gotta *want* the letters, you gotta *want* the names, because the more there are, the better your chance of finding the right one, finding the pearl in the shit."

Terry pushed the elevator button. "Shit," he repeated. "How come it doesn't bother you, Jose? How come you want the drudgery, how come you're not rooting for a dung pile of luck?"

"In *el barrio*," he replied, "you learn not to hope for luck, you learn to spend only the money in your pocket. And for us names, and letters, are money in the pocket." The elevator arrived, they stepped in. "Let's stop at Fire Prevention," Jose said, "see if they got some money for our pockets."

As the elevator doors on the fourth floor opened, Terry and Jose saw boxes and crates piled in the hallway. They had to edge by them to get to the office of the chief in charge of the Bureau of Fire Prevention.

A handsome, gray-haired man stood behind a paper-strewn desk. He was throwing single sheets of paper into an open carton by his side. He did not greet the two fire marshals. "After twenty-two years," he said gruffly, "they're moving me out to the Municipal Building in Brooklyn, can you imagine, taking fire prevention out of headquarters so they can rent the space to the Water Supply

Commission. The goddamn budget is bleeding all of us dry. I suppose you want to know how the Sophia got the certificate of occupancy?"

"Just curious," Jose replied.

"It's all informal, if you get my meaning. There's nothing down on paper. It turns out the building commissioner himself got a call from a guy named Lettington at the mayor's office. I don't know what the hell he is, a deputy mayor or something, a lot of clout anyhow."

Terry raised his eyebrows. "I talked to him after the fire, remember," he said to Jose. "He was pretty prickly."

"Who's going to take the fall?" Jose asked.

"No fall," the chief said, picking up a handful of memos. "The variance was given legally for the kitchen exit, and the sprinkler system was working. I don't think we'll ever find out who turned it off, maybe even the duchess herself."

"The Marchesa," Terry said.

"Yeah, so?" the chief replied.

"What are you going to do about it?" Jose asked.

"Listen," the chief replied, "you don't put Band-aids on a dead man. The thing is ex post facto, if you get me."

"I don't think the sprinklers were ever tested, Chief," Terry said.

"The report says they were operational," the chief answered. "What can I tell you?"

"You could give it to the Bureau of Investigation," Terry said, leaning against the doorframe.

"Listen," the chief said, "I'm going to Brooklyn. There are worse places. If I took it out of the department, I could wind up on the ass end of Staten Island, ferry boat and all. It's ex post facto as far as this office is concerned."

Terry walked out of the office, and Jose followed him. Edging through the box-filled corridor, Terry said, " 'Informal,' that's beautiful. The trouble with informal is that it doesn't stand up under oath. Either you know something or you don't, either you perjure yourself or you don't. What do you think we should do?"

"Nothing," Jose said.

"Nothing? This prick uses his influence like that and we do nothing?"

"Lettington isn't going anywhere," Jose said as he pushed the elevator button. "And don't forget, Lettington didn't *start* the fire. Somewhere in this city there is a creep who *did* start it, and *he* may be going somewhere." Jose stared at Terry. "He may even be going to start another fire. So let's do first things first, and like the chief marshal says, let's put on our hip boots and go to work on those letters. Because if we're real good boys tonight, we have the honor of a six-to-two."

"And if we're real bad boys?" Terry asked.

"Well, then, tonight we have the honor of a six-to-two." Both men laughed.

They spent the rest of the day checking letters, and when it was over, Terry could see why they needed the boots. Shit, nothing but shit. It wasn't until the quiet of the overtime tour that Terry could open the *Times* to the page that listed short biographies of the victims of the Sophia fire. He began to read aloud: " 'Giovanna, Marchesa di Totti Gambelli, fifty, was born in Cerveteri, Italy, where the Gambelli family had an estate of seventeen thousand acres and a castle. Never married, the Marchesa left Italy in 1977, after her brother had been kidnapped and murdered by Italian terrorists, and moved to France where she opened a discotheque called Mirage. As the club became successful among jet-setters, the Marchesa became an international celebrity in her own right. . . .' "

"All right, all right," Jose called across his desk, "I read it already."

"Hey, Jose," Terry said, putting his feet up on a chair and lighting a cigarette, "what do you think people find so interesting about discos, I mean other than there are a lot of men and women throwing themselves around?"

"Ya got me, I never been to one."

"I've been to small local ones, downtown and in Brooklyn, but I've never been to Orpheus and places like that. You know, where all the celebrities go. Why don't we go over there some night and see what the attraction is? Maybe see what all these victims died for."

"You suppose they let spics in?" Jose asked, smiling.

"I can prove I'm Irish, so I'll vouch for you."

"Well, just for that show of brotherhood, the spic is gonna get the mick a cup of coffee." Jose got up from his desk and walked to the coffee machine, limping like an old alley cat who'd been in a fight.

Terry watched him, going down easily on one leg and hard on the other. Jose hadn't limped when they first met, but right away he'd used the word *spic*.

They were introduced at the old department head-quarters in the Municipal Building overlooking the Brooklyn Bridge. It was Terry's first day on the job, and Jose said little to him until they got into the car on lower Broadway. It was before marshals were given unmarked cars, and Terry remembered feeling a little like a fire chief as he slipped into the red sedan with the dome light.

"You think the name is funny?" Jose asked.

"What name?" Terry responded, not knowing anything about the man next to him except that he was one of the more experienced marshals in the bureau.

"Jose Gillespie," Jose said. "Don't you think that's funny?"

"No," Terry said, "why should I? Maybe unusual, not funny."

"It's *funny*," Jose said, "and you know it. So lesson number one is don't bullshit your partner, ever. My father is Irish, my mother is Puerto Rican. I look like my mother. I think like her, too. Paranoid, you know what I mean? *You* can call *me* a spic if you want to, because I'm your partner now, and you can call me anything you want. But only you. And only me. All right?"

"Can I call you Jose?" Terry asked.

Jose laughed and put his hand out, palm up. Terry slapped it.

The phone rang and Jose picked it up as he walked back from the coffee machine, listened, and hung up.

"Captain Scalvone wants us to give him a hand in the Bronx for a little while. Most of the strike force is on surveillance tonight, and he got a report about a man with a gun throwing Molotov cocktails on Eagle Avenue. He needs the backup, and he asked us to meet him on One hundred fifty-sixth Street and Eagle."

"You tell him it's our pleasure?"

"Yeah," Jose said, "I told him that stabilizing neighborhoods was worthy of our participation. He said, 'Stop the horseshit.'"

"What time is it?" Terry asked.

"Nine-thirty."

"Christ, the night's falling away. We haven't had a meal since lunch."

Walking out behind Jose, Terry said, "If you love your job enough, you don't have to eat."

"Save a lot of dough that way," Jose replied.

O O O

They drove through the barren canyons of the South Bronx. Behind each open windowframe, Terry could not help thinking, lay the burnt-out, unfulfilled dreams of the city's poor. Once alive and moving with the hum of people, the streets—Kelly and Tiffany and Fox and the rest —were left by the politicians to die a slow death, because the costs of helping were great, and because the votes there were marginal and unpredictable. And the streets died, as the people died, of joblessness, of indifferent, even illiterate schoolteachers, of corrupted community leaders, of roaches and rats, of broken pipes and overinsured landlords, of poverty, and of fires, always the fires, the final muffling of the gasps of survival.

If certain neighborhoods of the Bronx were dead, others were still clinging to life with bloodless fingertips. The Eagle Avenue area was one of these, Terry thought, as they pulled into the block.

Captain Scalvone, a small, broad-chested man, entered the large H-type building, followed by Jose and Terry and two strike-force marshals. As obvious as billboards, the latter two wore bright red baseball caps as a matter of department policy, to give high-visibility protection against arsonists.

They walked up one flight and on the landing they saw a small soda bottle on the floor in front of a slightly charred door. The bottle was filled with a pinkish liquid that smelled like gasoline. Captain Scalvone held the bottle by the end of its neck, and he pulled a partially burnt paper roll from the opening. He spilled a little of the liquid on the floor and held a match to it. It flared up, and then extinguished itself as the heat consumed the last droplet. He turned to one of the men in the red baseball caps, said, "Make a note that the liquid appears to be gasoline and, after testing, it is concluded that the liquid is highly flammable." He leaned down to feel if there was any heat where the flame had burned the door paint. He continued, "Note also that there is charring on the apartment door at bottle level."

Terry knocked on the painted tin. The door was opened by a young, model-thin woman in a T-shirt and short black skirt. She held a can of beer in her hand.

"You the police?"

"We are the fire marshals," the captain said as the man in the red baseball cap picked up the bottle.

The woman's eyes widened as she saw it. She cried out, "You found another one?"

Leaving the door open, she ran into the apartment, yelling, "Goddamn it, damn it, damn it, they found another one in the hallway." The woman began to cry, large tears falling from large brown eyes, luminous and sad, the kind of eyes that might inspire a painting. The men followed her into the apartment. Terry slipped a chair behind her. As she sat, the can of beer fell to the floor. She put her face in her hands.

A window was open behind her, and dark curtains, with large red hearts appliquéd at random, swung up, blown by the winter wind. On the floor in front of the window Terry noticed another small soda bottle filled with pinkish fluid, its paper wick only slightly singed, probably blown out by the wind.

Terry and Captain Scalvone knelt by it; the woman turned to them. "That's the one he threw in here about an hour ago. My daughter saw him throw it. Her name is Virginia, she's only eleven, she saw him throw it. It was Herbert, the *mother* . . . you know what he is. My daughter saw him. He's a bootlegger, you know, and my old man takes credit from him, owes him some money, and today he put a gun to my old man's head and scared his shit right out. Well, my old man, he works for the Mafia, you know, and he don't take that shit, so him and his friends took the gun from Herbert, you know, and beat on him good. And now this Herbert is gettin' even with me and my kids for what my man did. It's real bad shit, man, you know?"

She was an attractive, even appealing woman, and Terry was moved by her, the situation she was in, and the rat den she called home.

The room had a makeshift doorway to the adjoining apartment, a hole hammered through eight inches of brick, and what served as a doorframe was jagged brick as rough as saw teeth. The adjoining apartment had evidently been confiscated by the unwritten rules of squatters' rights, and its front door had been nailed shut. Terry walked through the hole in the wall and saw a man with a vacant face sitting on a torn couch, staring out at the emptiness of the room, listening to Motown music coming from a portable phonograph.

"Do you know Herbert?" Terry asked.

The man did not look up, but continued staring at nothing. He was not, as many in the South Bronx were, desperately poor; his clothes, a black leather jacket, sharkskin trousers, and gleaming new wing-tip shoes, were expensive. He held an open bottle of beer in his hand, but it was still full to the neck.

The man seemed mesmerized, and Terry again asked if he knew Herbert.

Still without turning his head, the man sang more than spoke. "Shee-it, Ah dumped him t'day, this here Herbit. Took his gun an' everythin'. Shoulda hit 'im, hit 'im with his own gun." The man then paused for a long moment, and continued, "Shee-it, Ah works for the Mafia."

"Where's the gun now?" Terry asked. The man did not respond, and Terry asked the question again.

"The Eyetalian gots it," the man mumbled.

"What's his name?" Terry asked, twice.

"They cut my tongue," the man said, "if I tol' you that."

"What's your name?"

"Peter."

"Where do you work, Peter?"

"Hunt's Point junkyard." The man continued staring directly ahead.

"Is your boss the Italian?"

"Shee-it, no, he a Jew."

"Who's the Italian?"

"Man, you unnerstan'? They cut my tongue."

Captain Scalvone walked through the broken brick doorway, commenting to no one in particular, "Well, that's one way to get a bigger apartment." He was followed by Jose and the two men in red baseball caps, one of whom was carrying the two firebombs.

"What's his story?" the captain asked Terry. Terry told him.

The captain looked at his watch and then spoke to his group of fire marshals. "I've got to go to Bushwick yet, and it's already near midnight. Here's what we'll do." He pointed to one of the men in the red caps and continued, "This is your case. Jose and Terry will back you up. Take the little girl who can spot this Herbert character, and stake out somewhere across the street. Give him till two o'clock, and if he don't show, we'll try to get the cops to front the place till the morning."

Terry was about to tell the captain that if something more important broke he and Jose would have to take it in. But he thought better of it; the captain obviously had enough manpower problems already.

The fire marshals took Virginia to the building across the street which, like most of the neighborhood's buildings, had several vacant apartments.

The little girl, wearing a heavy oversized coat, took her place at an open window that faced the street and, with Jose standing next to her, began watching. At eleven, she knew only that her neighbor was trying to kill her, and it was her job to point him out to the Man.

Terry and the other two fire marshals sat on the hall steps talking of fires and of arrests they had made. All

around them were the familiar sounds of tenement hall-
ways, the pervasive rock music and laughter, the smells of
cooked pork and wine and urine.

A young man walked up the steps, and the fire
marshals made space for him to pass by. He looked affable,
smiled when he saw the three men before him.

"Hey," he said, "you guys cops?"

Terry answered hastily, "No. Fire marshals."

"Oh yeah, I seen you guys around, like you was
lookin' for a second base to play on."

One of the marshals lifted his red cap and pushed
it back on his head, saying, "That's the point, for you to
see us."

"Yeah, hey, can't you do something about this
building here, and stop the fires? Hey, I'll tell you something. I'm not afraid of bullets, and I'm not afraid of
knives, you know, but fire is something else, man, you can't
fight back, you know?"

"Well, I'll tell you," the marshal said, "we're doing
the best we can, but we need the help of you people, too.
You a member of the Devil's Rebels?"

"Hey, wait a minute, man, I'm twenty-seven years
old."

The marshal laughed. "Well, you're in great shape,
keeping your youth."

"The Devil's Rebels is my brother's gang. He's
doing two-and-a-half to five for them now. Hey, I even did
eight months for them, you know. When the cop came to
pick my brother up he got snotty, you know. So I rapped
him, and for that they give me a broken arm and eight
months on Rikers. No hard feelin's, though. Hey, it was
worth it." The young man did a little dance in the hallway.

"Well," the marshal asked, "do you know anything about who's making the fires around here?"

"No, man, I wish I did."

"Well," the marshal said, pulling a card from his

shirt pocket and handing it to the young man, "if you hear anything, let us know. Call this number. It might save somebody's life, somebody in the community."

"Hey," the young man replied, while pocketing the card and continuing up the stairs, "like I say, man, fire is something else."

The phrase "like I say" hit Terry. His father used it often; he'd used it in the only serious argument the two had ever had. They'd been to an off-Broadway play, and afterward had a few beers in a bar on Sheridan Square. The "few" beers turned into many. As always, the talk was politics; even breakfast talk at the Ahearns' was politics.

After an hour the old man had pulled a second ten-dollar bill from his pocket. "Like I say, when Petey Ahearn is nigger rich everyone gets a drink."

Terry was just drunk enough to challenge his father. What the hell, he thought, he'd been in the Army, he was earning his own freight at the docks, and he was waiting to get called up for the fire department. He was old enough now, damn it!

"How come you use the term *nigger*, Pop?" Terry asked, after drinking a half mug in one raising.

"Why not?" his father replied matter-of-factly. The bar was crowded, and the Ahearns were pressed into a corner, sitting on high stools with no backs.

"Jesus, isn't it obvious? I mean, you're always talking about the oppression of the workers and the in-equalities in the economic system, but when you're talking about the workers you're really talking about the poor, right?"

"Sometimes, yeah, but you couldn't call the steam-fitters poor, could you, or the electricians, or any of the construction trades for that matter, yet the bottom line reads that they're still gettin' screwed. Look at the prop-erty owner, he's gonna get an income from a building for fifty, maybe seventy years, but the most the workers are gonna get is a day's wage, and he's got thirty or forty years' wages to work for. His kids will be cashin' in his policies when the property owner's kids are still earnin' income off his ass, his investment that's left in inheritance."

"Yeah, okay, Pop," Terry said, "but don't jerk me around now, 'cause when you talk today about the oppressed in America, you gotta be talking about the blacks, right?"

"Whadya mean, jerk you around?" the old man said, putting a hand on Terry's arm. "I never jerk you around. You're my kid. But it's no fuckin' news that the niggers are oppressed. So's the wetbacks in California, the dumb fuckin' migrant workers down south, and the seventy-five percent of the workers in America that ain't organized. You're not gonna win no fuckin' Pulitzer prize with questions like that."

"There, you see, Pop? I think you are jerking me around when you talk about oppressed people and then toss around words like *nigger* and *wetback*."

The old man threw his head to one side, scrutinizing his son. "You gotta be kiddin' me," he said. "If you think callin' a man a nigger is oppressing him then you don't know nothing about the world. You go take a walk through all those men's clubs in the side streets off Park Avenue and Fifth Avenue, you won't hear none of them pricks ever use the word *nigger*, but none of them would ever invite a nigger in for a meal, or give them a fair shake either. Them's the oppressors, and don't you forget it. Like I say, it's not the words that come outta a man's mouth that means a shit, but what he does."

"I'll tell you, Pop," Terry said, signaling the bartender for refills, "I think that's bullshit. I think it's what a man says *and* what he does. Maybe in the thirties it was all right to *nigger* this and *nigger* that, but not today, Pop."

The old man stiffened. "You think it's bullshit, huh? You got a lot to learn, kid. You've had things too fuckin' easy, and don't give me no crap about Vietnam. You don't know nothin'."

Terry got off his stool, threw a dollar tip on the bar. "That's it, Pop, I'm leaving. Going home. You can't talk reasonably, and I'm not going to sit here and just take it."

The vessels in the old man's strong neck began to strain, and he hardly moved his lips as he replied, "Like I say, kid, you don't know a fuckin' thing. The poor niggers is like a cannonball aimed at the U.S. of A. But your sympathy ain't gonna give 'em jobs and education and decent apartments any better than the self-righteous men of manna in the fancy clubs uptown." Terry started walking out, but his father's words followed him out to the street, "Like I say, you remember it."

Jose ran into the hallway, startling Terry. "Okay, okay!" he said. "He's here. He's stopped in front of the building, talking to some dude. Put the red caps in your pockets, we'll casual him. Just two of us."

The child ran up behind them. "Can I go now?" she asked.

"You stay right here, Virginia," Jose said, "until we come back for you. Stay put, right?"

The little girl took in a chestful of the dark hallway air and sighed. "I'm just tired," she said.

The fire marshals decided that since Jose and one of the strike-force marshals looked like part of the neighborhood and spoke Spanish, they would go down and take the man.

The street was dotted with windblown garbage and the slush of the disappearing snowfall. Jose limped along quickly, speaking the high, animated tones of street Spanish, and gesturing energetically. He was talking about *cuchifritos*, how no one could make them like his mother, because no one else knew how to age the bananas in the right way. They moved between parked cars to the far sidewalk and down past the little girl's building, saw the two men just ahead, the one identified as Herbert wearing a blue beret. Jose kept chattering about *cuchifritos*, being as casual as he could until they were about to pass Herbert. Then, suddenly, Jose stopped short and lunged at him, pushed him across the hood of a parked car. The other marshal drew his revolver and yelled, "We're fire marshals. Now, take it easy."

Herbert cried out, "Don't hit me, man. I'm not goin' anywheres."

The other man put his hands up. "I was just talkin' to the man, officer, just talkin', and I did nothin' wrong, officer, honest, talkin', man, tha's all."

"Well then, get lost, brother," the strike-force marshal said, gesturing with his revolver. Hands over his head, the man sprinted around the corner of Eagle Avenue.

Soon all four fire marshals were around Herbert. After searching him, Terry said, "You were seen throwing a firebomb through the window of apartment 2E of *that* building." Terry pointed to it. "You're in a lot of trouble."

On his feet and trembling, Herbert said, "Man, that nigger owes me thirty-four dollars and he don't wanna pay me my money. What am I supposed to do, man, how else I'm gonna get my money?"

"You don't have to say anything, Herbert," Terry said. "We got you anyway."

The strike-force marshals put their red baseball caps back on their heads. One of them informed Herbert that he was under arrest and from a plastic-covered card began reading the rights of an arrested person.

As the strike-force marshals began walking Herbert to his building, where they would gather the evidence and take statements, Terry called out, "We'll take off now, guys. See you around, huh? And make sure Herbert understands how close he came to a homicide rap."

"Yeah," a voice came back, "thanks for the help."

Terry and Jose sat in the tired Ford sedan. As he turned the ignition key, Jose said, "It's late, we have an hour to knock off. To the office or should we take a meal break?"

"To the office," Terry replied. "Guys who love their work don't need food, remember?"

The car was speeding toward the Grand Concourse when Jose put his foot on the brake and slammed his left hand down on the chrome handle. They had not gone more than two blocks.

"The little girl," Jose said, "Virginia. We forgot her, we left her in the hallway."

Jose made a U-turn at the next corner and returned to Eagle Avenue. Both men went into the surveillance building, and when they reached the second floor they saw the young girl, her oversized coat pulled up over her ears, with her head against the grimy hallway wall, sleeping soundly.

"She's dead out," Jose said, leaning over her.

"Yeah," Terry said, moving in quickly to pick her up. He knew Jose would have trouble making the stairs with the girl in his arms.

Her eyes opened momentarily, and then her head fell into the warmth of Terry's neck.

"It's a hell of a place for this kid, huh?" Jose said, opening the vestibule door.

"Yeah," said Terry, as they walked across the filthy street. He looked at the child's worn, grimy face, shabby clothes. Then he thought of Melissa's clear, carefully tended skin, her shiny blond hair, her perfect teeth. "It's tough," he continued, "to go through this world when you start out on a street like this, where your goddamn neighbor is trying to burn you out."

Thursday

Late the following afternoon, walking through the tiled lobby of department headquarters, Terry heard footsteps behind him. He knew who it was without turning around. Joe Blanton, the department's press assistant, was the only person he knew who wore metal taps that covered half his shoe heels.

Terry pressed the elevator button just as the footsteps slowed and then stopped at his side. Blanton, a heavy black man, a political appointee, smiled casually.

"Hello, Terry," he said in an accent that bordered on Ivy League. "How're you making out on the Astor fire?"

Blanton was a minor department official outside of the uniformed force, and so Terry evaded the question. "I forget what progress means," he said. The press assistant would receive only as much information as the chief fire marshal wanted him to have, as far as Terry was concerned.

"I can dig that," Blanton said, pushing the large Windsor knot of his tie tight around his collar. "It's not a good day for me either."

"What's going on?" Terry asked indifferently.

"Fifty calls a day," Blanton answered, in a way that Terry thought was self important. "Every reporter in the city wants to break the story about the Astor fire, if it ever breaks. They call the mayor's task force, but this Sirkin guy puts them all off and then they call me. I got enough trouble with the daily fatal fires and the ghetto arsons, but they don't want to write about that. Uh-uh. Six black people burnt to death by a landlord in Harlem isn't news any more."

"I know what you mean. It's a crazy city, huh?" Terry managed a smile, then thought of the only definition of New York City he had ever heard that made sense: his father's. One night they were watching a television news report of a graffiti contest sponsored by the Department of Social Services. The city was as smeared and as ugly as a tattooed man, and here was this official graffiti contest on television! The old man sipped a can of beer as he quietly watched a horde of teenagers swirl felt-tip markers over specially built billboards set up in Central Park. When the winner of the contest was being presented with a one-year scholarship to an art school, Petey Ahearn just shook his head sadly and said, "New York is a riot."

Blanton was laughing as the elevator doors opened. "Gets stranger every day," he said. "You know my man Mike McDougal?"

Terry walked into the elevator and pressed the button for the seventh floor. "The one who writes the column in the *Daily Post*?"

Blanton nodded and pushed the button for sixteen, the commissioner's floor. "He got two fingers broken last night. Some hoods pushed him into a car and drove him two blocks. A finger each block. They told him next time they're going to drive him twenty blocks and go through his toes until they get to his legs."

"Christ," Terry said. "How come?"

"He told me he was scratching close to something in a real estate empire, but that's all he would say."

The elevator stopped at seven and Terry pressed his hand against the rubber safety mechanism to keep the doors from closing. "When you break people's balls the way McDougal does," he said, "I suppose you have to expect to take the heat."

The doors began to move as Terry removed his hand, but he shot his foot forward between them as he heard the press assistant say, "Yeah, look at the number he was doing on Lettington, that deputy mayor."

The doors sprung open again.

"What's that, Joe?" Terry exclaimed. "*Rodney* Lettington?"

"Yeah. McDougal ran three columns about him. Said Lettington knows as much about economic development as the pope knows about bordellos in Borneo, and that he got his job through the buy-a-friend pages in the *New York Times*. That's *chutzpah*, man, to write things like that."

As the elevator doors snapped shut, Terry chuckled and shook his head. It *is* a crazy city, he thought. Where else would a black speak Yiddish?

So here was Lettington again. Terry wondered what McDougal had on him that he couldn't print. Every reporter knew more about politicians than he could print. Guys like Lettington destroy a city, he thought, not crime and ghettos and garbage in the streets.

Terry sat at his desk twirling a pencil around his fingers. Maybe Jose was wrong. Maybe they *should* just get it out in the open that Lettington pressed for the certificate of occupancy for the Sophia. Maybe it *was* all legal but . . . Christ. The pencil snapped in Terry's hands, and he threw the pieces into a wastebasket.

Even if he went to the Bureau of Fire Investigation and laid it on the table, they'd simply look into the records. And, as the chief said, it was all legal. Questionable judgment maybe, but that didn't cut any cake in the City of New York. It was common knowledge that a certain judge sold work permits to illegal aliens, and that half the highway department inspectors sent their vacation bills to the gas and electric company. Confessed criminals still held their seats on the City Council. Would anyone get excited over a deputy mayor strong-arming the building commissioner for a certificate of occupancy? Even if forty-three people died?

Anyway, all anyone was interested in was who threw the bomb. And Lettington didn't throw it. There could be no doubt about that.

Terry got up, put on his trench coat, and left the office. At the corner of Church Street he bought the final edition of the *Daily Post* and began to walk toward the subway. Goddamn it, he thought, Lettington will probably never be touched. As the old man says, it's hard to screw the bosses. Yeah. But he also says it's not impossible. You can always drive a fork lift over them. That's what we need, Terry thought, a fork lift. Someone who's got that kind of strength. . . . Mike McDougal? Shit, why not?

He turned and went back to Church Street, to the corner Longchamps restaurant. Inside he opened the paper to McDougal's column, "The Concrete City." He quickly read today's story, about a teenage girl who was gang-raped in a Brooklyn social club on her confirmation day. It was a tear-jerker. If McDougal wasn't writing about corruption, Terry thought, he was pulling water from your eyes.

He went to the phone, dialed the number at the bottom of the masthead, and asked for the reporter.

"Yeah, McDougal." The voice sounded as if it was coming out of a mouth stuffed with landfill.

"Mr. McDougal," Terry began, "this is Fire Marshal Ahearn from the fire department. Listen, I think I got a story for you, if you can find the time to meet me somewhere."

"Mike," came the reply. "The name's Mike. What comes before Ahearn?"

"Terry."

"You wouldn't waste my fuckin' time, Ahearn?"

"Listen, I wouldn't call you if I thought I was wasting mine. It's about Deputy Mayor Lettington."

"Yeah, yeah, all right. You know the Grotto?"

"In Little Italy?"

"Yeah, yeah, meet me there in half an hour, but ya can't stay long 'cause I'm meetin' friends for pasta. Deal?"

"Listen, I just want ten minutes. I got friends too."

The restaurant was in the basement of a turn-of-the-century tenement on Mott Street. The walls were large pieces of polyurethane foam made to look like irregular Italian stonework. Thinking of the Sophia, Terry searched for the second exit. He saw it, a door at the rear of the room, and noticed that the exit sign was unlighted.

The room was crowded, although it was still early evening. Terry sat at the small corner bar to wait for McDougal. He opened the newspaper to study the reporter's photograph at the head of his column. It was a fuzzy picture, and Terry checked it against each male face in the restaurant. The Grotto was known to be a haunt of criminals and politicians, one of the few places in town where they could come together without much notice.

Sitting on the hard bar stool, he wondered what kind of guy this character was. He had asked for Terry's first name and then called him by his last. That was a snotty thing to do. Terry knew only that McDougal was read by the city politicians the way those in Washington read the editorials in the *Times*, and that he had a way of wailing against dog shit in the streets, graft in the City Council, rape, and murder with the same level of energy.

The old man liked McDougal, and Terry smiled as he remembered one of the reporter's columns that blasted the cardinal himself for being too pious. "Fuckin' right," the old man had commented.

Yes, Terry thought, McDougal had no sacred cows that Terry knew of, and the mayor would be hard pressed to cover for Lettington if McDougal wanted to do a number on him.

A curly-haired man appeared at the entrance. Tall and well-built, he was wearing a tailored gray woolen suit, with a black-and-white polka-dot tie and matching handkerchief, and a fur coat over his right arm. The man walked to the bar and took the stool next to Terry's. "How ya doin', Guido?" he asked the bartender. "How's the grape crop?"

His face was contorted when he spoke, and his lips pushed so far to one side that his nose shifted. Terry knew lots of people who spoke out of the side of their mouths, but he thought this was too deliberate a pose, an affectation.

The man did not wait for a reply from the bartender. Instead, he leaned toward Terry. "You Ahearn?"

Terry introduced himself, discreetly flashing his badge.

They moved to a table for four in the middle of the room and began to talk. McDougal kept his left hand in his jacket pocket. Terry wondered if he should make reference to the broken fingers, but quickly decided that it was none of his business.

There was no room for small talk; Terry related directly what he knew about Lettington, speaking first of the variance that permitted a second exit through the basement kitchen, and then of the certificate of occupancy that had been issued even though the sprinkler system had not been tested.

McDougal kept saying, "Yeah, yeah," each time Terry paused, as if he were in a Baptist congregation responding to a sermon.

"I think it's pretty sure," Terry concluded, "that these forty-three people would've been wet instead of dead if the sprinklers were working, if Lettington had kept his hands out of it."

"Yeah, if it wasn't him it would be somebody else," McDougal said. "You think they were turned off because of the ceiling? What's that about?"

He was cynical, Terry thought, but interested.

"New plaster, with oil paintings all over it," Terry replied. "It seems the Marchesa didn't want to risk having one of the sprinkler heads blow open accidentally and ruin the pictures. They weren't even finished yet; that's why she had silk hanging down from the ceiling to cover them. The oil paint, too, probably contributed to the quick spread of the fire."

McDougal laughed. "Art ahead of people, that's the history of royalty. It's a fuckin' shame, but it's like pigeon shit. It exists. You read my colunm on the fire?"

"Yes," Terry replied laconically. Actually he'd thought the column was irrelevant. McDougal had compared the victims with the Romans of Nero's time, listless and pleasure-seeking, a bad rap for forty-three people who'd died in the fire.

"Then you know," McDougal went on, "that I think there are greater tragedies in this city every day than that fire." He took his left hand from his pocket and put it on the table. The middle and ring fingers were wrapped in a hard plastic splint that was taped to his wrist. "I go after the real tragedies," he continued, "and I pay the dues."

"How'd that happen?" Terry figured he'd better ask, even though he knew.

"Well, I tap a lot of open nerve endings, so I'm not sure which these fingers are paying for," McDougal answered. "Did you read my columns about all the insurance money for those abandoned buildings torched out in Brownsville?"

Terry hadn't read them, he admitted reluctantly. "I usually read the *Times* in the morning; often I don't have time to read your paper in the afternoon."

"Yeah," McDougal replied, "well, you can't learn anything about the city in the *Times*. They only report the indictments after everyone else takes the heat." McDougal looked down at his fingers. "I did a story about Lloyds of London insuring eight buildings, abandoned buildings, out there. They laid the insurance off on a state-owned insurance company in South America, more than a million dollars worth, and then all eight buildings burned the same night."

"I remember the fire," Terry said. "It was a five-alarm; I wasn't working that night."

"Don't matter. I can't tell you what the country is," McDougal said, "but I learned that the insurance payoff is gonna lead to a fuckin' revolution down there. They were taken bad and they're pissed."

McDougal put a cigarette in his mouth, and as he struck a match his bandaged fingers stuck up in the victory sign.

"Anyway," he continued, "I want to write more about it, but I'm stuck. So you called me for help. That's fine, yeah, but the street goes two ways, right? These buildings are owned by the S and L Realty Corporation, I found out, with a post-office-box address."

"It figures," Terry said, waiting to see what he wanted.

"I know you guys can find the principals for a corporation if you call Albany, right?"

Christ, Terry thought, he wants me to dog for him. He could do that himself with the Freedom of Information Act. All he has to do is make an application, but he must know that.

"Albany could only tell you names," Terry said. "But if it's a dummy corporation, you'll find the principal is a little old lady on Social Security in Staten Island. And if it's an insurance scheme, you can bet your mother it's a dummy."

"My mother died a long time ago."

"Oh," Terry said, "sorry to hear that."

"Yeah, well how would you do it?"

That's it, Terry thought, he wants to use my badge. He knows that corporation records tell you very little, probably searched them already. Damn. I can't use my badge and go dogging for a reporter.

"If it's a post-office box," Terry said, keeping his

voice friendly, "I'd go to the post office and pull the card."

"I can't do that," McDougal replied quickly.

"I know," Terry said, thinking that a badge would get him in there easily enough. "But anyway, that would give you a name and address—a cousin, probably to the little old lady in Staten Island. So I'd go to the Department of Real Estate in Brooklyn and search the records in the registrar's office—building permits, mortgage transactions, liens, that kind of thing. I'd copy down all the names, the lawyers, brokers, bank officials, and make a chart. I'd search the fire records for that neighborhood. These guys like to operate in one neighborhood, consolidate their properties."

"How come?" McDougal asked, writing on a small pad.

"They can keep the insurance value up that way, at least on paper. So, I'd look at those fires and search those building records and put those names down on a chart. Sooner or later I'm going to find one name that keeps showing up. It might not be the owner, but it will be somebody close, like a lawyer or a broker."

McDougal stopped writing and looked up. He handed Terry a slip of paper with the building addresses and the post-office-box number. "Will you do it for me?" he asked directly.

Shit, Terry thought. He paused a moment and then said, "Look, I have a lot of work of my own."

"Yeah," McDougal said, "but the question is really what you want. All these guys are scumbags. They're destroying people, but they think well of themselves. Decent citizens. Members of the establishment. The politicians don't give a rap about them, because they fit into the grand idea of planned shrinkage for the city—let the buildings burn and force the blacks and Puerto Ricans up to Yonkers or out to Long Island. Yeah, saves money and increases property values down the road, five, ten, fifteen years from now. I want to get these pricks, just like you want to get to Lettington."

Terry smiled. It was no wonder his father liked McDougal's columns. He folded the paper and put it into his shirt pocket.

Terry knew the reporter would not print anything about Lettington on his word alone, and he was pleased that McDougal said he would look into it. So it would cost something. It wasn't a big deal to look for the name. You have to get the hose to the fire before you can open up the nozzle.

"Here's my number at home and at the paper," McDougal said. "Give me a call anytime you got somethin'."

Friday

The next afternoon, Terry sat at his desk deliberating about McDougal, waiting for the phone to ring. When it did, he grabbed it on the first ring. It was the call he expected. Paddy O'Leary, the fire marshal in charge of the major caseload, Brooklyn.

"You called, Terry?"

"Yes, Paddy," he said, pulling a pad in front of him and picking up a pencil. "What do you have on that Brownsville five-alarm last November? The buildings were owned by the S and L Realty Corporation with a post-office address."

"It's a bit thing. What's your interest in it?"

"Listen, Paddy. Remember I worked for you on Christmas Eve so you could be home with the wife and the rabbits."

"Yeah, and I owe ya. The thing is very hot now because the State Department is looking into it."

"I just need a name. But a live one. You did all the paper work?"

"It takes me three, four weeks to find a name. You want it on a telephone call?"

"Paddy, it's me, Terry! You remember? Who's the S and L Realty Corporation?"

"Christ knows, pal."

"All right. Who's close?"

"A lawyer named Moe Perritz, only one. And that's not much. He comes up as the attorney of record on these property transfers."

Terry wrote the name on the pad. "That's all I need. You're a prince among paupers."

"Terry, it *is* hot. The feds think the insurance deal is going to cause a government to come down for chrissakes."

"I knew that, but it's none of my business. You know what I mean? I love ya."

Well, that's that, Terry thought as he hung up. He walked to the coffee machine in the hall, thinking, What if McDougal blows the information in a column? O'Leary is sure to know it's me, then. Crap. I could just forget it, but that might let Lettington off the hook. Maybe if McDougal agrees to sit on it for a couple of weeks, though, then O'Leary couldn't connect it to me. And what about Burke? Christ, I can't let Burke know I've been talking to McDougal. He'd have me out on my ass if he knew that I gave McDougal a name. But the main question is, What will I get from McDougal for what I'm giving him?

Back at his desk, he set down the coffee, lit a cigarette. Maybe I should just forget it, he thought.

He sat for a long while without puffing at the cigarette; the ash grew long and fell to the desk. Finally he picked up the phone. I'll tell Jose, though, he promised himself, so someone will know what I'm doing and why. He dialed McDougal's number.

o o o

At the end of the week, Lieutenant Sirkin of the
Arson and Explosion Squad chaired the mayor's special
task-force meeting in the old State Office Building across
from City Hall on Broadway. Attending were the braided,
striped, and gold-starred officers of the police and fire departments, representatives from the district attorney's office,
the field investigation unit heads, Captain O'Connor of
Homicide, and Jack Burke. Terry and Jose sat at the back
of the room on metal folding chairs, along with three or
four police detectives. Scattered throughout the room
were other police personnel and fire officials, assistants,
deputies, aides, and underlings. Standing at the room's entrance was Rodney Lettington, impatiently chewing at the
end of his little finger. Terry noticed him and nudged Jose
with his elbow.

"Custom-made," Jose whispered. "Six hundred
bucks, not a penny less."

"He gets the best-dressed prize for the room; no
question," Terry replied.

A court stenographer sat at the side, gracefully
stroking his small machine. The press was barred, but the
minutes would be made available to them in an edited ver-
sion. It was a newsworthy conference.

Sirkin introduced Lettington as the representative
from City Hall. He turned and addressed the room, but it
was obvious to all that he was talking to the court stenographer. "The mayor of the City of New York," he said, "is
greatly saddened by the tragic consequences of the fire at
the Sophia Club in the Astor Hotel, and he speaks on behalf
of himself, his office, and indeed all New Yorkers in convey-
ing his condolences to all who lost family and friends in
that profoundly unfortunate occurrence. The city officially

mourns the loss of its citizens, many of whom were among the most prominent of New Yorkers. By official proclamation the mayor calls forth this special task force to investigate the cause of the fire. Every available resource will be . . ."

Terry whispered into Jose's ear, "I can see this will be as much a campaign as an investigation."

"Looks like it," Jose said, loud enough so that the chief of police turned his silver-gray head and scowled.

"How the hell can he go on like this when his own wife was killed?" Terry asked.

This time Jose whispered in return, "He could be a member of the polar bear club, you know what I mean?"

"Cold."

"Frigid."

When Lettington finished, the assistant district attorney, the police chief, and the fire chief committed the resources of their departments. After each speech, the speaker left the room, mumbling about another meeting to attend.

Then Lieutenant Sirkin took charge, pulling a mobile blackboard to the front of the room and drawing a large circle in its center. "This, gentleman," he said, "is the organization chart for this task force. We are all in this together. The Arson and Explosion Squad, Homicide, and the Fire Marshals are going to operate as one group during the course of this investigation. Thus far, we've been working pretty independently, although I've been in touch with Chief Burke and Captain O'Connor. Henceforth, we will work as a unit, and I've prepared special control sheets that will be filled out daily by each investigator. We have nothing concrete to work with yet . . ."

Here, Chief Burke glanced casually around until he made eye contact with Terry and Jose.

"Our labs are still doing chemical tests. So far we know only that the accelerant is not gasoline. We have psychologists doing profiles of the kind of people who might set this kind of fire. Our graphics office is doing schematics of the Sophia Club with body identifications. So far, the interviews with the next of kin of the victims have turned up zero in leads, although many of the victims were involved at the time in complicated business deals. The interviews with the survivors are incomplete, but so far have turned up nothing. Four guerrilla organizations claim credit for the fire, but it looks like they're all afterthoughts. However, I want to point out that this is the only area where there is any lead at all, so we'll try to get inside them as best we can. The chief of detectives will supply us with a few undercovers." Chief Burke again turned to look at Jose and Terry. It was the first mention they had heard of a guerrilla connection. Burke sucked one cheek into the side of his mouth. Sirkin went on to conclude, "Other than that, it's all hoof work."

The chief fire marshal lit a cigarette in the hallway and motioned to Terry and Jose. They walked to an alcove where they could talk privately.

"What he forgot to say," Chief Burke said, "is that the circumference line of the organization chart is represented by Lieutenant Sirkin. I don't know why the chief of detectives is letting him get away with it. Anyway, we might put a wall around him if we can get somewhere with the butyl nitrite. What's happening there?"

"Nothing so far," Jose said, "except that the distributor in Connecticut told us there are a dozen stores in the city that handle the stuff, no matter what the brand name. All sex shops, whips and boots and anus strings, you know?"

"Yeah, sure." Burke smiled. "Just don't do any personal shopping on Father Knickerbocker's time."

Jose laughed. "Cute. Real cute."

"I'm still waiting for a book of bottlemarks," Terry said, "but I don't have anything else on the shard yet. And we've been checking out a lot of names and letters. Nothing."

"Okay, guys," Chief Burke said, "I've got another meeting." He gestured toward an envelope Jose was carrying, and continued, "These work control sheets will be a pain in the ass for you, I know, but keep them as plain and concise as possible. Don't offer anything, but don't withhold either. We don't want to appear at cross purposes with these guys. For instance, if you interview someone at a sex shop, just record that you interviewed Mr. So-and-so, and the address. You don't have to say it's a sex shop, and the connection will be ours alone."

Jose and Terry nodded.

"Another thing," Burke went on. "There was a big meeting at the mayor's house yesterday, and I heard that it was this guy Lettington who brought up the subject of incorporating the fire marshals' work into the Arson and Explosion Squad. I wish I knew what the hell he's got to do with it. Just keep following up the leads. Every one, as if it were gonna be the one with the magic answer. Right now there's nothing else to do."

"Right," Terry replied. The task-force meeting was enough to convince him that the investigation was as much political as anything else.

O O O

The two men walked over to department headquarters on Church Street.

Terry stopped at his box at the Bureau of Fire Investigation. There were two messages: his sister and Lieutenant Mills of Engine Company 8 had called. He put the message from his sister in his back pocket.

Jose limped up beside him, opening a business envelope. "If this is what I think it is, we might have to work overtime tomorrow." Terry looked over Jose's shoulder at the list of fourteen New York stores that sold Jac-me, Push, Ou, and Ram.

"Damn it," Terry said. "I have a date tonight. Can we start at noon?"

"What the hell, we're making our own hours on special assignment, aren't we?" Jose said. "Noon's fine. You in love again?"

"Who knows?" Terry shrugged. "She's terrific, though. Beautiful. But she's from on top of the hill, you know? She even knew one of the victims at the Sophia, a woman named Hartfield. She's part of that crowd, around it anyway, and I can't get a handle on it. Want to meet her?"

"Why not?"

"Come for breakfast tomorrow. Say, eleven?"

"Man, that's lunchtime for me."

"So you'll have an egg sandwich," Terry said, walking across the large open room to an empty desk. Jose winked.

Terry dialed Engine Company 8. "Lieutenant Mills, please," he said. He could hear the fireman at the other end yelling through the firehouse intercom.

"Engine Eight, Lieutenant Mills," the voice came, after a few minutes.

"Yeah, Lou, this is Fire Marshal Ahearn."

"Ahearn? Look, I asked to speak to someone investigating the job at the Astor. Is that you?"

"Right. I talked to you at the fire."

"Well, listen, I don't know if it means anything, but I know in these things you guys can make somethin' outta little things, ya know. I remember you asked me if I noticed anything strange or peculiar at the fire. Was it you?"

"Yeah, Lou, that was me."

"Anyway, I remember a couple o' things when we was responding. I just tried hard to think about it, and then

I remember these three colored kids across the street from the fire, where the fountain is, ya know? I was running to the fire, but I saw them there for a moment, like the see-no-evil, hear-no-evil monkeys, with their hands around each other's shoulders."

Terry was writing on a pad. "How old were they, you think?"

"Teenagers, fourteen, fifteen, who knows? I don't remember clothes or anything else. Then, there was a cab that ran a light on Fifty-seventh Street and Park. That happens a lot when they hear the sirens, but this guy not only jumps the light, he makes a U-turn to boot. He cut three cars off when we was trying to get by."

"Was it a sedan, a Checker?" Terry asked. "Occupied, or unoccupied?"

"You know, I don't know. . . . I think it was a Checker."

Terry said, "That could be something. Keep trying to remember, okay?"

"Yeah, okay," Mills said. "And then there was this guy walking on Central Park South, maybe it means something, maybe it don't. He was wearing a tuxedo with a black cape over his shoulders. He was just crossing Fifth. He was walkin' pretty fast, too, 'cause I remember thinkin' he had somewhere important to go. I don't like to bother you guys, or anybody in this job, for that matter. I got almost thirty-one years on the job, ya know."

"It's no bother," Terry said, as he began taking notes. "As you say, you never know. Did you see what the guy looked like?"

"No, we were responding pretty fast."

"That must have been about nine-thirty, huh?"

"Thereabouts. The alarm time out was twenty-one twenty-seven. That's what bothered me, ya know. Was this guy comin' from the fire, and if he was, how come he didn't stick around for a little while at least, ya know?"

"Right, Lou. It all might mean something, like you say. What's your home phone in case I have to reach you?"

"Well, it don't matter, 'cause I'm leavin' in two days, Fort Lauderdale, Phoenix, I don't know. This is my last tour. I was going to wait till a new contract, but I figure let them shove their four percent. The Astor job was the straw, ya know what I mean? So I put the paper in. A man spends thirty years in this job and what does he have to look forward to except a couple years in the sunshine, ya know?"

Terry laid the phone down gently, thinking aloud. "Well, now we got a few more."

"What's that?" Jose asked.

"Three blacks, a U-turn, and a cape."

Terry looked to his pad, where he listed every lead—name, letter, fact—that came his way. There were sixty-four of them. So far, all nothings. Terry shrugged and listed them.

No. 65: *three black teenagers at the Plaza fountain.*
No. 66: *cab runs light at 57th and Park, makes U-turn.*
No. 67: *man in tux, black cape on Central Park South. In a hurry.*

Would these be nothings numbers 65, 66, and 67? Or would one of them be Something Number 1?

Saturday

Terry awoke in Melissa's bed the next morning. After showering, he crossed the hall to his own apartment and changed clothes. The message to phone his sister was still in his back pocket.

Melissa had followed him, wrapped in her blue silk robe, carrying a loaf of bread, a box of Ceylon tea, and a crock of English marmalade. Terry took eggs and bacon and butter from the refrigerator.

Melissa was amused at the fastidiousness of his apartment. "You'll make some woman a wonderful house-keeper—as well as sex object," she said. Terry laughed, placed a clean and pressed flag of the City of New York over a small, rectangular table and centered the sugar, salt, and pepper on the city seal.

"It comes from living in the projects," he said. "Working or welfare, you know if you live in one, you're poor, and unworthy. And so to prove to yourself you're *not*, you keep things extra neat and clean. At least that's the way we felt. I don't know if anyone feels that way any more."

"Probably not," she said. "I remember reading a monograph on the failure of project houses in Saint Louis . . . uninhabitable after just ten years. They dynamited them. The conclusion was that they would have been suc-cessful if people had felt a sense of belonging, of owner-ship."

"I don't buy that," Terry said, putting three mail-order place settings on the table. "A sense of belonging comes from the family, not from any building. As the family becomes less of a cohesive unit, so does the building, the neighborhood, and finally the city. I watched it all disinte-grate in Brooklyn. But my house was clean, 'cause my family cared."

He went to the bathroom to shave.

"Cohesive unit, eh?" she yelled in to him. "You sound like a sociologist."

"I work in a bureaucracy," he answered. "I pick up the jargon."

"Is your family a cohesive unit?"

The question stopped Terry. He had never thought about it before.

"I don't know," he said between strokes of the razor. "It was cohesive when I was a kid. I know that much. There was just me, until my sister came along when I was twelve. I did everything with the old man—ballgames, the beach, movies, trips to Coney Island—everything. When he was working, I used to pray every night that he would get laid off or fired so that he would be home more. I worshiped the ground he walked on, as my mother would say."

He saw her reflection in the mirror as she appeared at the doorway to the bathroom, and turned to her. "It was cohesive then, when it mattered, but now, probably not. God, it hurts to say that, but the folks and I don't speak the same language. I should say my father and I. My mother doesn't say much. Then there's my sister, who speaks still another language."

He turned back to the sink and spoke to Melissa's face in the mirror. "I suppose family cohesiveness is really important when you're a young kid. What about your family? Cohesive?"

She came closer, put her arms around his waist, and raised her chin up on his shoulder.

"Um, yes," she answered. "Almost as close as you and I are now. But not quite." She grinned at him in the mirror. "Of course Father, being a lawyer, worked impossible hours, still does, and Mother is still ambitious as hell, and if you're in international investment, and ambitious, you're flying all over the place all the time. Yet they both always seemed to have time for my brother Spence and me. We did everything together, too, except that instead of going to Coney Island, we went to Southampton. But you know it's more important that the family goes together than where it goes. Oh my, did I see some miserable broken families in Southampton, beach houses and all!"

He knew she was trying to bring them together, but he felt himself moving away. Southampton. He wasn't even sure where it was. On Long Island, somewhere between Coney Island and Montauk. He sure as hell had never been there. "Yeah," he said, "I suppose kids don't know the difference between Coney Island and Southampton, because they've either been to one or the other. They don't get to learn the difference till they're grown up. But then they learn. Boy, do they learn!"

She let go of him, looking hurt and trying not to show it. "And on that egalitarian note, may I say I made a date for us to have lunch with Father on Tuesday? He favored the University Club. I insisted on McDonald's because I knew you'd prefer it." She paused. "Hey, I'm being mean, and I'm sorry. I know how you feel, wish you wouldn't, but I understand. By the way, I told Father and Mother all about you, and all about us." She grinned. "Well . . . I didn't tell them *everything*."

Terry wiped his face with a towel. He was in a prickly mood. "Wanted to see if I'd pass the test, eh? And did I? Could you take me to Southampton? To the Universal . . . what's the name of that club? Did they approve?"

She slapped his face, lightly, lovingly. "Stop trying to pick a fight, it just won't work. To answer your question: the club is the University. Yes, I can take you to it, or Southampton, or anywhere else I feel like, and you'll do just splendidly. And I was not trying for their approval. They know I run my own life, and they approve of it, because they approve of *me*. And I approve of *you*. In fact, when you're not being so sticky, I think I love you." She leaned to him and kissed him on the mouth. He put his arms around her and pulled her close.

The doorbell rang.

Terry went for it.

It was Jose. "She loves me, I think," Terry whispered.

"Well so do I, I think," Jose whispered back.

○ ○ ○

It was a clear, bright Saturday, more like autumn than winter, the kind of day that reminded Terry of the neighborhood football games in Prospect Park that his father took him to before Maureen was born. After that, the old man would spend the clear weekend days pushing his daughter around Red Hook in the carriage or the stroller. It was that kind of day, anyway.

The two fire marshals went to the office first to sign the time sheet. "Burke says he can't approve the overtime," Jose said as Terry headed for a telephone. "But he can give us compensatory time."

"Big deal," Terry answered, sitting on the edge of a desk. "Straight time back puts a lot of food on the table, huh."

"It's the way it is."

"What shit," Terry uttered bitterly. "We got the biggest case in history, and we can't get the men for surveillance; over a hundred leads still unchecked; the department worries about our budget, while the police department tries to steal our authority."

"C'mon, Terry," Jose said in a soothing tone, "you know we could get all the surveillance we need if we worked through Sirkin. Burke says we have to buy time, so we buy it. Relax. There's time. And, there's the butyl nitrite."

Fourteen places in Manhattan sold butyl nitrite, by the trade name of Jac-me. Most, maybe all, were porno shops. Of course there were others in other boroughs, in the suburbs. But they'd start in Manhattan. Driving up

Eighth Avenue, slowly, searching for the first address, Jose said, "I'm glad I met Melissa. She's nice. Very pretty. Very classy. Sounds like Katharine Hepburn in those old movies."

"She's it, I think sometimes," Terry said. "It's time. I'm thirty-three years old. It's time. She's pretty, smart, honest. Maybe too honest. Maybe *too* classy. But special. The kind that doesn't come along very often. Maybe only once."

"Just don't end up in suburbia."

"I can only breathe right when the buildings are fifty stories." Terry laughed.

"Yeah, but when you have kids, you'll be looking at the schools, and unless you got four extra Gs a year, the schools in suburbia look good."

"At least that's something I don't have to worry about now."

"She's pretty rich, huh?"

"Yeah, pretty rich."

"Women that sound like Katharine Hepburn usually are. She looks it, too. Maybe she could pay the school bills."

"I'd pay my own school bills."

"Hey, it would be her kid, too. It's all right, that's what women's liberation is all about."

"C'mon, Jose."

"What, c'mon?"

"I don't want anyone paying the bills in my house but me, and I haven't even given her a pin yet, or an ankle bracelet, or whatever it is you give these days when you go steady."

"You breaking my horns?"

"Yep," Terry said, with a wink. "You'd like me to get married, huh?"

"I think you need kids. Everyone does. Life is all selfish if you don't have kids."

"Now you're breaking *my* horns, are ya?"

"No. After I got shot, you know, I had to ask myself what it all means."

It was rare for Jose to mention the shooting, and Terry let the grin fall from his face.

"Lots of people ask that of themselves," Jose continued, "but you can only ask it *seriously* when you come pretty close to being dead. Well, kids is the answer. What else could it be? Service? Doing good for others? Saving your own soul, like they tell you in church? Accomplishing something, getting rich, coming up with an invention? Uh-uh. Kids. That's it. Contribute something decent to the world through your kids and you've done something."

"Well," Terry replied, looking at the address numbers on the avenue, "I'd rather contribute something myself than wait for it to happen through my kids."

"What is it you'll contribute, Terry?"

"You don't have to have high hopes, Jose. Live a good life. Day to day. Every day. Pull up on the next block, across from Port Authority."

Jose parked beside a fire hydrant. The store had a large sign that read: TRIPLE X BOOKS AND MOVIES EMPORIUM, with another sign, attached by wires: LIVE NUDE SHOW.

A fat, unshaven man sat at a high counter in bored watchfulness over the browsing customers. Terry looked around. Two walls were covered by racks of books and magazines, the sections titled alphabetically according to the area of interest: Animals, Black Stockings, Children, Chocolate Women, Couples—Female, Couples—Male, Domination, Fruit and Vegetables, Gays, Mechanical Devices, Oral, Orientals, Penises, S-and-M, Silk Underwear, Teenagers, Vulvas. There were display cases of erotica throughout the store: playing cards, statuettes, key rings, sex guides to American cities, binding straps, vibrators of all shapes and sizes. In the rear was a curtained entrance with the sign: ALL LIVE, ALL NUDE, ONE MINUTE 25¢.

109 ○

Jose showed his badge to the counterman. "Is the manager in?"

"Yeah."

"Get him, would you?"

"Yeah." The man pressed a buzzer beneath the counter.

Curious, Terry walked to the racks and picked up a small glossy magazine titled *Babysex*. He flipped it open and saw a photo of three little girls standing naked before an exposed man, their eyes wide with shame and fright.

He threw the magazine to the floor.

"Hey," the manager yelled, coming from behind the curtain. He picked it up and put it back on the rack. "This is my merchandise. It costs seven dollars, and you got no right to do that."

Terry forced himself to keep quiet. He showed his badge, asked, "You sell butyl nitrite?"

"What's that?"

"Jac-me, Push, Piston, that kind of stuff."

"Yeah, I got it, it's in the back room. It ain't against the law."

"I know. Can we see it?"

They followed the manager past the curtain and down a long aisle bordered on one side by curtained compartments. Some were closed off by drawn curtains, and others were open. The only light came from dim purple bulbs. In each open compartment was a small window in the wall, covered by a sheet of thin metal, and next to the window was a coin machine, like a parking meter.

Terry asked the manager if he had a key. "You know," he said, "like bartenders have for juke boxes."

"You wanna see?" the manager asked.

"Just for academic purposes," Terry said. "We'll leave the curtain open."

"It's okay," Jose said, "he's single."

"Don't ya got a quarter?" the manager asked.

"What quarter?" Terry said. "I can get an egg cream for a quarter."

The manager put a coin into the machine, and the metal screen rose. Behind a pane of clear plastic Terry and Jose saw a young man and woman, both very thin and small, lying naked on a bed covered with soiled sheets. They were talking, although their voices could not be heard. The woman ran her hand up the man's thigh indifferently and fondled his scrotum as he caressed the tips of her small breasts without passion.

"College students," the manager said.

"Too bad they couldn't get a scholarship," Terry said, walking out of the compartment and down the aisle to the back room.

On an unpainted wooden shelf behind a small desk stood a dozen or so bottles of Jac-me.

"Is this all you have?" Jose asked, indicating the bottles.

"That's it," the manager said, sitting on the edge of the desk. "We don't get much call for it, so we keep it back here. Fags use it mostly, and we don't get too many fags in here."

"Do you know of anyone who comes to buy it regularly?" Terry asked.

The manager thought for a moment. "No."

"Do you remember anything strange about anyone who came in recently to buy this stuff?"

"There's something strange about *everyone* who comes in here to buy *anything*."

"I mean, particularly about this stuff. Someone buying it in quantity, or making a big thing about it, or like that."

"No. And I would remember 'cause I'm always

111 o

here. If I don't sell it personally, they buzz for me back here to cover the store while they come back to get it."

The two fire marshals entered another store called Tingle's Sex Shop, interrogated the manager briefly, and left without learning anything except, possibly, that discounts were available for men with badges at the company-owned massage parlor located above the store.

Then four more shops with the same result: nothing.

They walked east on 42nd Street to the seventh location on the list, a place called Leathersex.

The salesman, dressed in black leather pants and a black turtleneck, with a small gold phallus hanging from his neck, looked at Jose's badge and said gleefully, "Ooooh. Guns, and cruelty, and oppression. I love it!"

Terry ignored him and said, "I notice you have a display of Jac-me in your window. Do you sell much of it?"

"Hordes. It's all the rage." The man reached below the counter and came up with a bottle. He placed it on the counter. "Will one be enough, or are you having a dinner party?"

Terry said, "Don't take this too lightly, pal. I want to ask you a few serious questions: I'm not here for laughs, understand?"

"Pardon *me*," the salesman said with exaggerated dignity, and he sat on a high bar stool behind the counter.

"Do you sell other brands besides this?" Terry continued.

"No. A rose is a rose."

"Do you remember anything unusual regarding this stuff in the past few weeks, something strange about a person looking for butyl nitrite, or buying it in quantity?"

"Umm," the salesman murmured, placing a long index finger to his lips. "Not that I can remember. There was a man here yesterday, a perfect Adonis if you'll know the truth, who bought a bottle, but then I sold him a life-size replica of his you-know-what."

"No, I don't know."

"One of those," the salesman said, pointing to the display of rubber and plastic dildos on a table. "I made the mold myself."

"I'm talking about any time before last Monday night."

Again the narrow finger poised at the lips. "Last Monday night, huh?" He thought quietly for a few moments. "Say," he said expectantly, like a child in a classroom who suddenly thinks he has the right answer, "there was a man in here last Monday for Jac-me. I know it was Monday, because Monday night is my group therapy session, and that's why I remember him. I talked about him in the session that night. He was so humorless and trying *so* hard to seem straight, but *I* knew he was gay, I can always tell, the way Masons recognize each other by their rings. I can see it in the eyes; I could see it in his even though they were inflamed and bloodshot. Definitely gay, I told myself, but he wouldn't let on. That's what we talked about at group therapy. Closet people. No sense of humor. Afraid. Pretending. It's so counterproductive."

"Did he say anything in particular?"

"Not that I recall."

"What did he look like?"

"Forty, maybe. Your height, but not muscular like you." The man winked.

Terry looked at him sourly. "White?"

"Yes, very good. You get points for asking that question. It shows you're open, without prejudice."

"Listen," Terry said, stern-voiced and intent, "shove the asides. Can you describe him?"

"Well-dressed, well-spoken . . . no sense of humor."

Terry replied, "That describes half of the United States Senate. Anything else?"

"He was . . . *delicate*. Well-groomed. Brown hair, every hair in place. I think his eyes were blue—where they weren't red. His nose was thin and pointed. Maybe one hundred and sixty pounds."

"That's it?"

"Yes, except that he whistled his *s*'s. Like a lot of gays, even when they're trying not to. I normally love it when men whistle their *s*'s, but this one was too haughty."

Jose, standing to Terry's side, was writing notes.

"Do you think you could identify this man if you saw him again?"

"Yes. I'm very good at faces—men's anyway."

"What did he do? Tell me exactly."

"He came in, looked about a little bit, and asked for some Jac-me."

"By name? Or did he ask for butyl nitrite?"

"Jac-me."

"How much did he buy? And is there a name on the receipt?"

"Three bottles. I remember, because he gave me a ten and it wasn't enough. Names on receipts? Are you *kidding*?"

"Do you remember any others who bought the stuff?"

"No."

"Listen, Mr. . . . what is your name anyway?" Jose asked.

"Oh, I'm just known as Mr. Leathersex. That's the name of the shop, you see."

"Beautiful," Jose responded. He handed the man his card. "There's my name and number. If our friend with the whistling *s* and the red eyes comes in again, or if anyone buys more of that . . . Jac-me than you think is normal— if you'll pardon my expression—you'll call me, won't you?"

Jose stared at him. "What with all this stuff you sell here, I know you want to stay on the right side of the law."

"But of course!"

"Promise?"

"Promise."

As they were leaving, Mr. Leathersex blew them a kiss.

Walking in the 42nd Street crowd, Terry suddenly thought of Melissa. "I'm glad I like girls, Jose," he said.

"That's what I tell my wife twice a week," Jose replied with a laugh.

Seven down, seven to go, but now they had something. Jose headed downtown to check four shops in Greenwich Village. "Red eyes," he said. "Of course, they could have been red just that day. And a whistling s. The rest sounds ordinary middle-class fag—or straight, for that matter. Not much to go on. But more than before, partner, more than before."

"From now on," said Terry, "we get every suspect to say 'Mississippi.' "

WEEK TWO

The tail of Rodney Lettington's Meledandri pin stripe flapped in the wind as he raced down the steps of City Hall. Ever since someone had told him he looked like John Lindsay, he'd taken to Lindsayesque pin-stripe suits, had let his hair grow a little long, and had tried to lose weight to take on the long, lean look of the former mayor, though he was neither long enough nor lean enough. Still, he knew, he looked far more like the movies' idea of a handsome WASP mayor than most of the competition around the Hall did. And that was a good start, although he needed more than a good start. That he knew too.

He took the shortcut through the park, hurried south on Broadway for two blocks, walked into the delicatessen they'd agreed to meet in, went past the steam tables reeking of pastrami, corned beef, tongue, brisket, to the back, where he caught sight of Sirkin.

Every Monday morning, just before his regular meeting with the mayor, he'd been rendezvousing with the police lieutenant, working out their little plan, making sure Sirkin was his man. And the veteran cop seemed to be: steady, cold, a loner, smart—but not too smart—and hungry, hungry as an Eighth Avenue hooker.

Lettington didn't like this deli and its smells; it all seemed so . . . middle European. But he didn't want Sirkin in his office too often. Not yet. Soon, but not yet.

He glanced at his watch; today he wouldn't have much time for the lieutenant. He must not be late for the Monday meeting. Nothing ever happened, they were a waste of time; but to the mayor, promptness was a sign of loyalty.

Lettington sat down with the cop, who as usual started out by wanting something. "I need your help," he said as soon as the deputy mayor was seated. "If we're going to prove that switching fire investigations over to the police will save money, you gotta get those dollar figures from the fire department."

"Why can't you get them?" Lettington was annoyed, but he kept his voice down, because as he spoke the waitress was approaching with his cup of coffee. By now she knew enough to serve it as soon as he arrived, without his even asking. "I don't want my name on any request like that." He wanted to be the hatchet man without being known as one.

"Carry more clout comin' from the mayor's office. Besides, the firemen have a hard-on for me as it is. For you, too, as a matter of fact." Sirkin almost seemed to smile as he said it.

"Why me?"

"They know what you're tryin' to do. There are no secrets around the Hall."

Lettington's face, always pink and slightly flushed, reddened. "Try to do a job, try to save the city money—and

120 o

this is the thanks you get!" He wondered if Sirkin believed him.

"Listen, I'm on your side. But those firemen beef about how they'll lose the jobs, about how those men have families to support. About how you don't understand."

"Don't understand? I've got a family too, you know!" He blurted the words out, then had to face them. He had a wife, until a week ago. Penelope. Penny. But Penny died a week ago today. In the Sophia fire. He had made it to the door, and she hadn't. What could he have done? He kept asking himself that over and over. Gone back? Then they'd both have died. The fire had burst into the room with such frightening speed, and there was only the one remaining exit to get to—he'd known that, God had he known that. He was lucky, he was close to it. If he hadn't gotten right out, he'd have gone with dear Penny. He kept feeding himself that, kept trying to make it stay down.

But it kept coming up. The night he had to identify the body. The day of the funeral. It had to be a Jewish funeral—her father had insisted on that. He even had to wear a yarmulke—not that he minded. It couldn't hurt him with the public to have his blond WASP countenance showing under a Jewish skullcap. Still, he was stifling that memory pretty well.

What was harder to stifle was the nagging knowledge that he'd not exactly been heroic under pressure. Heroic? Hell, he'd panicked. Made for the door, not thinking of anyone or anything but himself. It was only later that he began the rationalizing, that it wouldn't have done any good . . . and so on. But he was even beginning to handle that, and soon he'd be left only with the blessed memory of Penny, and the fact—and the money—of Penny's father, Meyer Samuels.

Sirkin was telling him something during all this and Lettington was nodding, but he wasn't listening.

It was an axiom of New York politics that you

didn't try to run for mayor without real estate backing and without money, and Meyer met both requirements. Not to mention a third: he was willing to throw his weight behind his WASP son-in-law.

But Samuels never gave anything away; he wanted a quid pro quo, even from a son-in-law. And he was a shark. He owned, among other things, half the rundown buildings in the Times Square area. Half the porno shops could look to the millionaire philanthropist Meyer Samuels as their landlord. You'd think that someone with his money would be satisfied with the normal profit from the increase in the property values as Times Square was rebuilt. The normal profits would be enormous. But not enough for him. Certain of his buildings were worthless. And vacant. And heavily insured against fire. Suppose they burned down? Samuels would collect twice: from the insurance, and the normal increase in property values.

"Who's going to get hurt?" Samuels had said to his son-in-law. "It's safe; it's money in the bank . . . no, no, my boy—it's money in your campaign. I mean, what's the sense of my making you a deputy mayor if you can't take care of a harmless little venture like that for me?"

Samuels was never for a moment worried about Rodney rebelling; Rodney cared too much about suits being made for him at Meledandri, and you didn't buy them—and the lifestyle to match—on a deputy mayor's salary. So Lettington had to make it safe for Meyer Samuels's plans for the Great White Way.

The first thing he found out was that the fire marshals were fanatics. They apparently hated fires so rabidly they wouldn't listen to reason. Lieutenant Sirkin, on the other hand, would listen to reason. Of course he wanted something, too, and his reminder of it broke through Lettington's daydreaming.

"The promotion," the police lieutenant was saying when Lettington finally tuned in. "I was talking about the promotion. You know I never passed the captain's exam and it would take a directive from the police commissioner himself to make me a provisional captain at captain's pay. We talked about it before, remember?"

Lettington took a swallow of coffee and then pursed his lips, as if he had drunk poison. It was bitter, like Russian coffee, just the way Meyer made it. "No problem," he answered finally. "It might take a month, but I know I can guarantee it." It was getting late. "I've got to go. I'll talk to the mayor today about shifting the authority soon. He thinks it's a good idea so far, but I don't want to go too fast. We don't want any monkey wrenches in our machinery."

"Some people," Sirkin said, moving uneasily in his seat, "might criticize a change of authority in the middle of an investigation as big as this here discotheque fire."

"I don't think so," Lettington said, standing. "That's why I made sure you became the coordinator of the special task force. It makes more sense to run a ship from the helm, and we're going to make sure that people see the Arson and Explosion Squad of the police department as the helm."

Sirkin seemed satisfied then. Lettington left.

Twenty minutes into the meeting at City Hall, the mayor, an unimposing man who had started out as Bronx district clerk, was still pacing the floor of his office and ranting about fiscal responsibility. He was an expert on fiscal responsibility, but that was all he knew.

"Damn it, Rodney," the mayor said, "we've got to raise Standard and Poor's rating on the city bonds. We've just got to convince them that the city is a good investment, that we're manageable, cost-efficient."

Lettington smiled. The mayor was eating out of his hand. "Our management-by-objectives plan is being implemented," he said, "our indebtedness is being reduced, the unions are capitulating on all the productivity issues.

The rating will rise inevitably. Particularly as we weed out redundant services."

The mayor got up and sat on the front edge of his desk, as if to signal that the meeting was coming to an end.

"Speaking of that," Lettington continued, rising to his feet, "you remember I spoke to you about shifting the entire responsibility of fire investigation over to the police department?"

The mayor walked to the door. "You show me how much we'll save," he said, "and we'll do it."

Lettington smiled again. "The report will be on your desk in a week. All I need is your authority to have the fire department release its financial statistics to me."

"Done," the mayor said. "Just tell them I've approved it."

The deputy mayor went to his basement office. He looked at his watch again as he sat at his desk. It was 10:42. He had three minutes before the police commissioner was due for a brief talk. There was the Sirkin promotion to discuss, and anyway, it would help in the long run to be a little friendlier with the P.C.

All the little things helped when you put them together, and no one else was going to do that for you. A man had to work hard at making allies if he wanted to be mayor one day.

Lettington leaned back in his chair and propped his feet up on the desk. Like the Marchesa, he thought. Totti was a perfect ally. She knew all the right people: Mrs. Staravakos, the governor. She held hands with the money and the influence. And she liked me, he thought, she would have helped me. "Oh, Rodney," she had said that night when she took the Lettingtons to dinner at 21, "I am so, how do you say, dis-trouted?"

He'd had to laugh. That was so like her, so sweet.

"Distraught," he had corrected. "But what could upset anyone as charming as you?"

"The K of O," she had said. "The building department said they could not give to me this K of O with the exit that goes out through the kitchen. They want, madonna mia, to make a hole for a door, to break down a wall. It is crazy."

He felt pleased to have power. She seemed so flustered, and it was so simple a thing. "K of O," she kept saying. He told her the buildings department gave variances for such things every day, and there was no reason they couldn't do it for her, if a deputy mayor asked. He told her it was a C of O, and he got it for her.

She kissed him then, and threw her arms around him. "Angiollo from heaven," she cried. He would have done anything for her. The variance didn't matter. The fire came too suddenly, so fiercely. It couldn't have mattered. He told himself that many times.

Rodney Lettington, a deputy mayor of the City of New York, put his hands behind his head and watched the hands of the wall clock move to 10:45. "I've had some setbacks," he said to the empty room, "but things are on schedule."

Monday

Monday afternoon, one week after the Sophia fire, Terry walked briskly down Hamilton Avenue in Brooklyn. It was snowing lightly. He looked at his watch as he neared the waterfront housing project. There was still time to talk to the old man, to try to reason with him, before his sister came home from school.

Maureen had called him that morning, just as he

and Jose were leaving to interview more survivors on the invitation list. Terry asked her to have dinner with him, but she was busy.

"It's not that *you* and *I* have to talk, Terry," she said. "It's the old man. You've got to tell him to leave me alone. He's acting crazy—even crazier than before. I went away with Eduardo, you know, my boyfriend, for a couple days last week. He's a guitarist, and he's from Brazil, you know. And the old man is raving all the time about his daughter being the neighborhood slut. You know how he can be. Crazy. Eduardo asked me to go to Philadelphia because he was giving a recital at some church, and I went. It was no big thing. Who I sleep with is my business."

Terry listened to her without saying anything. "Terry, get him off my back," his sister begged. "You've got to talk to him. You've got to tell him that I wasn't born to suit his image."

Finally Terry asked, "Are you in love with this Eduardo?"

"What kind of question is that?" Maureen said. "I'm twenty-one years old, Terry. I haven't locked the rest of my life up yet."

It would have been a reasonable question, he thought, when he was his sister's age. There was a silence on the phone, a pause that grew out of the dozen years that separated them. Almost half a generation. "I'll talk to him," he assured her.

He walked up the stone stairwell to his parents' third-floor apartment and pressed the doorbell. Terry's mother came to the door, her face expressionless. "How are you?" she asked.

"Fine, just fine." He kissed her cheek.

"Your father is in the kitchen. Can I fix you something?"

"No thanks, Mom."

"Tea?"

"No. Thanks."

"Well, I'll see you later then. I'm just taking the wash to the Laundromat. Will you be here for dinner?"

"No. I can't. I'm sorry."

Petey Ahearn was sitting at the kitchen table, smoking a cigarette and drinking coffee as he looked at the *Daily Post* spread out before him.

"How are ya, Pop?" Terry said as he took a can of beer from the refrigerator. He snapped the lid open.

"How good could a man be," his father answered, "when he reads this shit. Ya know, there's a story in this newspaper every day about the rich dancin' their asses off at places like this Orpheus, havin' a good time while hard-workin' people are being raped and robbed in a city that's got no decency."

Terry sat across from his father and poured his beer into a clean jelly glass. The old man felt like talking, and Terry was sure the subject of Marxism would surface naturally enough.

"Look at the president we got now," Petey Ahearn continued between puffs of his cigarette. "A born-again Christian. No one believes a born-again Christian has any smarts, but everybody believes he's honest. After all those lies, we get a man who tells us just one thing, that he won't ever lie. And where are we? The fuckin' dollar is worth a quarter less since he got into office. So he ain't gonna lie, and we're goin' broke."

"Ahh," Terry said, "the inflation isn't so bad that you can't make it. And remember, Pop, you always want it both ways, a labor socialist president and a good economy at the same time. It doesn't work. At least this guy is a man of the earth. He isn't living off an inherited fortune, but since you can't find any class reasons to cut the guy, you bring up his religion. You're hot shit. Really."

Petey Ahearn sat back in his chair. "Did you ever hear me say I was rich?" the old man asked.

127 o

"No, Pop, I never heard you say that."

"That's 'cause I'm poor," Petey Ahearn said, sitting straight again and turning a page in the newspaper. We're poor, but it's not a big deal. I pay the rent, put food on the table, and I usually got ten bills left for a couple of drinks. But a lot of time goes by before I get a big one in my pocket, and *then* I'm rich. Spend it like a nigger before the bastards find ya got it."

The old man got up from the table and looked out the small kitchen window, holding the curtain to one side. "Your mother and me don't have much, but we never really cared about money, you know that. We got it, we spend it. If ya spend it, it shows you don't care about it, but you're in fuckin' moral quicksand if ya go around to banks to get somethin' ya never worked for, an you're only connin' yourself if ya buy life insurance that pays off at your death. The working men of this city sweat their balls off to put money in the bank so they can run to the suburbs to get away from the minorities. Even the minorities run from the minorities. They get theirs, and they turn their backs on the unorganized and ignorant. It's all fuckin' humiliatin' today. There's no dignity."

"What about me, Pop? Don't you think I have enough dignity? Don't you think my job has dignity?"

"Ha! You can believe that if you want. Doin' the politician's penance for the politician's sins. I just hope they never bring ya home to me wrapped in wood."

"C'mon, Pop," Terry said, "my job's not so bad. I'm happy, right? And I know plenty guys who came right out of this neighborhood who got it made out on Long Island. They got a backyard with flowers, the schools are good, their kids aren't being mugged in the streets, they can deduct their mortgage instead of givin' it away to a landlord."

Petey Ahearn turned and said, "You're dreamin' again, kid. I'm sayin' that until workers get an equal distribution of the profits they make with their muscles and sweat, they'll always be in the shit. You can't have dignity at the same time you're bein' screwed."

The old man lit another cigarette. He threw the newspaper down. "What can ya expect, huh?" he asked. "Take this newspaper. It's got no competition, it's a god-damn monopoly, and it tells everybody that it's a good thing to dance your ass off while the city's burnin' down. Brooklyn is a fuckin' no man's land to this newspaper. Nobody wants to be serious. Except maybe this Mike McDougal. You read his column about that fire you went to at the Astor?"

Terry was going to tell the old man about Mc-Dougal, but he realized it would be pointless. It would only lead to another argument. Anyway, the old man didn't wait for a reply.

"He at least has more sympathy for the people who are bein' wiped out day to day than for the Brahmins who got soldered to the floor in a rich man's dance parlor," Petey continued. "He cares about the Bronx and Brooklyn. And we're part of the destruction here, livin' in it. Everywhere around the projects here you can see the shells that're left after all those guys bought the fuckin' con job of the suburbs. Well, we're not leavin'. They're gonna have to burn us outta here, me, your mother, and Maureen."

Petey Ahearn paused and stared down at the table as if he were trying to remember something. He opened his mouth to speak, but then closed it. Terry thought he was ready to talk about his sister. He was right.

The old man said, "Speakin' of Maureen, you know she's been acting like a real hooplehead lately, like a kid they let outta Creedmoor by mistake. She comes in here the other night with this banjo player from the Amazon jungle. The guy looks like a fuckin' walnut tree, and talks like he was born under the fence on the Texas border. So I ask him, I say, '*Seenyore*, what kinda work you do?' Now,

I called him *Seenyore* 'cause I forgot his name and figured it was better than callin' him fuckin' Pancho or Jesus Rodriguez Lopez, right? So Maureen jumps up like I stuck a pin in her ass an' tells him he don't have to answer the question. I thought I was in a fuckin' courtroom, so I came in the kitchen here to have a beer and left them alone. Ya know, I can't figure out what kinda scramblin' is goin' on inside her head. She knows she irritates me, and goddamn it, I wish she'd straighten out an' marry some clean Irish kid that'll take care of her. Like I say, stick with yer own an' ya won't get hurt. Ya might not be happy, but ya got no reason to expect to be happy to begin with, ya know? Anyone who tells ya different is givin' ya a hand job. I told her just this mornin' she'd be better off in a tenement with an American bus driver than in a penthouse with a fuckin' musician from South America."

"What did she say to that, Pop?" Terry asked between sips of beer.

"She said nothin'. She just stormed outta here like the place was on fire. She hadda come back for her coat."

"Christ, Pop, I think you're a little hard on her."

"Hard," the old man shouted, "I didn't do nothin'. She don't know what hard is. I never laid a hand on that girl in my life."

"What I mean, Pop," Terry said, "is that you're on her back, you're needling her, and if you'd just let her alone, give her her head, as the cowboys say, she'd be all right. I mean it, Pop. She's not a young kid any more, and she has to figure what's best for herself."

"Are you gonna tell me I don't know what's good for my own daughter?"

"Yeah, that's it, Pop. Maybe I am."

"Well, kid," Petey Ahearn said, "that's like when the bosses tell ya you're already overpaid. There's not much to talk about after that."

Terry could see that his father was hurt. He wouldn't look into his son's eyes, even as Terry spoke.

"C'mon, Pop," Terry said. "I know that you care a lot about her, and she'll be all right if you just leave her alone. She's not in love or anything with this guy. I don't think so, anyway."

Staring at the yellowed white enamel of the refrigerator, the old man said, in a near whisper, "No daughter of mine would go away to Philadelphia with a man for two days unless she loved him. That's somethin' I hafta believe."

Terry heard the motor of the electric wall clock. The air in the room was heavy and silent. His father was right, he thought. There was not much more to say, at least not without crashing through the barriers that lay within the old man. He left the kitchen table, grasped his father on the shoulder warmly, saying, "Gotta get back to work." He waited a moment as the old man took a long swallow of coffee and lit another cigarette, but Petey Ahearn made no reply. He was still staring into space as Terry put his coat on and left the apartment.

Tuesday

It was three o'clock when Terry walked into the headquarters office. He threw his trench coat over a chair, and took the mail out of his box. He felt tired. Thinking about the talk with his father drained him.

He sat at an empty desk across from Jose and began to sift through memoranda, department orders, and letters that made up the day's mail. He became suddenly excited by one of the return addresses and ripped open the envelope. It was from the American Association of Bottle Manufacturers.

He took the glass shard from the office safe and held it between two fingers as he went through the pages of punt marks. There were diamonds and squares and rectangles with one or two initials centered in them, and there were names and single initials, and some strange combinations like cattle brands. Yet, not one punt mark resembled the bizarre slope of the M or N or W on the shard. He looked through the booklet again, more slowly this time, reading the description of each registered mark. Most were indicated to be on the bottom of the bottle, others on the side or neck. He studied each one again. Nothing.

"Shit," he said, loud enough for Jose to hear.

Jose was dialing the telephone. "*Qué pasa?*" he asked.

"I'm dead on the bottlemark," Terry replied. There was a hint of disgust in his voice. "I need more information, I guess. How's the telephone doing by you?"

"No better than that book of marks did by you. Nobody's ever home. But one thing we never run out of is names—the guest list for the opening night at Sophia, the employees of the place, and of course all the other names the names on the list gave us. We're maybe halfway through, and the damn list keeps growing as we keep checking. Sometimes I think we're further from the end of it now than when we started." Terry picked it up and stared at it.

There were two hundred names and, from their best estimates, there'd been about that many at the party. They couldn't tell exactly, though, because some of the guests had gotten out of the burning room and gone straight home. Terry knew a guest list was a funny thing, because lots of people accepted and never showed, others came who weren't on the list, either with someone or as crashers. So it was tricky, but it was the best they had.

"Okay," Terry said wearily, "let's get in that wreck the boss calls a car and ring a few doorbells."

"The only good thing about this list," Jose said as

they headed for the car, "is that almost every name on it has an East Side address. Look at this: Park Avenue, Park Avenue again, Fifth Avenue, East Seventy-second Street, East Sixty-fourth Street. We won't have a lot of driving to do."

"Damn considerate of them," Terry said. They drove off.

Eleven names later they hadn't done much driving; nor had they gotten much information. Some weren't home; some would hardly talk to them; some didn't have much to add. One young woman, on East 73rd Street, off Fifth, broke down as she told them how her boyfriend had lifted her and literally thrown her over a pileup of people so she could escape—and then had died himself. The two men had stood there, not knowing what to do or to say. She was still crying when they said goodbye and left.

Now it was near the end of their tour, time for them to start the drive downtown. Jose looked at the list and said, "Hey, this next one's only a few blocks away, on Sixty-seventh. Why don't we knock it off before we quit?"

"You know how much paperwork we've got to do before we can leave the office," Terry replied. "If we don't get started, we'll never get out."

"Ah, hell, one more," Jose said.

Terry smiled. "Talk about gung ho! All right, one more. What's the name?"

"Leland Quimsby."

"Leland Quimsby, please," Terry said to the door-man. The partners had an unwritten rule: each man took on the things he could do best. Many East Side doormen were Irish, and when they spotted one, Terry took the lead. Invariably where Hispanics and blacks were involved, Jose stepped forward.

"Don't think he's in. Is he expecting you?"

"No. We're fire marshals." This time it was Jose who spoke, showing his badge.

"I'll ring up for you." The heavy doorman walked slowly to the board, rang Quimsby's apartment, waited. "No, I guess not," he said. "He usually comes home after I'm off duty."

"What time do you go off?" Terry asked.

"Four."

"And the elevator man?"

"No elevator men. Self-service. They got rid of the old elevators ten, eleven years ago."

"But you know what this Leland Quimsby looks like?"

"Sure." He looked at Terry. "About your height and build. Maybe five years older. A little swishy. Quiet. Goes off to work in the morning and that's the last I see of him. For me it's one-way traffic. I see 'em go, I don't see 'em come back. But I know they come back, 'cause next morning I see 'em go again." He laughed and looked disappointed when the two men didn't join in.

"Ever see him wear a cape?" Terry asked and then realized it was a pointless question, because this doorman saw people only in weekday morning business dress.

"Cape? No, he's a pretty fancy dresser, but never a cape. At least not that I remember."

"When does the afternoon guy get here?" Terry asked.

The doorman looked at his watch. "It's four. He should be here now, but you know those . . ." He looked at Jose and stopped short. "He's a good guy," the doorman added quickly. "But new, been here a week or so."

"Was this . . . whatever . . . working last Monday night?" Jose sounded angry. Terry knew that he'd guessed what the doorman had been about to say.

"Last Monday? Yeah. I remember they brought him in on the weekend to show him the ropes when it wasn't so busy." The doorman looked at Jose. "He's a good guy."

And then the afternoon doorman was there. His name was Carlos, and Terry saw that Jose was right, the first doorman had been about to say "spic."

Jose took the lead. "I'm a fire marshal," he said, and again showed his badge. "How you doin', *amigo*?"

The Puerto Rican doorman was nervous. "Okay, just learnin' the people."

"Do you remember working last Monday, what it was like?"

"Oh yeah, I sure as hell remember. It was my first regular day on the job, and I was scared as hell. Didn't know nobody. Didn't know who to stop; I mean, I couldn't stop everybody, so I just tried to keep an eye on suspicious ones."

"See any suspicious ones?" Terry asked.

"Not that I remember."

"Know a Leland Quimsby?" Jose asked.

The Puerto Rican looked to the other doorman for prompting. "Well-dressed all the time; not very friendly. A little you-know-what."

"Nah, I don't think I know him," Carlos said.

"On that Monday night," Terry said, "that first night you worked, do you remember anything unusual, anything out of the ordinary?"

The man thought for a moment. "No, like I said, I was too worried about doin' the job."

"Do you remember seeing a man with a cape?" Jose asked.

"A what?"

"Cape." Jose repeated. Then in Spanish, *"Capa."*

Carlos's eyes lit up. "Yeah! Oh, yeah! Some people were in the lobby, asking me to ring up to see if somebody was home, and I was about to do it, when out of the corner of my eye I see this cape swirling by, and I figure we got fuckin' Batman coming to visit. But he waves his hand at

135 o

me as if he belongs and heads straight for the elevator, and anyway I'm busy with these other people, so I let him go." Carlos shrugged.

"Can you describe him?" Terry asked.

"Man, all I saw was the black cape flyin' out behind him and his back. Could've been a tall, skinny girl for all I know."

"How tall, how skinny?" Terry asked.

"Oh, taller than me. Not as tall as Mike." Carlos looked at the other doorman. "Maybe as tall as you." This time he looked at Terry. "And on the thin side. But nothing special. That's it."

"That's plenty, *amigo*," Jose said. "One more thing. Can you remember about what time you saw Batman?"

"Yeah, that's easy. 'Cause when those people were asking me to work the switchboard, which I couldn't do too good, I remember looking at my watch and thinking, Thank God the super comes to relieve me for a coffee break at ten. So it was just a couple of minutes before ten."

"Hey man, that's good, really good," Jose said. "Now I'd like the two of you to do me a favor. Forget we were here. Don't mention it to anyone. Not anyone, okay?"

On the way back to the office, Terry said, "We got a guy coming into the building, wearing a cape, just a little while after the fire started. And we know Leland Quimsby, on the party guest list, lives in that building. We don't know that the guy with the cape *is* Quimsby. But it wouldn't be a bad guess, because if he got out of the Sophia when the fire started, that's just about when he'd be getting home. Of course, even if it *was* Quimsby in the cape, and he *was* at the opening, that doesn't mean he was the man the lieutenant saw hurrying along the street. And it sure as hell doesn't mean he set the fire. Quimsby sounds like a fashion plate to me; if he wears a cape, there must be others who wear one, too. Who knows, maybe a dozen other people at the Sophia showed up in capes." When Terry looked over, he saw Jose grinning.

"Don't get *too* happy, partner," Terry said. "Maybe we've got something. The question is how much."

But Jose kept grinning. When he spoke, he sounded excited. "Sure, maybe a dozen men arrived at the Sophia with capes. Maybe *two* dozen. But how many of them *walked away* from the Sophia that night with their capes?"

Terry got it at once and got excited, too. "Sure! They *arrived* with capes. And they *checked* them!"

"Right!"

"And the fire started right near the checkroom. Remember the poor girl who worked there?"

"Right!" Jose repeated, this time louder.

"And when the fire started they all went for the kitchen exit. And they sure as hell didn't, *couldn't*, get anything from the checkroom!"

"Now hold on," Jose warned. "Don't *you* get too excited. It's possible that Quimsby went in a cape and never checked it, wanted to keep it on to look sharp. Or maybe by some miracle, he could get it from the checkroom. But this I tell you, partner, Señor Quimsby is worth another visit."

Wednesday

Terry and Melissa walked past St. Patrick's, the winter sun bouncing in dazzling reflection off the cathedral's bronze doors, as if on celestial command. The day was perfect; the girl he was holding seemed perfect, too, but Terry was not happy. Lunch with Melissa's father, it turned out, was not to be at the University Club *or* McDonald's. It was not to be.

"Don't be angry, darling," Melissa said. "I know you're taking it personally, and you mustn't. He does it all the time, because he's so busy, so much depends on him at the office. And he lives through a crisis a day—some days two. He is *awfully* sorry; he asked me to be sure you know that. He wants to meet you just as soon as he can. Which means today you'll have to suffer lunch with only me, in the most darling little French restaurant. Do you think you can bear it?"

Terry smiled. "I guess I'll have to bear lunch alone with the most beautiful woman in the restaurant. In *New York*."

He let her lead him to the French restaurant; he'd spent a long, boring morning slogging through the life-insurance data of the forty-three Sophia victims. Next to each name, the amount of insurance and the names of the beneficiaries. It seemed his life these days was spent either making lists or investigating them.

The restaurant was charming; everything about it was unassuming except the prices. It was miles from the grubby offices of the Bureau of Fire Investigation, which delighted Terry; yet as soon as he sat down, all he could think of was the fire. What triggered him was the smell of the roses on the table. Their sweetness reminded him of the butyl nitrite he'd smelled at the Sophia.

Why butyl nitrite? It was an extraordinary accelerant, of course. . . .

"Terry," Melissa called.

But gasoline is so much easier to get, and cheaper. So is naphtha. And benzene. Why?

"Terry!"

Of course, it could be a homosexual. Butyl is so common among them. It was in that fag bathhouse that we found it, after all. But there's got to be others who use it besides them. People today are willing to shove anything down their throats or up their noses to turn them on to something other than their own lives.

"Terry," she called a third time, tapping his arm lightly.

He looked up at her then. "I'm sorry, Melissa," he said. "I was just thinking about the job."

"Yes," she said, leaning toward him. "What about it?"

Burke had warned him to keep quiet about the butyl nitrite, yet the idea of sharing this secret with Melissa appealed to him.

He told her about Sirkin, too, and the move to put the fire marshals out of business.

"That's rotten," she said. "Is it just to save money?"

"That's part of it; a grandstand play. They can only save pennies. It's also interagency jealousy, goes back a long time." That's what it looked like on the surface, Terry thought, but there had to be more to it than that.

"Sure it's not simply a rumor?"

"Rumors don't start with the commissioner." He let his shoulders drop.

"Can't you do something about it?"

"That's the whole point, that's why it's confidential. If we can bring this one home, this case, they'll have to think twice. And so at the moment we have this nagging question of why this particular chemical was used."

Terry lit a cigarette and Melissa signaled the waiter to pour some more wine. "God, I hope you catch the madman who did that—to poor Lucy Hartfield and all the others. It's just horrid, and I don't want to sound flippant but . . ." and her eyes took on the glint they often did when she was about to tease, "if butyl nitrite is the favorite of gay men, then how come you and Jose recognized it? I mean you two aren't . . . are you?" She winked at him. He grinned back.

"Only when you're not available," he said. This was good for him, he knew; thinking of nothing but the case would drive him nuts. Yet he went back to it. "We first smelled it at a fire, three or four months ago. You must have read about it: the Macedonian Bathhouse on Eighth Avenue, a bordello for homosexuals."

"I *do* remember," she said. "Some people died, didn't they?"

"Four. Jose and I had the job, and we got the kid who made the fire within three hours, a towel boy who had an argument with the manager. It was a big news item, as if the city suddenly realized there were tons of homosexuals huddled together like Chinamen in opium dens, and because it made big news it became another reason for the police department to turn against us."

"Why?"

"Because they had nothing to do with bringing the guy down. They weren't mentioned in the papers. The fire marshals got all the credit. Anyway, as we found out, the fags like to take this stuff, sniff it just as they're climaxing. It speeds up the heart, puts them on an erotic roller coaster. We found some of it around the Macedonian Bathhouse. It's dynamite, bursts into flame when a match comes within an inch of it, and it was soaked into all the mattresses in the joint and most of the towels. One guy I interviewed told me the fire ran across a mattress like an army of frightened cockroaches."

Melissa laughed. "What a lovely lunchtime simile! But it's not funny, is it?"

"Not if you've ever seen an army of cockroaches in the sink when you turn on the kitchen light. It always scared the hell out of me."

○ ○ ○

That afternoon Terry and Jose continued through the invitation list. They knew that Sirkin's office was working from the same list, and that most of the people would be interviewed again by the police detectives. They were just one step ahead of Sirkin, but it wouldn't be long until the police would isolate butyl nitrite as the accelerant. We still have the shard, he thought. And the butyl. And maybe Quimsby. They waited until evening to drive over.

At Quimsby's building, Carlos the doorman greeted Jose like an old friend. "Have you found out who Quimsby is?" Jose asked, smiling.

Carlos smiled back. "Yeah! 14D. He came in about a half hour ago."

"Was he the man in the cape?" Terry asked. This time Carlos looked disappointed. "Can't tell. Could be. Could be no."

"We'd like to see him," Terry said.

"Want me to phone up?"

"No," Jose said. "Thanks, *amigo*, we'll just surprise him."

As soon as Quimsby opened the door, Terry sized him up. About the same height as he, same weight. Not as muscular—Terry remembered "Mr. Leathersex" saying that. But his eyes were not red. Blue, yes. Watery—definitely. But not red. Terry was disappointed and had to remind himself not to hang this guy just yet. They still had a lot to find out.

The eyes narrowed and grew cautious as Jose identified himself and explained why they were there. Then Quimsby's head cocked to one side, he took a deep breath, and sighed more than spoke: "Oh, ye sinful wights and cursed sprites."

"I beg your pardon?" Terry thought he'd heard it, but didn't understand it.

Exasperated, Quimsby said petulantly, "Oh, never mind! Nothing. Nothing at all. You wouldn't understand."

It sounded like poetry, Terry thought, but what the hell would he be spouting poetry for? Peculiar. He let it go. Didn't want to, but he let it go.

"You were a guest at the Sophia opening," he said. "Would you tell us what you remember of the night of the fire?"

"I beg *your* pardon," he answered coldly. "I was *not* a guest at the Sophia opening. I only know about it what I read in the newspapers or saw on television."

Terry hated the man's arrogance to the point where he didn't believe anything he said, but he knew he mustn't let that get in the way. He pointed to his clipboard. "We have your name on the invitation list, and we have you checked as having accepted. Is that wrong?"

"No, it is not wrong, but at the last moment I was feeling a bit under the weather and decided not to go."

Well, well, Terry thought. If Quimsby was telling the truth, then some other guy who *happened* to live in this building and *happened* to be wearing a cape, just *happened* to be coming in on the night of the fire, just when he would have *if* he left the Sophia when the fire started. Strange. In fact, startling. He wondered if this guy were queer. He sure as hell could be, Terry thought. Or just an upper-class effete WASP snob. He had to remind himself: Don't hang the guy yet.

"Did you call anyone to cancel, Mr. Quimsby?"

"No, it was a last-minute decision; I knew how busy dear Totti would be—poor Totti! Besides, it's done all the time. One is not ostracized for it."

"Did you tell anyone you weren't going?"

"Oh . . . let me see . . ." Terry could see the machinery whirring in the man's head. "Oh yes, I did call

Lucy . . . Mrs. Hartfield—poor Lucy!—and told her I wouldn't be coming. She was *so* sorry. Now of course I'm the one who's sorry. Poor Lucy! Such a dear, *dear* friend. Gone. And to think, if I'd been there with her. . . ."

He bowed his head. Terry wondered if he could believe this show of emotion. He also wondered about Quimsby knowing Lucy Hartfield—that was the name of Melissa's father's friend. He wondered if Melissa knew this guy, too.

"On the night of the Sophia opening, Mr. Quimsby, did you go out at all, anywhere, for a newspaper, to the drugstore—anywhere?"

"No, I did not. I was really feeling quite ill."

"Did you go to work the next day?"

"Oh no, I just couldn't, because you see in addition to dear Lucy—poor Lucy!—my business partner, Jenks Monroe, died in the fire, too."

"What business are you in, Mr. Quimsby?"

He seemed surprised that they should have to ask. "I am the editor and publisher of *Design and Discourse Weekly*. Perhaps you know of it as *D and D.*"

"I'm afraid I don't," Terry said. "Is it a newspaper?"

"It is a *magazine* that *you* might mistake for a newspaper because it is printed on newsprint."

Terry let that one go, too. "Did anyone call you, or write or visit, to threaten you—or Mrs. Hartfield, or your partner, Mr. Monroe, for that matter—recently?"

He pursed his lips, thought for a moment. "No, no one that I'm aware of."

"Do you know of anyone who might wish to harm you or, insofar as you know, any of the guests at Sophia that evening?"

Quimsby looked thoughtful. "No, no, I can't think of anyone."

"Mr. Quimsby, you own a tux, I guess," Jose said.

143 O

"A tux? You mean a dinner jacket? Why, yes, of course."

Terry could have decked him just for that. Jose took it better; he ignored it. "When you wear your tux in the winter, Mr. Quimsby, what do you wear over it?"

"I wear a black overcoat with a velvet collar, designed especially for me by Ralph Lauren. I have always championed American designers, you see, and the coat was a little thank-you from Ralph."

"Do you ever wear a cape?" Jose asked.

"A cape? Why in the world would you ask that?"

"Oh, just trying to get a little education in style, Mr. Quimsby. Do you?"

"No. But it's not a bad suggestion. A cape is a classic, you know. It doesn't depend on trends." Now Quimsby sounded like he was playing with them.

"Do you own one?" Terry asked.

Quimsby stopped playing. "No, I do not." He said it icily.

Terry looked at Jose, who shrugged. "Well, that's all, Mr. Quimsby. Thank you for answering the questions. We appreciate your help. You see, the Sophia fire was the worst in this city since the Triangle Shirtwaist back in 1911, and we're trying to find out what started it. . . ." Terry was careful not to say "*who* started it." "If you think of anything that could help us, please call. Here's my card."

"Well?" Terry asked when they got back in the car.

"Well, I could see you couldn't stand the fuck, and I don't blame you. But don't let it get in the way. I also think he's a faggot, but that doesn't make him guilty."

"Yeah, he could be swish. Or he could be just another upper-class hard-on who looks down at people. And he says he has no cape. . . ."

"Believe him?"

Terry shrugged. "Don't know. He got pretty cool

around then. And he says he didn't go at the last minute."

"Believe him?"

Again, Terry shrugged. "All I know is, it's damned convenient—for him—that the one person he told about not going, Lucy Hartfield, died in the fire. But I'm glad he mentioned her name, because it gives me a new pipeline to him, maybe. Mrs. Hartfield was a friend of Melissa's family."

"I think it was a good interview. The best yet. We're a long way from locking him up. Or even being sure he did it. But he's the only name we haven't crossed off the list so far." Jose held up two crossed fingers.

"Yeah," Terry said. "Even his s's whistled a little, but so do mine. Too bad his eyes weren't bloodshot."

O O O

When Terry stepped into her apartment, Melissa said, "Surprise, we're having dinner here tonight, prepared by yours truly, the noted cook. I want to show you there's something solid and down-to-earth beneath this gleaming exterior."

She took the raincoat off his shoulders. He reached down to pat her behind. "I know there is."

She giggled, sidestepped his hand. "Maybe *too* solid."

"Uh-uh, as perfect as the exterior."

"Let me get you a glass of wine." When she walked into the kitchen, Terry slipped the pistol and holster off his belt and put them in his raincoat pocket. Melissa returned with two glasses and a bottle of white wine.

"Pouilly Fuissé," she announced. "The dealer said it would never be this cheap again, so I had to buy a case, of course."

"I thought you said this would be down-to-earth? Don't get too fancy for me; I get nosebleeds from heights."

She laughed, went back into the kitchen.

"Music?" he called after her.

"Up to you!" she shouted back.

"How about this record of Mozart horn concertos?" he said.

"How about Cole Porter?" she countered.

"You said it was up to me," he said. He put on the horn concertos, picked up the glass of wine, sat on the sofa, and put his head back. He was not used to being this comfortable. He usually felt a little uneasy with her, with her classical music—he'd forced himself to put the Mozart record on—and her heavy books. He looked at her bookshelves and saw names like Skinner, Chomsky, Lévi-Strauss. Deep, he supposed. What does she want with me? But right now, at this moment, he felt easy.

Dinner was an omelet with delicate herb seasoning and a salad made of Boston lettuce and arugola. Without wanting to, Terry found himself talking about the fire.

"Do you know a man named Leland Quimsby?"

"I think . . ." she hesitated. "Yes, he's the editor of that chic weekly, *Design and Discourse*, but I don't know him."

"He says he's a dear friend of Lucy Hartfield."

"I suppose it's a small world, yet a big one. I'm sure Lucy knew hundreds of people I never met; and I'm sure Quimsby knows *everyone*. He'd probably know me if I wanted to put in the time at those dreadful parties his magazine writes about all the time. But I don't like the people at them."

"What kind of people do you like?"

"I like *you*. I like Jose."

"Me? That's bad judgment." He said it, laughing. "But Jose—is a great guy." And he told her how they'd met and how Jose had been shot on the roof of an abandoned tenement. "I'm glad you like Jose," he said. "It's important to me."

"Then I'm doubly glad I like him."

"Why?" he asked. "Why do you try so hard to please me? Frankly, Melissa, I don't understand what in hell you see in me."

"Shall I tell you?"

"Yes!"

"First, more wine." She refilled her glass. "For you?"

"I'd rather have some coffee."

"Yes, sir!" She walked to the kitchen, came back with a cup of black coffee. He really wanted it light, but he didn't say so.

"Shall we sit on the sofa while I tell you?"

They walked to it and sat facing each other, she with her legs curled up in front of her.

"I've had just one serious love affair, which lasted fourteen months. An English professor at the New School. Landon. He was bright, considerate, handsome, intellectual, even smoked a pipe. He came from the right family, the right prep school, the right college. Life was so tidy; too *damned* tidy. We would sit together every evening. I'd work on my papers, Lanny would sit there devising new ways to test his students on the significance of the four-teener in the poetry of Barnaby Googe or something like that. French movies, Italian restaurants, Russian novels, German operas. Walks to the bookstore on Sheridan Square. Off-Broadway theater, because it's honest. The Museum of the City of New York, because it's honest. Buying bread at Balducci's, because it's honest bread. I realized I was getting more of what I was brought up with: everything right, everything orderly. Sure, a little more intellectual than I was used to—we didn't exactly sit around the fire discussing the romantic poets—but essentially more of the same. Landon would have fit in so perfectly, they'd never have noticed when he arrived. It was so right it was dull.

"Then I met you, Terry, and I must say you *are* different. You carry a gun, God help me, and aside from the Freudian implications of that, you work on the dark side of the world, one that I know nothing about. You're in it, guts and all, and I like that. I like it that I can't predict what you're going to say next, that you look at the world with a simple honesty that's refreshing after the sophisticated bullshit I'm used to. I even like it that you're shocked when I say a dirty word. And so I want to make you happy, the way you make me happy."

He leaned forward. "You do, Melissa, you do."

She clinked her glass against his coffee cup. "Here's to making each other happy."

Melissa kissed him hard, put her hand to the back of his neck to press his mouth to hers. When she let go and sipped her wine, he suddenly thought of something.

"Tell me more about this English professor," he said.

"Oh, no," she said, pausing to sip the wine. "I've said enough, too much. No rummaging through the details."

"Do you still talk to him?"

"If we meet at school we chat, yes." She stared at him, the teasing look in her eyes. "Jealous?"

"No, not jealous. I was just wondering if he could help me. Could you ask him?"

"But what can he *do* for you?"

"He knows poetry, right?"

"Does he ever know poetry!"

"You know this guy Quimsby spoke a very peculiar phrase today, and I think it might be from a poem. I don't know what or where, but maybe your professor might know." Terry got up and went to his jacket for a pen. He wrote the line down on a small piece of paper and handed it to Melissa.

" 'Oh, ye sinful wights and cursèd sprites,' " she

read it aloud. "Whoever wrote it is a *lousy* poet, I can tell you that. But otherwise I don't have a clue."

"It might be nothing," Terry said. "Maybe Quimsby made it up. But if it is a poem, even a lousy one, do you think he might recognize it?"

"Landon?" she said. "He knows literature the way some men know baseball statistics. And even if he can't spot it, he'll know where to look. I'll ask him tomorrow. I love the idea of helping you," she said, and kissed him again.

"You've got another chance, sweetheart," he said, stroking her cheek. "Jose and I want to go to a top-shelf discotheque, as classy as you can get. . . ."

"Orpheus," Melissa interrupted, "but it's hard to get into."

"We do have badges, you know."

Melissa reached for the wine bottle. "Let me take you. Father keeps a membership for visiting clients, although he's never been there. We'll sail right by them at the door."

Terry laughed. "Yeah," he said, "that's terrific. Just like the carriage trade."

"Not like," Melissa kidded. "We *are* the carriage trade."

"If you say so." He kissed her again.

Again she refilled her glass, this time with the last wine in the bottle, and to pour it she had to tilt the bottle so that's its bottom was pointing right at his eyes. He was forced to stare at it.

"My God!" he said suddenly and seized the bottle. This time he examined the bottom carefully. It had a deep concavity, and in it he could see the bottlemark, a star within a circle. It was nothing like any of the punt marks in the book he'd been sent.

Of course not!! This time he said it to himself. This was a *European* bottle. It had a deeper indentation underneath than American bottles. Which would explain the U-shape of the shard he'd found, and explain why the print wasn't in the book of American marks.

"What's the matter, darling?" she asked.

"I just couldn't believe we'd gone through that whole bottle, that's all."

"Not *we. I*, darling. I got you in here for wine, women, and song. Shall we go on to the second now?"

If he was different for her, Terry thought, she sure as hell was different for him. He had no business being with her, drinking . . . he couldn't even pronounce the name of the wine to himself. But he knew he didn't ever want to let go of her. He put his hands on her shoulders. "What would you say to having your child baptized in a Catholic Church?"

Misunderstanding him, she laughed, touched his cheek. "Don't worry, darling," she said. "I took my pill this morning."

Thursday

Next morning the sky was a solid curtain of gray clouds. It had rained all night; ice clung to the branches of the trees on 13th Street.

Terry was standing on the brownstone stoop, waiting for Jose and thinking of Melissa. And of the weekend ahead. He would spend it with Melissa and her parents in Connecticut.

Jose pulled up in the battered sedan. "Your sister called," he said as Terry got in. "She wants you to call her." He handed Terry the message.

"Thanks." Terry leaned back and sighed. "She's got troubles. I feel for her."

The car began to move toward Seventh Avenue. "What's her problem?"

"Christ knows. For one thing, she's involved with a musician. But it's more than that. It's always more than that." Terry paused. He didn't want to talk about his father. He changed the subject. "Last night a clue was shoved right under my nose."

"What's that?" Jose asked, stopping at a red light.

"The bottle. It's got to be European. I already called Washington, and they're sending me an international register."

"They could've done that the first time."

"Yeah," Terry answered resignedly. "I could've asked too. Where we going?"

"Downtown," Jose replied, making a left onto Seventh Avenue. He reached up and took a memo from under the sun visor's rubber band. "Here," he said, handing it to Terry, "read this."

It was a confidential memorandum to the fire commissioner from the office of the deputy mayor for economic development: "Please forward all pertinent data regarding the Bureau of Fire Investigation to this office by the end of the business day on Friday. Such data will include budget allocations, overtime disbursements, records of all expense vouchers for the previous twelve-month period, all court appearance records, records of major caseloads, and case dispositions for the previous thirty-six-month period, and current personnel roster."

"We expected it," Jose said. "But still . . . the pricks gave him just two days to get all that together. He's keeping it quiet, 'cause the troops will mutiny, you know. He wants us to give him a hand."

"What about the fire? I wanted to do a background on this Quimsby and make up some reports for Sirkin's meeting tomorrow."

"Fuck it. We'll do that in the morning. And you

can call the FBI on Quimsby's profile—take you ten seconds."

"Yeah, screw it," Terry said, fingering the memorandum. They drove in silence. After a while Terry asked, "This from Lettington's office?"

"That's it, pal."

"What gives with this guy?"

"He's a schmuck. Rich and connected schmuck who thinks the city oughta make a profit. I asked around about him. All he knows about New York is what's east of Central Park, and below Eighty-sixth Street."

"No, I don't mean that," Terry said, letting the memo fall to the seat. "I mean, doesn't he understand that firemen are the only ones motivated enough to do the job? We know it. Shit, we live it, and they want to make arson no different from a pocketbook snatch. It's a twelve-billion-a-year industry and they're gonna take fire investigation away from the firemen."

"Yeah," Jose said. "But I think this goes back a long time. The P.D. has always been lobbying to do us in, and they finally found a receptive asshole—Lettington."

"Yeah, but why?"

"Ego, man. They want the whole ball of wax."

"What bullshit. It's really frustrating to think that they might be able to get away with this."

Jose laughed. "Now you're thinking like a Puerto Rican."

"Sì, amigo," Terry said in return. "Speaking of that, how'd you like to go dancing tonight?"

"I'm in, man," Jose laughed. "I feel I could salsa my way to another life."

They were passing Sheridan Square then, and Terry ordered, "Stop the car, Jose."

Jose looked quickly to the pedestrians on the street as he pressed down on the chrome handle. "Qué pasa?" he asked.

"The phone booth," Terry said, pointing to the corner of Christopher Street. "I gotta make a call. The Lettington thing is annoying the bejesus out of me."

McDougal was not at his office, but he answered on the third ring at his home. "I gotta see you," Terry said.

"Yeah, listen," the reporter said, "I'm squeezed for the day, but I could meet ya tonight after eight. Maybe we could eat something."

"Shit," Terry replied forcefully, making sure McDougal understood his displeasure. "I'm busy, I'm going out."

"Well, where you goin'? I'll meet you there."

At least he was being cooperative, Terry thought. "Orpheus. You know it?"

"Yeah. A little chic for a civil servant, ain't it?" came the reporter's reply. The tone was good-natured and Terry smiled.

"It's for the carriage trade, pal," he answered. "That's me. See you later."

O   O   O

There was a knock on his door, and when he opened it Melissa handed him a thin, leatherbound book. *The Day of Doom*, by Michael Wigglesworth.

"Who's this?" Terry asked.

"A pre-Revolutionary poet," Melissa answered. "Wigglesworth Hall at Harvard is named after him. Landon thinks the poem you're looking for might be in there. It's a start, anyway."

"Thanks," Terry answered, opening his apartment door. He threw the book onto his bed and returned to the hall. "I'll take a breeze through it later. But first—Orpheus!"

Jose was waiting for them. As Melissa slid into the front seat of the battered sedan, she laughed. "I thought the city gave you guys Mercedeses!"

Jose smiled. "You can park it anywhere you want."

"They won't tow it away?"

"Uh-uh."

"Then it's as elegant as you can get." Melissa winked mischievously. "But isn't it against the rules to let me ride in it?"

Terry slid in next to her and slammed the door. "We're stretching all the rules lately," he said, taking a quick look at his partner.

They drove up Eighth Avenue to Central Park West, where Jose parked the car in a bus stop. A line of people stretched from the marquee of Orpheus, in the center of the block, nearly to the corner. Many of them wore full-length furs. One couple in chartreuse roller skates was standing taller than the rest. To the side of the line, a small group of autograph hounds waited anxiously to see if someone recognizable would step from a cab or limousine.

A brawny bouncer stood, Sphinx-like, by the door. In front of him was a short, ferret-faced man in a V-neck pullover with a silk scarf around his neck. Melissa recognized him as the owner of the discotheque. "I made reservations for three," she said to him. "The name is Melissa Reid."

The man gave Terry and Jose a glance and then looked at a small pad he was holding. He said, "Yes, Miss Reid. It will be about twenty minutes. If you'll just step to the end of the line."

"But we have a membership," Melissa protested.

"So does the Ayatollah," the man replied sarcastically, "but he'd have to wait tonight, too."

Jose reached into his hip pocket for his badge and turned his back to the line of waiting people. He flashed his badge to the little man, saying, "We won't be long."

The man's face soured, as if he had just bitten into something rotten. "Listen," he said, "I can't take care of all of you guys."

"We're not asking you to take care of us," Jose said, holding the badge a little higher. "Take a closer look, and ask yourself how many people above occupancy are inside. We pay our own bills wherever we go."

The man gestured silently to the gorilla, the door opened, and Terry, Melissa, and Jose went into Orpheus.

Walking through the lobby, they could hear the heavy thumping of the music growing louder and louder as they neared the inner doors. It was a large place, an old movie house that had been stripped to the bare brick walls. As they entered, they were momentarily stunned by the quick-flashing strobe lights and the loudness of the sound system. Melissa started to move with the beat.

Terry looked at several women dancing wildly before him. One wore short velvet pants with a single black-leather legging, another was in an apache blouse, with one breast almost fully exposed. Still another wore transparent pajamas, with nothing underneath.

Melissa, in a green satin pants suit, was noticing too. "I feel positively Victorian," she yelled into Terry's ear, "in comparison with this crowd."

Terry laughed and squeezed her, saying, "Sweetheart, you're royalty. Where should we sit?"

"If you want to dance, we'll sit down here," she replied. "If you want to look, we should go up on the balcony."

Terry gestured upward.

"You've been here before?" Jose asked, leaning close to her ear.

"Just once, and we didn't stay long. It's not bearable after a half hour." Melissa held onto Jose's arm, leading him toward the balcony stairs. Terry hung back, watching the dancers. A shirtless man in luminescent coveralls started to pass him, winking seductively and running his tongue across his lower lip. Terry looked the other way.

Suddenly the stage lit up in a film image of roaring flames. The room darkened, the strobe lights stopped flickering, and a cloud of perfumed smoke began to drift through the room. Terry made his way to the side of the room, to where Melissa and Jose were standing. Everyone had stopped to watch a magician and a naked woman who had appeared on the stage in front of the fire-filled screen. The music thundered, a shock wave of sound, and a group of women, screeching like purged sinners at a gospel meeting, delivered the words above the rapid beat of the drums. "Fire! I'm on fire!" they sang, as the naked woman entered a raised oblong box centered on the stage. The magician conjured a flaming torch from out of nowhere. "Fire! I'm on fire!" the song repeated again and again as the oblong box was covered and as the magician swept the torch across it, igniting it into a burning bier. The sides of the box were lowered, and the room exploded into applause as the flames danced across the woman's body. "My body's in flames, take it, take it, my body's in flames."

"It's perverse," Terry said, as they sat down at a table adjoining the balcony balustrade.

"It's fun, Terry," Melissa answered. "The crowd loves it. Don't be so serious."

An overweight waitress in a low-cut bodystocking came to the table and took their order. Terry noticed she was wearing a tiny silver spoon on a chain around her neck, and that it was caught between her heavy breasts.

Terry leaned his head against his fist. "Maybe you're right, Melissa, but I don't see the entertainment in it."

"The entertainment is in the people," Melissa said. "Stars, bankers, congressmen, weirdos. Everyone. It's a zoo."

"The zoo is healthier," Terry said.

"You're right," she said. "I haven't been there in a while."

"We should do that one day in the spring," he said, taking her hand.

"It's a date," she replied.

"I'll tell you what I think," Jose said.

"Yes, tell us, Jose," Melissa said.

"Well," Jose continued, "I don't like the song or the act, 'cause it's a little close to our work. Lighting a fire on someone's body may give them relief, it may be fun and games to *them*, but I think it's in bad taste, you know? Me, I get my relief by playing with my kids." He paused then, before adding, "Anyway, my wife wouldn't let me make a habit of coming here without her."

The music again became piercingly loud, and the strobe lights flickered so that the dancers on the floor seemed to move in slow motion.

"It's all business, partner," Terry said, looking down over the balustrade.

"Yeah, but on our own time. I wish I had a nickel for every free hour I've given the city."

"Should you get paid for this?" Melissa asked.

"We won't," Jose replied.

"Hey, Jose," Terry interrupted, "you don't know how to whistle, do you?"

"Not loud. Do you?"

"No. And I see Mike McDougal down there looking for me."

Melissa leaned across Terry, saying, "Listen to this."

Terry leaned back. "No kidding," he said, surprised. He pointed. "The guy in the tweed jacket, the red handkerchief hanging out."

Melissa tightened her lips over her teeth and listened for the downbeat of the music. The reporter looked up, as did others, when he heard her shrill whistle, and Terry waved at him.

"You're terrific," Jose said to Melissa. "Where did you learn to do that?"

"At the horse farm. Sometimes you have to catch them before you can saddle them."

Horses, stables, Terry said to himself. Christ, the little things that separate us get bigger every day. And Jose, he's lucky if he can send his girls roller skating once a week.

"How're ya doin', Ahearn?" McDougal said as he neared the table. The words bled out of the side of his mouth.

"Not bad for a civil servant," Terry said, standing to greet the reporter. "Yourself?"

"Yeah, right," McDougal said, sitting at the table. "I feel like I'm slumming in this joint." He did not shake hands in greeting, and he kept his left hand in his jacket pocket. When Terry introduced him, he nodded at Jose and winked at Melissa.

"I read your column," Melissa said.

McDougal said, "Yeah, thanks." He turned to Terry, continuing, "Slummin' is an interesting word, you know? It began when the fuckin' rich used to prowl the tenements to get laid."

He didn't have to talk like that in front of Melissa, Terry thought.

"Now it's vice-a-versa," McDougal continued. "Yeah, I guess you could say I'm slummin'—lookin' for the tenderloin, as they used to say. How ya makin' out with the discotheque fire?"

"No change," Terry said. "Waiting some stuff out, biding time. What about the information I gave you?"

McDougal looked around the table and then at Terry. "Maybe we should talk downstairs."

"It's all right," Terry said.

McDougal said, "I was gonna call you, but I keep getting waylaid. This Lettington thing keeps developin' like a fuckin' paramecium. Every time I look there's another tail falling off. You know who his father-in-law is?"

"Who's that?"

"Meyer Samuels. You know who Meyer Samuels is? He's very cute, Meyer."

Melissa broke in. "I know who he is," she said. "His wife is on the committee for every benefit and dinner-dance in town."

McDougal turned to her. "Yeah, how'd you know that?"

"The society column, Mr. McDougal, in your newspaper."

Terry smiled at her. Even his mother read the society column, though he never understood why.

"Shows you what dough can do," McDougal went on. "He's a very respectable investor, firm of Penny Investments, but I shoveled pretty deep and found he's weighted down with real estate, dirty ground cover in the area of Times Square, whorehouses and jerk-off shops. And he tries to hide it, eight dummy labels at least. Yeah, all his dollars have black edges."

His bandaged fingers still concealed in his pocket, McDougal managed to light a cigarette.

"And you know what?" he said.

"What's that?" Terry asked.

"You did fuckin' terrific with this Moe Perritz, 'cause you know who Moe Perritz is? There's a Meyer and Moe act going on in Brooklyn and on Times Square. This fuckin' Perritz is the counselor for Penny Investments. It's a dynamite story, yeah, but I have to go easy, make sure everything fits right. I'm gonna sit on it until I see the first fire in Times Square."

Sit on it, Terry thought. Shit, everyone wants to sit on things. We're sitting on butyl nitrite, sitting on the glass shard. Burke is sitting on Sirkin and the move to undermine our office. We're sitting on the whole goddamn case, waiting for the hammer to slam down and the bell to ring. Why can't we just be out in the open about things?

"What about Rodney Lettington?" Terry asked. Then he added, "You want a drink?"

"I'll drink yours," McDougal answered, reaching for Terry's glass and holding it up, studying it.

"Vodka and Perrier," Terry said. "You don't get heartburn."

"Yeah," the reporter answered. "Where you from, Los Angeles?" He sipped the drink and said, "Meyer bought the mayor's advertising bill in the last campaign, which is how he bought little Rodney his present position."

"To protect his investments, you think," Jose shot in.

"Yeah, prob'ly, but I don't see the connection yet, only that Rodney likes to throw his weight around, like for the Marchesa dame."

"Are you going to write that story about the Marchesa?" Terry asked, reaching over to take a sip of scotch from Melissa's glass. She let her finger slip across his hand as it wrapped around the glass.

"Yeah, small shit at the moment, unless you can get the buildings commissioner to swear that Lettington put the arm on him for a certificate of occupancy."

Christ, Terry thought. I give him Moe Perritz and he's going to give me diddly on Lettington. Maybe I should've never talked to him. "Why don't you just write the thing and let the pieces fall wherever they fall? You said the street goes both ways, and I want Lettington's role in this fire out in the open. I don't want to sit on it, you know?"

The reporter spread his right hand out on the table. He studied it a moment and then clenched it. "Yeah," he said finally, "give it some time, Ahearn. I want to dig a little more. A poke here, a poke there. It's a big package, and I want to fill it first, you see."

Terry didn't see, and he thought for a moment about telling the reporter about Lettington's memo to the fire commissioner. But that connection was too valuable to give away now that he knew about the deputy mayor's father-in-law. If it was Lettington's plan to control fire investigations, Terry thought, I'll have to sit on that too, damn it, until the time is right, when the rug begins to slide.

"I gotta go now," McDougal said. "Before all the action goes home with their hairdressers."

"It was nice meeting you," Melissa said.

"Yeah, sure," McDougal replied. He stood and began to turn away.

"Leland Quimsby mean anything?" Terry asked.

McDougal turned back. "It's familiar," he said.

"Editor and part owner of something called the *Design and Discourse Weekly.*"

"The *D and D*, yeah. It's a slop sheet for rich people who like to read about themselves. I met him a few times at those things you gotta wear tuxedos for. Tall and skinny. He's a three-dollar bill, but hangs around moneyed broads for a beard. If I find something, I'll call ya. Keep in touch."

As the reporter paraded from the table, Melissa asked, "What's a beard?"

"It's a cover," Terry explained. "If a married man like Jose were having an affair with you and wanted to take you somewhere in public, he'd have me come along as the beard. A fag would bring a woman as a beard."

"Gay," Melissa corrected. "You said fag the other day too."

Terry suddenly remembered the argument he had had with his father over the word *nigger*. She was right.

"Homosexual," he said, thinking at least that was more honest than fag, more realistic than gay. What the hell are they doing to my language?

"Anyway," Melissa continued, "what would it mean if he's a homosexual?"

"If he's a homosexual, it means that he would probably know about butyl nitrite."

"Right," Jose broke in. "And you know something else?"

"What's that?" Terry turned to him.

"The connection McDougal was talking about. I just figured out why Lettington is interested in the bomb squad. He wants to be wired into it."

"Why would he want that?" Melissa asked innocently.

Jose wanted to end the conversation. He stood, reached his hand toward her. "I'd really love to dance," he said, "and take our minds off business."

"Right," she said, "there's nothing to keep us from being part of the joke, huh? If our beard will excuse us!"

"Let's go," Jose said. "I'll teach you the one-hop step."

Melissa was laughing as she and Jose left Terry alone at the table. Jose's self-deprecation brought a smile to Terry's face. It's a good partnership, he thought. Jose is as smart as they come.

Christ, it made sense to be tapped into the office that was responsible for fire investigation if you were going to make a fire out of Times Square. Those seedy goddamn buildings would profit terrifically from the insurance just as they profit from the sex industry. Jose is right. That's Lettington's angle in sticking his nose where it doesn't belong, same as his father-in-law's—to protect his investments.

Terry looked over the balustrade at Melissa and

Jose. He was still smiling as he watched Jose, doing a sort of twist, all of his weight on his left leg, dancing more with his arms than any other part of his body. But his smile changed. Then he remembered when Jose could claim the title of mambo king of the fire department, and he stopped smiling.

He looked at Melissa. Her hair was swinging from shoulder to shoulder as she rotated her body. She looked good. Classy. The kind of woman he would pick out of a room at first glance. It was strange to watch her move, letting herself loose with the wild music within a wild crowd. Yet, even within the wildness, the roar of the music, the flickering of the strobe lights, he thought he could see an elegant restraint in her, as if she were pointing out she didn't really belong.

The waitress came and Terry ordered another round of drinks. He began to think about what McDougal had said about Quimsby. So Quimsby was probably a homosexual. Which meant he *might* know about butyl nitrite. And the cape? The doorman saw a cape man in his building. Was it the same cape the lieutenant from Engine 8 saw? But Quimsby said he didn't own a cape. Christ. We need something stronger. If we could only get enough to justify a search warrant, but what do we really have? A guy who *could* know about butyl nitrite because he's a homosexual? Shit. At least we have the butyl nitrite, and we wouldn't have that if it weren't for that gimpy guy Jose, out on the dance floor. If it weren't for Jose and the Macedonian fire.

There must have been forty or so little cubicles, each one with a bare mattress. That's where it started, in a mattress. He and Jose were on the still-steaming second floor, at the end of a long, narrow corridor.

They interviewed the officer of the engine company which was first to arrive and learned that there was nothing out of the ordinary—no two separate fires or empty fuel cans or cloth or paper streamers. They talked to the manager of the bathhouse, who told them that there were no significant incidents lately, no arguments with customers, no reason for anyone to set the fire; that the premises were not overinsured; that he owned the building, it was profitable, its taxes were paid.

They couldn't find anyone who'd profit in revenge or in money by setting the fire. They folded their notebooks and walked down the corridor. Just another cigarette, another mattress, another fire. But four men had been caught in the shower room—it didn't matter what you called them—they had died needlessly. Horrid deaths in a dirty dungeon where they had gone looking for a little happiness.

As Terry neared the stairs at the end of the corridor, his foot suddenly slipped forward as if he were kicking a football. He fell back, losing balance, and was about to drop to the muddied floor when Jose caught him beneath the arms.

"Three points," Jose said. "Notre Dame takes it ten to seven."

"Holy Saint Gobnet," Terry cried, "what the hell was that?" He did not know who St. Gobnet was, but he remembered his father crying out the name when he'd been stung by a bee in the Ebbets Field bleachers.

Looking down, Terry saw the small bottle he had slipped on lying in the debris. He picked it up and read the label to Jose. "'Jac-me, for that heightened feeling. Butyl Nitrite, no prescription necessary.' What is this shit, Jose, you ever heard of it?"

"Nope," Jose replied.

Terry twisted the cap off and raised the bottle to his nose. "Christ," he sneered, his nose puckered into his face, "it smells like Bayonne."

Jose took the bottle and sniffed it. "It is powerful," he said. "Butyl nitrite, huh? Let's give it an open-cup test for the hell of it."

They walked down the stairs, and as they came into the light of the reception area Terry noticed that his Stetson shoes had mud rings above the soles. He cursed beneath his breath as he grabbed at a stack of folded towels by the counter. There was a white stain under the mud on the shoes, and Terry continued cursing as Jose toweled the countertop and poured a capful of the Jac-me onto the dry surface. Jose smiled at Terry as he lit a match.

"Hey, what're you doin'?" a resting fireman said.

"It's a fundamental technique for fire marshals," Jose answered. "It sounds impressive in a courtroom, but it's as simple as lighting a match. It's called the open-cup test."

The fireman grinned.

"If it were gasoline," Jose continued, "the vapors would ignite when the match was half an inch from the liquid." But the match was still more than an inch from the Jac-me when the liquid burst into flame. "Man," Jose yelled, "it almost bit my goddamn finger off."

And Jose remembered the bathhouse and the butyl nitrite. So it had to be a homosexual who threw that bomb down into the Sophia Club. Who else would know about butyl nitrite?

Christ, he thought, there are lots of others who might know about butyl nitrite. You're looking for a break, Ahearn, and you're trying to build one in your mind. Yet . . . yet, there was something about this Quimsby, cape or no cape, something in his eyes, bloodshot or clear, something cruel, in an indifferent way. Something. Not enough for a search warrant, though.

Melissa and Jose returned to the table. The music

seemed to have grown even louder; the drums resounded in Terry's ears.

"Whew," Melissa said, falling into her chair. "That was fun."

"Ready for more?" Jose said, snapping his fingers in time to the music.

"Not yet," she answered, taking a sip of her drink. "They even rest horses between races, don't they?"

"I was born and raised on Lexington Avenue." Jose laughed as he sat down and loosened his tie. "The only thing I know about horses is what they tell you on the scratch sheet."

Terry smiled. He reached over and stroked Melissa's forearm. Looking beyond her he saw a young woman, seated at a table, in the dim light of the balcony corner, lower her head into the lap of a man. Was she stoned, he asked himself, or was she making it? Or both? The man closed his eyes as the woman's head bobbed behind the table linen. God, the place had a reputation for things like that, but he hadn't believed it until now. The music was blaring. The strobe lights began blinking erratically in red and blue. His head was throbbing.

"Could we pack it in?" he asked Melissa.

"You mean leave?"

He nodded.

"Of course," she said. Terry raised his hand for the check.

On the way out they saw the ferret-faced owner of Orpheus counting tickets in the checkroom. The attendant, a young black woman, handed him a thick roll of dollar bills.

"Thanks for the hospitality, *amigo*," Jose said.

The owner frowned. "You're lucky to be in here at all," he said nastily.

"Yeah," Terry shot back. "And make sure you tell the IRS about all that cash."

The three of them were grinning as they walked out into the cold night air.

Friday

The following morning, Terry was about to pre- pare the reports he would need for the meeting at Sirkin's office later that afternoon when the phone rang. He cursed under his breath as he picked it up.

It was Jose. "Listen, Terry, Burke and I are over at City Hall seeing what we can do about saving our asses and the bureau, you know what I mean?"

"Yeah, who are you talking to?"

"A couple of councilmen Burke knows, but then we have to go out to Queens to talk to the borough presi- dent. Burke knows him, but it seems like pissing in the wind. By the way, I may not see you for the rest of the day."

"What's up?"

"There's a cop I know, my neighbor, wants me to do him a favor and take an arson bust. It's a personal thing and he doesn't want to give it up to the detectives."

"What about Sirkin's meeting?"

"You go."

"You gonna make the bust alone?"

"Listen, Terry, it's no problem."

"Where is it?"

"Ninth Precinct. Noon. But listen, Terry, I'll do it alone. The man asked me to do him a personal favor."

"I'll be there at noon."

Just before twelve, Terry walked through the Lower East Side. In the narrow corridor of tenements that was 7th Street he could feel the heavy smell of burning wood in his nostrils. Up ahead, toward Avenue A, he could see smoke swirling through the sky; just another fire in an abandoned building.

He turned into the flat, concrete entrance of the 9th Precinct. Jose had not arrived yet. Terry showed his badge to the desk officer, a sergeant, who sat on a high platform, fronted by an unshined brass bar and looming like a judge's bench. Terry said, "I'll hang around. I'm supposed to meet someone here."

The sergeant nodded, and Terry walked to an old oak desk, apparently unused, in a corner of the large reception area. It was a room made bright by bare fluorescent tubes overhead, yet deadened by the dark green paint that covered the walls. The only other people in the room were a patrolman at an information desk near the door and, across from him, near a pay phone hanging on a wall, a young woman perched on a hard wooden chair. Terry noticed that she would face one direction for a minute, sigh audibly, then suddenly move her arms and legs the other way. She kept moving and sighing like a wind-up doll. Terry thought as he watched that something was building inside her that would soon explode.

The woman was not much older than his sister, Maureen. Christ, he should take some time to think about his sister. His mother had called to tell him she had not been home again the night before. "Your father," his mother had said, "keeps calling her a bag o' bolts."

That was funny, Terry thought. The old man used to call her "sweetie-pie," and now it was "bag o' bolts." Christ. Whatever money the old man used to squander over the bar he also used to blow on Sweetie-pie. "Buy her a new dress tomorrow," he used to say to Terry's mother.

"She doesn't need a new dress, Petey."

"Buy her a new dress, goddamn it."

When the old man used to come home drunk, ready to sing another song or start another argument, all his wife had to say was "Shh, or you'll wake Maureen," and the old man would put his slippers on.

He wanted his little girl to be the one with the straight back, with her chin raised just a little more than the others. He made sure she did well in grade school, and made sure she got a scholarship to a good Catholic high school so that she would be prepared to mingle with the best of them, maybe marry one of the best of them. She was his princess, his sweetie-pie, until the last year at Queen of Angels grammar school, when she began to notice boys. The worst kind of boys, the old man said. From then on Petey Ahearn took it on himself to be the protector of his little girl's innocence.

"Where you goin'?" he would say whenever she approached the door of the apartment. "Be back here in an hour," or "before nine o'clock," he would say.

She would beg. "Everybody except me stays out until eleven."

He used to curse then. "If they jumped off the fuckin' bridge, would you jump too? And don't let me see you on the street with that oily-haired kid again."

It's no wonder Maureen became a stranger in her own home, Terry thought. He wished there were something he could do to help her.

Then Terry was startled by the desk sergeant's strong baritone bellowing into the telephone. "Yes, he's here, ma'am, he's a prisoner. . . . Now calm down a little. . . . I don't know what he did, we're just lodging him." The sergeant yelled to the patrolman at the information desk, asking if the wagon was coming. The patrolman shrugged, and the sergeant spoke into the phone again. "If the wagon comes, he might be in court tonight. If not, it might be tomorrow. . . . Hold that. Tomorrow's Saturday. Make it Monday. . . . No, I'm sorry. We're not permitted to call prisoners to the phone. . . . That's okay, ma'am. Sorry I can't help you more."

The patrolman fed another call to the sergeant, signaled to the young woman near the pay phone.

"Ma'am, it's for you."

About twenty-five, she was trim, but her face showed a hard life, bitterness and contempt. She looked up. "What you mean, it's for me? What's my name?"

"I'm sorry I don't know your name," the sergeant said, "but it's about your children. It's the social service. If you want your children, pick up the phone there at the information desk."

"I'll get my children," she replied with anger. "They're right here, and I ain't leaving without them. I'll answer a phone when it's for my name."

The sergeant raised his eyebrows, and he looked through a pile of papers bunched in front of him. Pulling a report, he looked at it and said politely, "Miss Banks, the phone is for you."

Raising her head in small triumph, the woman got up and walked to the information desk. She held the phone to her mouth and said, "What the fuck do you want?"

There was a silent pause throughout the reception room until the woman slammed the phone down and walked back to her seat.

The phone rang again, and after listening a short time the sergeant said to the patrolman, "Transfer this to the squad. Miss Banks's problem just became the detectives' problem."

Just then two patrolmen escorted another woman into the reception room. She appeared to Terry to be in her late thirties and was attractively dressed. He heard one of the patrolmen saying that she was being arrested for shoplifting. The woman looked up at the sergeant and snarled, "You wanna get laid too? Do I gotta screw you too, like these guys made me screw them on the way over here?"

The sergeant looked at her with an expression

that showed years of experience, shook his head just a little, and said, "The judge will love to hear that story, lady."

After booking her, the cops took the woman up the creaking wooden steps at the back of the room. They passed a detective who had come down to take Miss Banks upstairs. "Are my children up there?" Miss Banks asked defiantly.

The detective was hard and brisk. "Just come on," he said. "Don't give me a hard time." Miss Banks followed reluctantly.

A few minutes later, a patrolman came from a back room with two small boys. They walked through the room and out the precinct doors.

The sergeant shook his head slowly as he watched them pass, commenting to the clerk, "She abandons her kids for three days and then breaks our horns. There ain't enough years in a lifetime to explain what people do."

Jose came into the reception room then, and Terry signaled to him.

"Sorry I'm late."

"No sweat. It's an education here. Queens?"

"Yes. The borough president's a master at the hand job, said he would do what he could with what little influence he had at the mayor's office. We got tied up in traffic. Donnelly, that's my neighbor, is supposed to be on a meal break. I hope we didn't miss him."

"It's not one yet. He should still be on lunch."

"The detectives will go bananas, you know. Arson always looks good on the score card, but they stole an armed robbery from him last week so he wants to give us this one. It's just down the street, I think."

They walked up the worn, wooden stairs of the precinct house, and down a long, dusty corridor to a glass-paned door. The glass was clouded and someone had printed on it with a felt-tip pen, DINING ROOM. Beneath these words, someone had written in longhand, "When shit becomes valuable, the people of the 9th Pct. will be born without assholes."

Jose opened the door, looked about the narrow room, and saw his friend Donnelly sitting on a stained couch that looked as if it had been taken from a sanitation truck. His close-collared uniform was open, exposing a red-and-black hunting shirt. He was eating a sandwich with one hand and holding a lighted cigarette in the other.

Jose introduced Donnelly to Terry, and the fire marshals sat on wooden school chairs as the patrolman related the incident. He read from the small leather-covered journal all policemen carry in their hip pockets, and Jose took notes.

As they were leaving, the patrolman said, "Thanks, Jose. I really appreciate it."

"Right," Jose replied. And to Terry, "What the hell else have we got to do, anyway?"

O O O

The two fire marshals entered a deteriorating tenement building at 7th Street and Avenue B. The hallway seemed colder than the outside air, and Terry threw his wool scarf around his neck. Jose, carrying a legal-sized briefcase, limped quickly behind him.

"Colorful place, huh?" Jose said.

"Modern art," Terry returned. The walls and the apartment doors looked like the side of a New York subway car. Garish, emblazoned names from floor to ceiling: Chico, Pepe, Iron Man, Simbu.

"Simbu," Jose said. "That's our man. He lives on the fourth floor. We gotta see Mrs. Nieves first, though." The stairs were hard for Jose, and Terry slowed his pace as they climbed to the fourth floor. The hallway ceiling was blackened.

An old woman opened the tenement door. Her neck was bent with the weight of a head filled with too many years of sorrow.

"Mrs. Nieves?" Jose said.

"Police?" she asked apprehensively. Terry showed the woman his badge, and she waved them into her kitchen. The walls were uneven and fallen plaster had left them pockmarked, but they were painted a bright glossy yellow. "She reminds me of my grandmother," Jose whispered. "Her railroad flat in *el barrio* was always clean and orderly, just like this. 'Come in from the bad streets,' she used to say to me."

Mrs. Nieves pulled chairs out from a worn wooden table, and she sat, gesturing for the men to sit also. In surprisingly good English she said, "The man there across the hall is crazy. He's all the time yelling, or making those crazy marks on the walls. You saw them? The landlord painted over once, but this crazy man painted them again. It's terrible to live here, but where can an old lady go? To a welfare hotel? It's worse there, I know, I have friends. This morning this crazy man brings a bag of matches in hallway, a big bag, and he yell and he scream and he make them on fire. The super *a Dios gracias*, was upstairs in hall and he run to my apartment and get a pot of water and throw it on the fire. The crazy one, he went to throw more matches on the fire. He have another bag, and the super hit him. I am so afraid, I call the police. The man run back to his apartment and lock his door. When police come, he is gone."

"And the super?" Terry asked.

"He clean up mess. Then he went away also. He takes care more buildings. You can to find him. He live next door, number six-five one, the building with glass broken out of the front doors."

173 o

"What's the super's name, Mrs. Nieves?" Terry asked, writing on a legal pad.

"Perez. Hector Perez."

"And the man across the hall, what's his name?"

"He don't have a real name. Is called 'Simbu.' Phony name. You do something, officer?" The woman put her hand on Jose's arm and began to whisper again. "I am too afraid to go asleep at night with this one. I have no one to take care of me. Is enough bad without this crazy man near my door. You can help me?"

Terry put his hand on hers and said, "I hope so, Mrs. Nieves, but we will need a statement. Will you sign a statement for us if we write down everything you told us?"

"Will I must to go to court?"

"No," Terry said, "nothing like that. You see, Mrs. Nieves, we are fire marshals, and we can take a sworn statement from you, under oath. The police can't do that, but we can."

"That's all right. I don't want to go to court. Is terrible."

"It's all right, Mrs. Nieves. Let me ask you just one thing. Did you see this man Simbu light the fire in the hall?"

"Oh, yes, I see. He yelling so much I open the door just a little, with chain on. He take one book of matches and light the whole thing, and then put it in the bag and it begin on fire. When the super cleaned up, we see there is nothing in the bag, just matches. Hundreds."

"Thanks, Mrs. Nieves," Terry said, and began writing a statement. Jose began to talk with the old woman in Spanish, explaining what their job was, Terry guessed, and reassuring her. A cockroach began to walk up the front of the refrigerator, just next to them. Jose turned his head away. "I don't mind," Mrs. Nieves said, getting up. She took a sponge from the sink and killed the roach as it tried to hide on the field of enamel paint. "There's nothing you can do about it," she said, "you just live with them."

After reading the statement aloud, Terry asked the old woman to raise her hand and swear to its truth. It seemed strange to administer an oath. Here, he represented the law. And it made him feel good.

The old woman signed the statement and Jose witnessed it. As Terry began to place the papers in the briefcase, there was a loud barreling noise from the hallway. It sounded like someone running down the steps two by two from the floors above. The noise stopped and was followed by the sound of a turning lock.

"It's him," Mrs. Nieves whispered, crossing herself, "it's that crazy bastard."

Jose whispered in return, "Do you know if he owns a gun, Mrs. Nieves?"

"I think so," she answered, "but who knows anything in this building, in this city. I know only he's a crazy man."

"Thanks," Jose said. "You just stay in your apartment, now, okay?" He opened the door quietly, and he and Terry stepped into the hall. Wordlessly, they walked to the door on the far side of the hall, each silently wishing he had a back-up team to cover the top and the bottom of the rear fire escape.

His revolver drawn, Terry looked at Jose, thinking, No problem, pal. We're together. You're not alone on some godforsaken roof in the Bronx.

They paused at the door a moment, listening. Terry thought he saw sweat glistening on Jose's forehead and wondered if it came from fear, from the memory of looking straight into the dark circle of his own revolver. Christ Almighty, Terry suddenly thought, does he have it? Will he be there if I need him?

Jose drew his own revolver, and reaching over

from the side of the doorframe, he knocked heavily on the door.

They heard a small rustle from inside the apartment, and then a high voice, an incongruous voice. "Yeah," it said.

"Simbu?" Jose yelled.

"Yeah," the man answered, his voice echoing as in a room without furniture.

"We're from the fire department, Simbu. We want to talk to you for a minute."

"Eh, man," the voice came through the door, "you got the search warrant?"

"Ah, c'mon, man, Jose called out, "we can get a search warrant and come back tomorrow. What are ya gonna do, move? We just want to ask you some questions."

"What about?"

"About the fire that was here this morning."

"There's no fire, man."

"Open the goddamn door, Simbu," Terry yelled, "and talk to us face to face."

"Okay," the voice said resignedly. "Wait a minute, one minute." Then there was a pause. "Come on in, the door is not locked," the voice came finally.

Terry looked at Jose, who was nodding his head, reached for the doorknob, turned it, and pushed as hard as he could. The door swung open, and Terry and Jose rushed simultaneously into the apartment, their revolvers held high in front of them. There, directly before them, stood Simbu, a small man, bent over, back to them, his Bermuda shorts and underwear pulled down to his ankles. He was looking, upside down, through his legs at Terry and Jose, and laughing. "Like you said it, man, face to face."

Jose limped forward quickly, and standing on his good leg, he kicked out with the other, connecting solidly between the sides of Simbu's hairy buttocks, sending him hard against a bare wall. Terry could see that Jose's leg hurt like hell, but he was pleased he had connected.

Simbu fell to the ground.

Jose limped over and grabbed the man roughly by the arm, saying, "Get up, hard-on. We'll see what's funny about starting fires in a building with babies and old people." Shoving him against a bare wall, he continued, "You're some kind of prick. No heart, huh? Nothing serious to you, huh? You're under arrest."

Jose released the man's arm.

Simbu looked defiant. Reaching down to pull up his pants, he said, "You're a motherfucker, know that?"

Terry breathed easily, relieved that the possibility of gunplay was past.

Jose smiled at the light-skinned, undersized Puerto Rican and looked directly into his cloudy eyes, set deep into his face and framed by curly black hair and a few days' growth of beard.

"Don't let your mouth get you into any more trouble," Jose said dispassionately, pulling a card from his breast pocket. "Here's your rights, Simbu," he continued, reading the *Miranda* guidelines. "One, before we ask you any questions, you must understand your rights; two, you have the right to remain silent; three, anything you say can be used against you in court; four, you have a right to talk to a lawyer for advice before we ask you any questions and to have him with you during questioning; five, if you cannot afford a lawyer, one will be appointed for you before any questioning if you wish; six, if you decide to answer questions now without a lawyer present, you will still have the right to stop answering at any time. You also have the right to stop answering at any time until you talk to a lawyer."

He then handed the card to Simbu, who threw it on the floor. At least, if the question arose, he could tell the judge that he had formally handed the card to the accused. "You can't arrest me, man," Simbu said. "I'm an artist, man. Artists got freedom."

Terry put the man back against the wall and searched him. "Not to set fires in people's houses, they don't."

"What were you doing up on the roof?" Terry said as he took a penknife from the rear pocket of the man's Bermuda shorts.

"Flying my pigeons, man. I don't do nothin'."

Terry looked through the three small rooms and the bathroom, each covered with light purple paint, saddened to see the condition of the rooms. Simbu had little of his own in this world, one of thousands in New York who lived at the borderline between subsistence and starvation. He opened the refrigerator; in it stood a container of milk and a jar of peanut butter. The kitchen also held a rusted table and two chairs. In the living room, there were just four unmatched wooden chairs, in the bedroom a single bed. No lamps, no bureaus, no tables, no pictures on the walls; Terry saw only the bed, a closed metal closet, and, stacked against the fire escape window, four green plastic garbage bags and six large brown grocery bags, each filled to the top with matchbooks.

Terry counted the bags and made a notation in his notebook. He returned to the living room.

"What's the story with these matches, Simbu?" he said.

"They're bad, man, dangerous," the man answered. "I pick 'em up everywhere. They call me 'Smoky the Bear' sometimes. I tell people they shouldn't have matches. I take 'em from everyone, man, 'cause they shouldn't allow matches to be everywhere where they are." His tone had changed, the insolence was gone, and he seemed to believe what he was saying.

"That's funny, Simbu," Terry said. "You collect matches because they're dangerous, and then you light a fire in the hallway when there are people living upstairs. You ever realize you could kill all the people upstairs?"

"No, man, I wouldn't kill no one," he replied. "I'm a gawd. No shit. I'm a gawd. A gawd wouldn't hurt no one, and you can't arrest a gawd either."

"You're right, Simbu," Jose replied, "we wouldn't arrest a god. Maybe just send him on a trip to Valhalla, you know what I mean."

"Hey, man, you're making fun of me and I ain't lying to you, I swear I ain't." Simbu began to walk through the purple of the living room to the bedroom. "You don't believe me, man," he continued, "I'm gonna show you."

Terry followed him. The man looked strange wearing Bermuda shorts in the middle of winter. He reminded Terry of a scarecrow; his legs were severely bowed, and dropped down beneath the plaid shirt and green-and-black striped shorts like dead grapevines. "Just be careful," Terry said, realizing the man was about to open the metal-closet door.

"Nothing here, man," Simbu said, "no tommy gun or nothing. Just proof." He reached into the closet and pulled out a bright green uniform with a patch on the sleeve that read SANDFORD SECURITY.

"Holy Christ," Terry said, "you're a *guard*."

"That's right, man," Simbu replied, flashing a gold-capped smile. "See, I ain't lying to you."

"It doesn't mean anything, Simbu," Terry said resignedly. "You're going to have to come along with us."

Simbu threw the uniform on the dirty flooring. His smile vanished, and he began clenching his teeth so that his cheeks vibrated. "Bullshit, man," he said. "I'm here to help the people, to protect the people. You don't know how the people live here. You just come with a badge and think you can do anything you want with the people. The *people* are on fire, man, and you give me bullshit about lighting a fire in a building."

179 ○

"Forget the speeches, Simbu," Terry said. "Just put a coat on, and come along with us for a while."

"Listen, man," Simbu said, bent over and cowering, "I don't want to go with you. It's no big thing, man, a little fire in the hallway. But I've been to Rikers before, and *that's* a big thing. Oh no, man, I ain't going back there." The man began to scream, and Jose joined Terry at the doorway. "I'm not going nowhere with you, man. *Nowhere.*" He began prancing back and forth.

Terry looked around. The man had no escape. He was cornered. There were two windows in the room, one leading to the fire escape, but both were shut tight. Nailed, probably, Terry thought. There wouldn't be time to open one, in any event.

The man pranced, gesturing wildly. "I been there, man, some badass come every time in the bathroom, the showers, anywhere man, and they tear your cheeks apart, man. Same thing, man, at Rockland, you're alone and they tear your cheeks if you don't got a knife." His eyes began to water. "The man do nothin' for you. He look away, and Simbu gets stuffed 'cause there ain't no knife, and the man don't help. Bullshit, man. And who's gonna feed my pigeons, man? Who's gonna take care of them?"

Holding his hand in a calming gesture, Terry said, "Take it easy, Simbu. No one said anything about Rikers Island or Rockland State."

Simbu kept pacing back and forth, his eyes widening, becoming glassy, as if he had seen something unbearably frightful. Terry saw fear turning the man's face into a grotesque mask. He moved toward him. "Easy, man, easy."

But Simbu's eyes rolled slowly upward until the pupils were lost behind the leathery lids. He began to shake, a strange gurgling sound came out of his mouth. As Terry moved near him, Simbu fell to the ground; the shaking turned quickly to short, rhythmic convulsions, his stomach rose, his head and feet hit hard against the linoleum floor.

Then his back crashed down to the floor as his head and feet lifted. It looked like some kind of violent swimming exercise, as if he were drowning, fighting for air.

Terry rushed to him, knelt by his side, pulled the frayed belt from around Simbu's Bermuda shorts, folded it in half and shoved it between the man's chattering teeth. He opened the shorts, loosened the waist.

Jose knelt next to his partner. "Try to calm him."

Terry put his hands on the man's shoulders and pressed against the convulsions, looking down at the red veins running through the whites of his eyes. "Relax," he said. "Relax."

Simbu's legs jerked out furiously in a final, desperate kick against death. His bladder emptied, the urine soaking through his shorts and down the side of his leg. Simbu twitched, and then lay perfectly still. The urine puddled at Jose's knees.

Terry put his hand at Simbu's thin neck and felt for the carotid artery. He pressed his fingers deep into the neck, hoping to feel the slow, surging movement of blood. Nothing. Simbu was dead.

"Christ," Terry said.

Jose got up and stepped over the lifeless form, kneeling again on the other side. Terry raised Simbu's neck, pulled back on his head, opened his mouth, and pinched his nostrils together. He leaned over, forced two breaths into the mouth and throat of this man who only moments before had been one of thousands of low, mindless, criminal enemies, part of a collective of city scum.

Then he raised his head from the kiss of life-giving breath. He closed his fist tightly and hammered it down into Simbu's sternum. The force of the blow shook the body. Terry hoped it would defibrillate the heart, shock it back to movement. Again, he felt the carotid artery. Again, nothing. And again, he raised the neck, pinched the nose, and brought his lips down over Simbu's.

Jose leaned over the body. "One, two, three, four," he counted aloud as he pressed his weight down on Simbu's chest with each number. On "five," Terry blew another breath.

The two kept at it for several minutes, both strangely calm. They had done it before, and both knew they were doing all they could, all they had been trained to do, to challenge the death they had witnessed.

Jose suddenly left his position and ran out of the apartment. He returned in a little more than a minute, saying, "Police emergency squad or Bellevue, whoever gets here first."

Terry was performing the single-man technique of cardio-pulmonary resuscitation. He was on his third round of fifteen heart massages when Jose resumed his place, counting, "One, two, three, four."

In less than twelve minutes the Emergency Medical Technicians of the Bellevue ambulance corps arrived and did what they could, using a mechanical resuscitator, a portable EKG, and an electric defibrillator. They talked by portable phone to a doctor less than a mile away in Bellevue's emergency room. They gave Simbu two injections. Nothing worked.

Fifteen or twenty minutes passed before one of the EMTs looked at Terry and said, "Forget it."

Simbu was beyond help.

Terry looked down at the spindly creature. "*Requiescat in pace,*" he said, "you poor fuck."

Mrs. Nieves was standing in the doorway. "Is he all right?" she asked.

"No, ma'am," Terry said, passing her, "it seems he had an epileptic fit and then a heart attack. He's dead."

"*Jesu, Maria, Jose,*" the old woman said, crossing herself.

When the police arrived, Terry and Jose gave them a statement that officially documented the death as they had witnessed it. They waited while the EMTs carried the covered stretcher through the garish hall and out into the street. As the ambulance pulled away, Terry said, "I guess Mrs. Nieves will sleep a little better now, huh?"

"Who knows?" Jose answered. "These tenements have changed since I was a kid. You always have to sleep with one eye open now."

"Yeah."

They walked to the car. "And you know what?" Jose said. "Now I'm really sorry I kicked him. There're a lot of crazy people in this city, but sometimes you forget, and you treat them like they were normal."

Saturday

"I've never been in Connecticut before," Terry said as Melissa drove them into the driveway of her parents' house. "Can you believe that? New Jersey a thousand times, but never Connecticut."

"Then welcome," she said. "I'm delighted that your first time is with me. I'm also delighted to show our house—I love it so."

They had driven through tall granite gateposts, onto a paved driveway that seemed never to end, bordered by rows of old maples, which finally gave way to a huge, sloping lawn.

"Is all this yours?"

"Used to be lots more," she replied. "It's only thirty-five acres now. It once was five hundred, but the taxes got so unbelievable, we sold most of it off after World War Two."

Only thirty-five acres in Greenwich, Terry said to himself. He wondered what it would be worth at—what?

Twenty thousand dollars an acre? Thirty thousand? A million just for the land wouldn't be too wild a guess, he figured.

The driveway curved as it went into a slight rise, and then he saw the house. He'd expected some kind of Southern Colonial mansion, pillars and all, and what he saw was a modest white house with black shutters, looking surprisingly small.

As if she'd read his mind, Melissa said, "It's a lot larger than it looks; it goes back and back and back and has more bedrooms than we've ever been able to use. But I like it, that it doesn't look too big when you drive up, don't you?"

"I like it," he said.

Terry carried her suitcase and his into the large entrance hallway, where they were met by the housekeeper, whom Melissa introduced and then hugged as if she were a member of the family. "Your mother and father aren't here," the woman said. "They weren't sure when you would arrive, so they went off to do some antiquing. They'll be back soon, and your mother said for you to take your old bedroom, the gentleman the red one."

The woman leaned to pick up a suitcase, but Melissa took it from her. "Lord, child," the woman laughed as she began to lead them up the stairs, "a person can't do anything for you."

Following her, Melissa whispered to Terry, "Don't worry about the rooms. There's a connecting door."

Terry smiled. "Does your mother know that?" he whispered back.

"Of course," she answered.

As soon as they were in their rooms, Melissa unlocked the connecting door, took his hand, and led him into her room. "I think this may be my most treasured place in the whole world," she said.

Terry realized that in the bosom of her own home

she was taking on a girlishness he'd never seen in her before. It was endearing. The wallpaper in her room was a delicate blue-and-pink floral pattern, and the bed was high and canopied.

"Same bed I've always had," she said, sitting on it. "All little girls want to be the Queen of England, and that's how I've always felt in it. You can be my Prince Philip."

Terry smiled. My father should hear that, he thought, with his tirades about how the British are destroying human rights in Northern Ireland while nobody—not the UN, not the U.S.—will do a damn thing about it. "They're all castle-conscious whores, sleeping in English beds," the old man once said.

Terry knew that he did not want to be Prince Philip, but he did want to sleep in that bed with her. And yet, and yet, he had to laugh to himself as he thought of it, for there was a great temptation to sleep in his own room, the big airy bedroom he'd been formally assigned for the night, just one of the many big bedrooms in this house.

"It's too much," he said, laughing. "If I took you to my parents' for the night, you'd sleep in my bed and I'd sleep on the living room couch. And, there'd be no connecting doors."

"Well," she said playfully, "there's a sofa downstairs, if you'd prefer. And I can always lock my door. . . ."

He sat, put his arms around her, and gently pushed her back on the bed, kissing her. "Nope," he said. "I'd rather sleep in this bed, if you don't mind that I refuse to play the Prince."

"Okay," she replied. "If you don't mind if I refuse to do much sleeping."

He ran his tongue between her lips and moved his hand to her breast.

"Umm," she sighed. "How about right now?"

"That's what I had in mind," he said.

"In that case," she answered, rising from the bed, "I *will* lock the door."

When they'd finished making love, and showered and dressed, they went downstairs, arm in arm, and saw the Reids sitting in the library, sipping martinis.

Terry felt a little embarrassed, but the other three handled it so naturally, he relaxed.

Agel and Pamela Reid were both tall, both angular, both fit-looking, and handsome in a way that Terry thought belonged to "the horsey set." He could almost see them being played by James Stewart and Grace Kelly, except that Mrs. Reid was older than Grace Kelly and not as beautiful. Terry noted how they immediately, gracefully, brought the conversation around to him, to what he "did." Which suited him fine, because if Reid knew Lucy Hartfield and Leland Quimsby knew Lucy Hartfield—well, this little social excursion into the Sophia set might yield him more than days of lists and phone calls and parking in the bus stops and ringing doorbells.

He was happy to talk about his work. "I'm assigned to only one case now, the Sophia fire. Melissa tells me you were invited and decided not to go at the last minute. Luckily! And she said you had a good friend who died in the fire. Or was it more than one?" Terry figured if there was more to learn, he might as well put in for it right away.

"Oh, I knew many of the people there slightly," Reid said, "but only one good friend—Mrs. Hartfield. She was a client, too. But mainly a dear friend."

"What kind of woman was she?"

Reid sensed what was going on—Terry could see that—and asked: "Should I be under oath?" But he smiled the most pleasant kind of smile. Terry figured he was about to be stonewalled—with high-class manners—and it made him angry.

"I guess I'm off base, Mr. Reid," he began. "But

I'm only a kid from Brooklyn and therefore very weak on social amenities. And very bothered by what I'm working on—a fire that killed forty-three people—horribly. A fire that was deliberately set by some madman, who is still walking the streets. Who maybe will set another fire—God knows when. Maybe tomorrow. Unless we catch him. And at this moment, we're not close. We're bogged down by all sorts of politics and shortages of money and manpower—and other problems I'm not going to bother you with. But my partner and I spend all day, every day, phoning people and chasing down leads, and ringing doorbells—trying, trying. Our problem is we're outsiders looking in at the social big leagues. Then out of a clear blue sky, this woman I'm crazy about . . ." he looked to Melissa, "who is way above my head, I'll say it before you do, happens to have parents who know one of the victims. And since I often make the social error of taking my work with me on weekends, I just figured I might save a few steps, maybe help my chances of catching this guy before he starts another fire. All right, I'm off base. I don't want to spoil the weekend for anybody. Forget I asked."

Agel Reid looked serious and intense. "I feel properly chastened, Terry—I mean that. And, by the way, I hope you'll call me Agel. I'll tell you what I can. Go ahead."

Then he smiled at Terry; Terry smiled back. "I guess I get on my high horse sometimes . . . Agel . . . and I'm properly chastened, too. I appreciate your help. What can you tell me about Lucy Hartfield?"

"That she is . . . was . . . a fine woman, a lonely woman who wanted love, wanted friendship, and didn't seem to know any way to get it other than to try to buy it, something she could do endlessly, because she had virtually endless amounts of money. As her lawyer, and someone who really cared for her, I tried to protect her from her 'friends' and, believe me, sometimes it wasn't easy. She'd meet all sorts of people who pretended to be crazy about her for

herself but inevitably had some sort of wonderful deal waiting for her to put money into. The latest was control of
a chic . . . rag, that's all I can call it . . . pretentiously
called *Design and Discourse Weekly.*"

Bingo! Jackpot! Goddamm it, Terry thought, that's
it! He could hardly stay calm, but he gave it a good try.
"You mean Leland Quimsby's magazine?"

"You know him?"

First Terry looked to Melissa, warned her with
his eyes to shut up. Then he answered. "I've met him, but
I don't know him. He was supposed to be at the Sophia
opening, like you. And like you, he was one of the lucky
ones who didn't go. What can you tell me about him?"

"That he became Lucy's dear friend and soon
enough suggested that she buy the controlling interest in
Design and Discourse Weekly from Quimsby's partner,
Jenks Monroe. . . ."

"Who died in the fire!" This time Terry was not
quite as calm.

"Monroe," Reid went on, "was about to sell eighty-
five percent to one of those English media barons, Lindsay
Barrett. . . ."

"Who died in the fire!" Terry had to control his
voice. "If it was a fire set for revenge, it sure worked . . .
for . . . for somebody."

"Barrett apparently wanted to get into the New
York market and wanted a prestigious publication. His
wife—his widow now—had social ambitions. His price for
Monroe's interest was irresistible, and Monroe was about
not to resist. The problem for Quimsby was that he and
Barrett hated each other, and so he tried to get Lucy to
outbid the Englishman."

Reid paused, taking a sip of his martini. "I guess
I was the bad guy in that. I prevailed upon her not to stay
in the bidding. She'd gone to six million, which I thought
overpriced. Barrett apparently went to six-two, and he and

Monroe shook hands on it. Lucy was disappointed. I was delighted. I understand Quimsby was absolutely *furious* with me."

"Jesus!" This time Terry couldn't keep quiet. "And you were supposed to be at Sophia, too! All his enemies . . . at one party. Lucy Hartfield, Jenks Monroe, Lindsay Barrett. And you. He got three out of four. And came close with you."

"I guess I'm lucky."

"So far."

"Should I worry?" Reid was so cool-looking Terry couldn't tell if the man was *really* worried or just joking. "What do you suggest?"

"Don't go to any big parties," Terry said, and didn't know if *he* was really worried or just joking.

WEEK THREE

In the two weeks since the fire, Leland Quimsby hadn't once been to the office of Design and Discourse Weekly. The weeks had been long, upsetting, vacant; the staff understood his distress and had muddled along without their editor and publisher. Also of course without the chairman of the board, Jenks Monroe—but that had been no loss.

Now, although still distressed, he was back. "Good morning, Mr. Quimsby," the receptionist said. He barely nodded as he walked by, headed for his office. She was a fleshy cow, bosoms always dripping out, skirt slit too high, showing her bulbous thighs. He was sure Jenks had hired her. All Jenks was interested in was tits and ass—and money.

"Welcome back," she called, but he was far

enough past her by then to be able to ignore her. He was no sooner seated at his desk when she buzzed.

"What is it?" he asked petulantly.

"Mrs. Fields is on the line about the American Revolution Costume Ball this Wednesday."

"Tell her I'll get right back to her."

He was in no mood to talk to that silly bitch about the ARC Ball.

He remembered he was to have gone with Lucy Hartfield, and he remembered the last time they'd spoken about it, about a month ago, over dinner at the Palace. They'd been discussing it, at least Lucy had, but he'd been too busy thinking of what he'd say this time when she asked him to come up to her apartment for a brandy when the evening was ending. Usually the invitation was accompanied by her hand on his thigh—it made him positively shudder with revulsion, which of course he couldn't show.

In a city that abounded with wealthy, lonely women, Lucy Hartfield was one of the loneliest, and the wealthiest, and he was always pleased to accept her invitations to the ballet, opera, symphony, theater, museum openings, charity dinners. It was good business—good for him, good for the magazine—to be seen with a woman like Lucy. She was warm, generous, pleasant—and valuable.

Before, when she asked him to come up to her apartment, he'd always made some excuse. But tonight would be different. What he saw during dinner would make it different. Actually, Lucy had seen it first, and with her eyes gestured toward a far corner table.

"My, my," she said, "there's Totti Gambelli."

He looked and what he saw made his heart pump faster. There indeed was the Marchesa—with Jenks Monroe and Lindsay Barrett. It's not that he was surprised, there was little Monroe could do to fool him. He'd heard about it first a few days ago and confronted slimy Jenks, who'd said he'd been just about to tell Quimsby, and that of course he would not sell his eighty-five percent interest without consulting Quimsby.

Well, he wasn't going to let Monroe go unchallenged on that! "What do I hear about your selling to Barrett?" Of course Monroe had said no, but Quimsby hadn't liked the look in his eyes as he said it.

And now there Jenks was, sitting and talking with that disgusting little Cockney satyr, who would turn D and D into another of the rags that he owned all over the world.

"Totti is a marvelously vital woman, isn't she?" Lucy said. "I hear her new disco is going to be scandalous, Leland." She tittered behind her hand—how thirties MGM! Leland thought—and added, "I can't wait for the opening."

He didn't even answer that, he was too busy watching Monroe whispering to Barrett, just knew they were planning the sale of D and D. His D and D. His life, his genius, his sense of style. Monroe had raised the money. But he'd given birth to it, nurtured it, made it the magazine of consequence for people of consequence. It represented twelve years of his life and he wasn't going to stand by and let a money-grubber and a repulsive Cockney take it away. But how? You don't fight money with indignation. You need money. But where?

Why here! Right across the table from him. Lucy could buy D and D a hundred times over, if she wanted to. Well, it was up to him to make her want to. And then, sometime later, to get her to give him more of an equity in the magazine than the fifteen percent he had now, enough of an equity eventually so that no one could sell his magazine out from under him.

So tonight when she asked, it would be different. And as always, with a hand on his thigh, she asked. This time it was in her garnet-colored Bentley on the way home from the restaurant.

"Leland?"

"Yes, Lucy."

"Will you come up?"

"Yes, Lucy," he said, looking into her eyes. "Yes, I shall."

Could he do it? Quimsby wondered. Could he put his arms around this woman and be aroused by her scent, by the touch of her flesh, by the heat of her body, the moisture of her mouth? Upstairs, in her large, ornate bedroom, he held her tight as he closed his eyes and thought of Howard Bates—his Howard. "Yes, Lucy," he whispered, "you are a wonderful woman."

"Undress me, Leland," she said.

He walked behind her and slowly began to undo the buttons at the top of her dress. You had better do this properly, he cautioned himself. And he bent to kiss her neck. He lowered the dress down her back over her hips. He knelt, she lifted her feet over the garment around her ankles; she turned and faced him. He placed his fingers under the elastic of her silk half-slip and slowly gathered it until it reached her waist. He brushed his cheeks against her thighs and kissed deeply. She sucked in her breath sharply and sat on the edge of the bed. "Oh, Leland," she moaned. Go on, he said to himself, go on. He forced the pantyhose down her flabby legs, rolling the nylon carefully, caressing her thighs and legs with his lips, all the way down to her feet. He bent over her and nudged her to lie down. He raised her arms and kissed her shaven armpits while moving the rolled slip up her torso and over her head. He let his lips touch hers for a moment, brush her eyelids and ears, and then, lifting himself, turned her over and removed her bra. She was running her hands over his body and sighing.

"Kiss me there, Leland, kiss me there again," she begged.

He knelt again, drawing her forward to the edge of the bed. He kissed her there over and over, not for present ecstasy but for future security. The present ecstasy was hers. "Darling," she cried, "darling, darling, darling, darling!" He kept on until he felt her thighs go into spasms and then relax completely. "Oh, Leland," she sighed, "I never expected . . . oh, darling!"

Now it was her turn to deliver. She had to agree to his plan. Everything, he thought, has its time and its place. Now was the time and place to approach her. She was sated, vulnerable. She would feel like it now. Letting his hand slide gently across her nipple, he said, "Lucy, do you know why Barrett and Jenks Monroe were together at Totti's table this evening? It's because that Cockney is buying D and D."

"Oh. Don't stop, please."

"It will be awful for me. Awful for the magazine."

Lucy cuddled against him.

"You could buy the company, Lucy. It could change your life. And you and I could work nicely together."

"Yes," she said, kissing his cheek, "we could, and we have."

"I love you, Lucy," he whispered, although the closest he had ever come to loving anyone was with Howard Bates.

Things went well for two weeks. Lucy was going to buy D and D, and she was looking forward to it: "A lady of leisure is so anachronistic these days," she had said. And Quimsby spent most evenings with her, even managing to perform sexually in ways he had never imagined possible with a woman. Each time Barrett raised the ante—driving Lucy up from her original bid of five million in increments of two hundred thousand dollars—Quimsby would drop by her apartment just to be sure she was prepared to top the offer. Finally, Lucy reached six million, which was in fact a tiny fraction of her net worth, but her lawyer, Agel Reid, that stuffy bastard, said, "Stop." And Barrett went to six point two.

Lucy was on the telephone with Reid when Quimsby, shaking, was led into her living room by the butler. "Yes, Agel," she said, blowing a kiss to Quimsby and motioning him to sit down beside her on the chaise, "yes, I'm listening to you. . . . But you know how much I want . . . yes, I understand, but . . . I realize that, but I'm sure . . . Agel! You know perfectly well I'm in complete control of my senses. Romance has nothing to do with it! . . . Oh, Agel. Yes, I suppose you're right. Oh, I am so disapopinted," she said, reaching out to pat Quimsby's hand.

But he jumped up without a word, stormed to the door, slammed it behind him. How could she? After all he had done for her, been a prostitute! And how he'd hated it!

And so they all deserved to die—Monroe, Barrett, yes, even Lucy—they stood for everything vile and sinful . . . sinful wights, they were, and cursed sprites. Money lovers, fallen by the deceits of money. Letting Howard die had been a mistake. He was honest and courteous and delicate. Not like those flaming faggots who were after him all the time. Not like the pansy in the sex shop who had sold the Jac-me to Quimsby the day he raged out of Lucy's apartment and paced the city streets, formulating the perdition of his enemies. "Let me help you, dearie," that shit in the sex shop had sung. "Jac-me? Three bottles? Oh, my. You must be entertaining the National Football League." His tittering and fluttering had made Quimsby furious.

Howard was quiet, strong, yes, manly. He missed Howard so! Every time he thought of it, he'd say aloud, "Howard, why did you disobey me?"

In a sense it had been Quimsby's own fault, born of his wanting to be good to Howard, who'd been really hurt and jealous because of all the evenings Quimsby spent with Lucy Hartfield. Howard, that silly twit! How could he have been jealous! To make it up to dear Howard, Quimsby got Totti to invite him to the Sophia opening.

But that was before the . . . plan. When the

plan went into effect, he told Howard, and only Howard, that he wasn't going. And he begged Howard, ordered him, not to go. Did everything but tell him about the plan— which of course he couldn't do. Howard promised he wouldn't. But he was still jealous, Quimsby knew that, and probably decided to show Quimsby. So he went, and was caught by the . . . plan—the one man Quimsby wanted most of all not to be caught by it.

The other mistake was Reid. But that wasn't really Quimsby's fault. Reid should have been there! He said he would be there!

Two mistakes. Poor Howard couldn't be corrected. But Agel Reid . . .

The receptionist walked in, startling him.

"Please knock!" he said angrily.

"I'm sorry," she said, looking flushed and upset by his snippiness—not that he cared. "I only want to give you your mail."

"Yes. All right." He wanted to tell her her breasts were too big and her thighs too soft and the slit in her skirt too high. But he didn't. He'd have her fired soon enough, now that Monroe was no longer around.

"Mrs. Fields asked that you call her back as soon as you can, because she's leaving for lunch in half an hour."

"Yes, yes."

As soon as she'd gone, he dialed Mrs. Fields's number. "Muffie, darling, how are you? The ARC Ball? So soon after the Sophia tragedy! But yes, you're right, it is for a good cause . . . and the show must go on. Tell me who's going to be there."

As he listened to her rattle off the acceptances, he wasn't sure if the idea came with the name or if he started listening for the name because the idea had come first. But he did know that by the time he heard "Mr. and Mrs. Agel Reid, Miss Melissa Reid and escort," his mind was made up.

"Of course I'll be there, dear. Wouldn't miss it for the world!"

Two mistakes. Poor Howard couldn't be corrected. But Agel Reid . . .

Monday

Coming out of the subway at the Brooklyn Bridge stop, Terry saw Lieutenant Sirkin walking toward City Hall. It was too late to avoid him; they almost collided.

"Listen, Ahearn," the lieutenant said gruffly, "I'm glad I ran into you, 'cause I wanted to talk to you and Gillespie anyway. I think you're jerking us around. Your daily reports are bullshit; you know what I mean. You're just filling in spaces, and you didn't come to the task-force meeting on Friday. Either you're on to something or you're doing nothing."

"C'mon, Lieutenant," Terry answered, folding his arms across his chest, "we're doing our job, talking to everyone we have to. We're doing the best we can with what we got."

"Look," Sirkin said, in a more conciliatory tone, "you gotta remember we're in this together. Whatever the differences between the police department and the fire department, they were created by politicians, long ago. You and me had nothin' to do with it. I figure maybe you guys are still pissed about the letter you found after the cathedral bombing, but I'll tell you this. There's a reason I didn't tell the press you found it. I got twenty-five men in my office who work their asses off, and I had to make sure they'd read about *themselves* in the newspapers after that explosion, not anyone else. I've got to keep them motivated, you know, 'cause there ain't no money incentives in the Arson and Explosion Squad, if you know what I mean. I wasn't just being a lying prick about it."

"That's all under the bridge," Terry said, "believe me. We're doing everything we're supposed to do. I think it'll take a long time. I mean there are all of those business dealings of the victims that have to be checked, and the interview list keeps expanding with everyone we talk to, new people who might have something to say, and we're still waiting for the lab reports."

"That came in just this morning," Sirkin offered. "It's a nitrite. Either amyl or butyl nitrite was the accelerant, and I'm going to the Hall now to ask for a few more men so's we can track it down. Amyl will be tough going. It's a prescription and there's a lot of drugstores in New York. Butyl will be easier, because there's not much of it around, as I understand it."

"Yeah," Terry said, beginning to walk away. "Well, I got a lot to do myself, so I'll see ya, huh?"

Terry had taken six steps toward Church Street when Sirkin called to him. Terry turned.

"Listen, Ahearn," Sirkin said from the steps of City Hall, "just remember, and tell all of them in your office. We're in this together. I can have your badge if it goes any other way."

Terry nodded and began to walk toward his office. But he stopped suddenly, asking himself, What kind of bullshit is this? "Going to the Hall," Sirkin had said, about manpower. Lieutenants don't go to the mayor's office. Commissioners do, and even they have to tread lightly.

Terry turned around and went to the City Hall door. He noticed that Sirkin did not make a left toward the mayor's end of the hall but went down the stairs. He followed Sirkin at some distance and waited while the police lieutenant went through a wooden door at the end of the basement corridor. Shit, it figures, Terry said to himself as he walked just close enough to read the lettering on the door: THE OFFICE OF RODNEY LETTINGTON, DEPUTY MAYOR OF THE CITY OF NEW YORK.

At his own office, Terry picked up his mail and messages. His mother had called. "Damn it," he muttered beneath his breath. She never called with good news.

Continuing to look through his mail, he went to his desk. Suddenly, holding up one envelope, he threw everything else onto the desk. The phone message fluttered unnoticed to the floor. Terry whistled, and Jose turned and smiled as Terry waved the booklet in the air. It was the international registry of glass manufacturers' punt marks.

The manufacturers were listed by country in alphabetical order, from Australia to Venezuela. Terry scanned the booklet. Like the American booklet, the punt marks were clearly drawn opposite the company name and address of each listed manufacturer. He laughed aloud as he got up and walked to the office safe, mentioning to Jose as he passed, "They don't make no bottles in Zambia, old pal. I'm making progress."

He searched eagerly through the safe for the glass shard he had found, like a man who held a long-shot ticket and saw that the horse was three lengths ahead at the break. The booklet had brought optimism.

Terry carried the manila envelope to his desk and pulled out a photo enlargement he had made of the shard and then the shard itself. For a moment, the Marchesa's cheek, the smooth shell surrounded by crisp and black and split skin, flashed through his mind, and he closed his eyes and shuddered.

He stood the photo against the bulbless lamp, placed the shard before it, and opened the booklet. He studied the punt marks for Australia. There were just three of them, nothing like the picture of the N, M, or W, squat and broadened, in front of him. He went on. There were five marks for Austria, three for Belgium, two for Brazil, and five again for Bulgaria. Nothing. There were just three in Canada. Nothing. Suddenly there were sixteen marks for Czechoslovakia. But nothing except strange symbols and rigid, straight initials. Whatever that letter was on the shard, it was at least clear that it flared out fancifully.

Even France, with forty-six punt marks, nothing. Nor did the eighteen marks of the German Democratic Republic or the twenty-eight of the German Federal Republic come close to matching. After an hour of this close studying, Terry began to skip around through the alphabet. Still no luck, so he went back to the methodical search. Finally he came to the thirty-five punt marks registered to Italy. There, just about halfway through the listing, he came to the wide, sloping ⌒⌒ of the Montini Glass Company of Salerno. "Gotcha," he yelled. Everyone in the office turned to see what the noise was about.

Jose came as fast as he could and looked over Terry's shoulder.

"Damn it, Jose," Terry exclaimed, "there's no doubt about it. Just look. It even says it's located on the 'in-swept base position.' That accounts for the curvature of the shard. Goddamn. Who do I have to talk to for approval to call Italy? And what time is it there?"

"Jack Burke, I guess, but he's not around. Six hours in front."

"What the hell am I gonna do?"

"It's your ass, pal, if nothing turns. But then what are they going to do that you can't take?"

"Right," Terry said as he lifted the phone. "The biggest arson case in years and I'm worrying about a seven-dollar phone call. What bullshit. International long distance, please, operator."

He was connected to the Montini Glass Company but was unable to find an English-speaker at the other end.

"Shit," he said to Jose as he hung up. "So near and yet so far. I'll have to find an Italian-speaking fireman and try again."

He looked up at Jose. "That's the bad news. Now let me tell you the good news. Let me tell you what I learned over the weekend." He told Jose about Jenks Monroe's plan to sell his controlling interest in *D and D* to Lindsay Barrett, about Lucy Hartfield's refusal to outbid Barrett on the advice of Melissa's father.

"Jesus!" Jose shouted. "Do we have a motive for Quimsby! I always knew some good would come of your hanging out with the top shelves! It's crazy, man; just crazy. See, I told you, you beat your brains out, following up leads, names, letters, that go nowhere, and then one just falls into your lap. It's the man upstairs, evening it up for you." Jose raised his eyes upward. "And I don't mean Burke!" He laughed. "But you know," he went on, "now Burke can really do something for us. We've got a motive now; what we need is a search warrant, to get into Quimsby's apartment, to look for the butyl nitrite, or a cape—or something."

Jose picked up the phone. "God," he said as he dialed, "a guy like Quimsby, if he's as sick as he seems, never runs out of enemies, and if he got such great results out of setting *one* fire, think of what the hell might be in his mind when he gets some new enemies."

"He's got one *old* enemy left," Terry said. "Melissa's father."

"Right! Shit, right!" Jose yelled, then spoke into the phone. "Chief Burke? Jose Gillespie. . . ." He explained the situation, listened, protested a few times, and hung up.

"No?" Terry asked.

"Not quite. But because of Sirkin and Lettington, he'll only go to one particular judge, who'll give us the warrant on the q.t. If the judge is sitting tomorrow, we got it tomorrow; if not, the next day."

"Well," Terry shrugged, "that's not so bad."

"It's not so good. You never can tell about a guy like Quimsby." Jose picked up the phone. "What did you say the name of Quimsby's rag was?" Terry repeated it. Jose looked it up and dialed the number. Making his voice sound as chic as he could manage, Jose said, "When does Mr. Quimsby go to lunch, please? We have a package we *must* deliver while he's in the office." Pause. "One to three, indeed," Jose went on. "That long? Thank you so much!" He hung up. "Let's get to the rag when he's not there. There's somebody in every office who's got a hard-on for the boss." Jose smiled. "I don't mean that literally."

O O O

They arrived at the magazine at 1:30. A sexy young brunette sat at the reception desk. "Wow!" said Jose to Terry, quietly but enthusiastically. "Will you look at that! If I were single, man, watch out!"

"Shame on you," Terry whispered. To the receptionist he said, "Excuse me, ma'am, but we are fire marshals . . ." he showed his badge, "on official business. We'd like to speak with Mr. Quimsby. Is he in?"

"Out to lunch, I'm afraid. May I help?"

"Well, we'll just wait, if you don't mind."

"You'll have a long wait, he takes a *long* lunch."

"We'll give it a try, that is if we're not disturbing you . . . or keeping you from going to lunch. . . ." Jose ended the sentence indefinitely.

"I have to eat early," she said glumly.

This girl is bored, Terry told himself. This girl wants to talk.

Jose got her going with idle chatter that circled around Quimsby, in smaller and smaller circles. "It must be fun to work for such a busy man," he said.

She was thoroughly relaxed and conversational by this time. "Eh . . . he's so snotty . . . you know how *those* people are."

"Those people?" Terry asked. She was a New York girl, Terry could hear, probably grew up on streets like his.

"Oh, you know what I mean. In this business, there are so many. . . ." She shook her head, tried not to smile.

"Don't say another word, honey, I gotcha," Jose told her. "He must be plugged in to the whole chic world, am I right?"

She laughed. "Plugged in . . . yes. The calls he gets! If telephones could talk!"

"They can, honey, they can!" Jose said.

She giggled. "Oh, you know what I mean." Terry could see she was delighted to talk with the neighborhood guys; he'd bet they didn't come in here very often.

"So it must be very tough," Jose went on, "to handle his calls. I'll bet that drives you crazy, to know which to let through and which to put off."

"Oh, are you right! And do I get into trouble!"

"So you gotta learn the rules," Jose offered.

"There was only one rule: when Howard Bates called, the call must *always* go through. But since poor Mr. Bates died in the fire, there are no rules, and Mr. Quimsby is worse than ever. He and Mr. Bates were . . ." She shrugged.

"Gotcha," Jose said.

"Things are pretty rough," Terry said.

"Oh, I'm ready to quit! I'm only here because Mr. Monroe was my friend, but he died in the fire, too, and since then . . . it's just rotten. If it hadn't been for Mr. Monroe, I would have quit long ago, because Mr. Quimsby hated me from the first. By the second week I was here, I got to hate the sight of those bloodshot eyes first thing in the morning."

"Bloodshot eyes?" Terry and Jose said it almost together.

"You mean Mr. Quimsby's eyes were bloodshot *every* morning?" Terry asked.

"*Were* bloodshot. Until he went to a new eye doctor, who gave him some medicine; he calls them 'my miracle drops' and his eyes have actually been clear most mornings. But he's no better."

Jose got to his feet. "Miss, I don't think we can spend any more time here. It's been a real pleasure talking to you. And cheer up. Things are gonna change."

"Likewise. I hope so."

"They're going to change," Terry said. "You can count on it."

Downstairs in the car they were exultant. "Bloodshot eyes!" Jose yelled. "We got the bloodshot eyes!"

"But how about Howard Bates?" Terry asked. "If he was Quimsby's boyfriend, why did he die in the fire?"

Jose shrugged. "Maybe a falling out, most likely beyond his control: after all he killed forty-three people, and they weren't *all* his enemies. Kill forty to get three, that's okay with him."

"We're closing in," Terry said. "It feels good."

"It'll feel better when I hear the cuffs go *snap*. I don't like this guy Quimsby," Jose said. "He's an amateur and he's nuts, and with that kind you never can tell what they'll do next."

Tuesday

It was Tuesday, a few minutes before noon. Terry hung up the phone, smiling, turned to thank the fireman next to him. "Dominic, you speak Italian like a native."

Dominic laughed. "That's because I *am* a native."

"Well, I appreciate it, *paisano*. And any time you want Gaelic translated . . ."

"That'll be the day," Dominic said, and they laughed again.

Terry turned toward Jose's desk. "Hey, partner, get this: The Montini Glass Company supplies just three wineries. Two of them do no exporting to the U.S.A., and the third has an eastern distributor in New Jersey. The distributor sells it to four Manhattan liquor stores. One in Spanish Harlem—you guys got taste!—one in Inwood, one at Madison and Sixty-ninth, one on East Twenty-third. I say we try Madison and Sixty-ninth first. The wine is called Arghilla Rosato, and it comes in special straw coverings called *fiaschi*, which is rare because *fiaschi* are normally made for half-gallons and these are fifths."

"Terrific," Jose said, looking over Terry's shoulder. "Let's see what's doing." He jumped out of the chair. "Burke just walked in, and he doesn't look like he won the lottery."

The chief fire marshal sat behind his desk in the enclosed office at the corner of the large, open room. "Lieutenant Sirkin," he said to both of them, "just made a complaint to the fire commissioner, saying that we are not cooperating with the mayor's task force. It seems they got to a company in Texas that makes butyl nitrite and were told a list of distributors was sent to the fire marshals' office two weeks ago. To be precise, he's pissed; nothing about butyl nitrite was mentioned in any of the daily reports."

"Shit," Jose said, "we're very close, Chief."

"What did the commissioner say, sir?" Terry interjected.

"Sirkin asked us to give a full explanation at the task-force meeting on Friday, and to make sure you're there this time. The commissioner assured him that it will be given. If you can't wrap it before Friday, we'll have to go to them hat in hand. Can you?"

"We're closing in," Jose said.

"I know. You've done great work. But by Friday? We don't want to let it get away from us."

"Chief," Jose said, "Terry's got the poop on the bottle. Made in Italy, just four stores here in New York. It's a wine bottle."

Standing now, the chief fire marshal said, "Jeez, that's terrific. By Friday?"

"We'll see," Jose said. "Maybe, maybe not. What about the search warrant?"

Here Jack Burke paused. "Yeah. Well, it's using a big credit card to go to a judge and ask him to go out on a limb for a warrant, especially if you don't want anyone to know about it. I don't know if I got that much credit. Check this bottle out, maybe that'll salvage it. If not, I'll pull out the stops tomorrow and go for it. We've got to have something by Friday. We got less than three days."

It was raining when they left the building on the Church Street side. The air was cold and moist, and Terry noticed Jose wince as the two of them ran for the Ford sedan.

"Christ," Jose said, getting into the car, "it's days like this that I think I should have taken a disability pension and moved to Puerto Rico."

"Your kids don't even speak Spanish," Terry said.

"French. Can you imagine that, my kids speaking French?"

Terry looked out to the gray, gloomy streets and said as much to himself as to Jose, "I wish I could speak French."

Their first stop was Madison and 69th, the Murray Liquor Shop.

"It's not very big," the owner said. "We order

maybe a couple of cases every six months, sell it by the bottle."

"Any special customers?" Terry asked.

The owner shrugged, thought. "Nope. We don't sell enough."

"Would you remember offhand," Terry asked, "if you have a customer named Leland Quimsby?"

"Not a good customer, a regular customer. I'd remember the name."

"Do you have your own charge accounts?" Terry asked.

"Yup."

"Mind if we look through the names?"

"I can tell you right now nobody buys enough Arghilla Rosato to even write it down, we only do that with cases. But if you want to look through them, be my guest."

Terry and Jose sat down at two file drawers, went through maybe three hundred names. An hour and a half later they'd come up with nothing.

"Well," said Jose wearily as they headed south in the car, "next stop East Twenty-third. After that, Spanish Harlem. The culprit will wind up to be some downtrodden spic busboy, just my luck."

"Not giving up on Quimsby, are you?" Terry asked.

"No, I just expected that liquor store to be the one; it's only two blocks from his house."

"Cheer up, partner," Terry said. "We've got till Friday."

At Wines East, on 23rd, it started the same way. The owner had never heard of Quimsby. Then things improved. He'd sold a couple of cases of Arghilla Rosato in the past few months. "Not personally, mind you, my clerks did, so I don't know to who."

"Might it have been to a customer with a charge account?" Terry asked.

"Might have."

"Could we look through your file of charge customers?"

"Help yourself."

This time they had real luck, because the name Bates comes at the beginning of the alphabet.

Terry found it. "Bates, Jose!" he shouted. "Goddamn Howard Bates! Sure! He lives—he lived—down here! Yeah! All right!" He yelled at the owner, "Any way you have of knowing if this guy bought the Arghilla Rosato?" He waved Bates's card in the air.

"Just look at the back of the card."

Terry flipped it over. "Yeah!" he shouted, even louder. "Not one case, baby! Two cases! For delicious evenings at home with Leland."

"Hey, mister," he said to the owner, "got any of that wine in stock?"

"Wait a minute." The man went to the back of the store and in a few minutes said, "Yes, three bottles."

"I'll buy 'em," Terry said.

He took one, tore the straw off, held it upside down. "The punt of the Montini Glass Company—better than in the book! We'll be able to cut duplicates from these bottles that will impress any judge in the city!" He looked at the owner. "How much are these?"

"Six-fifty a bottle. Plus sales tax. Twenty-one-oh-four altogether."

Terry took out a twenty, a one, a nickel, and a penny, dropped them on the counter. "Money well spent," he said. "Just give me a receipt, please, for Father Knickerbocker."

When they got out on the street, Terry said, "I know a nice restaurant down here; dinner's on me." They went to French's on University Place, and over a glass of wine—cheap Burgundy, not Arghilla Rosato—talked over the case.

"We got the bottle," Terry said.

"But we got no proof Quimsby has, or had, one," Jose countered.

"We know he's gay," Terry said.

"But that ain't a crime," Jose replied.

"We know a gay guy with red eyes bought Jac-me from our pal at Leathersex."

"But that doesn't mean it was Quimsby."

"We know a guy with a cape returned to Quimsby's house the night of the fire at just the right time."

"But we can't prove it was Quimsby."

"We know Quimsby's got the motive."

"But that doesn't mean he did it."

"Boy, are you making me blue, Jose. What do we have to do? Catch him in the act?"

Jose smiled. "That's the best way. Next best is to get a search warrant and find the Jac-me bottles. Find the wine bottles. Find the cape. Stuff like that."

"Goddamn it," Terry answered. "*Tomorrow* we get the warrant. After all, we've got till Friday."

O O O

It was after eleven when Terry got home, opened his apartment and found a note from Melissa under his door.

Please see me, darling. I have a fun surprise.

Actually, he hadn't wanted to. He'd come upstairs silently, so she wouldn't hear him. Why? He wasn't sure; he'd heard her record player—Mozart, he thought. But he didn't really know. She'd want a man who'd know. Who'd been in Connecticut before, and to Southampton instead of

Coney Island. Lovemaking wasn't everything, no matter how good it was. He had to think about all that—sometime when he didn't have till Friday to lock up a maniac.

But he rang her bell.

"I was afraid I'd miss you, darling." She leaned forward, kissed him. "How would you like to go to a costume ball tomorrow night?"

"What?"

It came to him as if in a nightmare that he struggled to awaken from. Melissa saw the look on his face and asked, "What is it? You look sick. What's the matter?"

All he could manage was, "A ball?"

"Yes, the ARC Ball, American Revolutionary Costume Ball—proceeds to various historical groups to preserve our heritage—it's a silly thing, but kind of fun. It used to be that everybody stuck to costumes of the period, 1776 and all that, but now they go in the most outlandish things, mixes—last year, someone came in eighteenth-century knee breeches and a space helmet!"

"You went last year."

"It's the only thing I go to; Father buys four tickets every year, two for him and Mother, two for me. It will take your mind off all this. Please go! I know it's last minute, but they just told me about it."

"Your father's going too?"

"Of course, everyone is entitled to one silly event a year. Besides, Mother is a member of the DAR. Don't get stuffy, dear, they *did* fight the British, you know."

She hadn't quite finished when Terry pushed past her into her apartment. "Do something for me, please. Call your parents, right now. I must talk to your father."

"It's a bit late. Father . . ."

"This is *important*! Please!"

She dialed the number, got her father. Terry almost grabbed the phone from her. "Mr. Reid, I'm sorry to bother you so late at night, I wouldn't if this weren't so urgent. Would you by any chance know who's going to be at the . . ." he turned to Melissa, questioningly.

"ARC," she prompted.

"ARC Ball, Mr. Reid?"

"Oh, all sorts of people," Melissa's father answered. "The society columns will say *everyone*."

"No, no. I mean an actual guest list."

"No, of course not."

"Who'd have one?"

"Muffie Fields runs the thing."

"Would you give me her phone number, please?"

"Yes, but . . ."

"It's urgent, Mr. Reid, important, critical, life-and-death. Maybe . . ." he started to say maybe yours, but he decided against it, for he suddenly had a cynical thought: he *needed* Reid there to smoke Quimsby out.

But Reid wasn't waiting for the sentence to end. He was getting Mrs. Fields's number. He read it to Terry.

"Thanks, Mr. Reid . . . Agel . . . see you at the ball." He hung up and dialed the Fields's number. An unyielding answering service said Mrs. Fields would not be available until ten the next morning. He left a message, asking her to call him as soon as possible. But nothing would happen between now and ten the next morning; he didn't even know if Quimsby would be there, and he sure as hell couldn't go through life from now on panicking every time someone had a fancy opening or dance. So he decided to say nothing. He could always warn Melissa once he knew Quimsby was going—*if* he were going. If he warned her now and she warned the Reids, the Reids might warn someone else, and Quimsby might be warned off. Then it would just be more of the waiting game, and after Friday there might not be any fire marshals to do the waiting—Quimsby's co-conspirators, Lettington and Sirkin, would see to that.

They weren't really coconspirators, Terry reminded

himself. Not in this particular crime. But, he said to himself, in this world you were either for fires or against them, and those two seemed to be for them. Especially Lettington; you'd think that son-of-a-bitch would care, what with his wife having died in a fire—but, Terry guessed, ambition was number one in his mind.

"Okay, then, you got yourself a partner for the ball. What kind of costume should I wear?"

Melissa looked happy. "I'm delighted," she said. "Let's see now: anachronism seems to be what they're doing these days; I'm going to wear a Martha Washington ballgown with a twenties cloche hat and boop-boop-be-doop makeup, you know, red spot cheeks and Cupid's bow mouth? I know it sounds silly, but it'll be fun. So anything you wear —with a powdered wig, for example—will look fine. Of course a lot of people play it straight and come in authentic Revolutionary costume, too, so you could do that."

Terry thought for a moment, said, "Okay, I've got it. I'll wear a powdered wig, and for the rest come as what I am. I'm a fireman, and I'll dress like one."

"You mean with the high boots and the rubber coat and hat?"

"No, I think just the dress uniform. It hasn't changed in over a hundred years. It's *me*, and it's the only costume I have."

"I think that's a *wonderful* idea. Anyway, it would be very difficult to dance with those big rubber boots."

Terry had to laugh at that. "I've got news for you, sweetheart. The way I dance, no one could tell the difference. Besides, I don't know how much dancing I'm going to do."

"Oh, Terry . . ."

"Never mind, sweetheart, we'll worry about that tomorrow night."

"All right, then," she said, brightening up again. "You'll be the fireman. I'll get you the wig. And the mask."

"Mask?"

"Of course, darling. It's a masked ball."

Jesus, he said to himself. Just another little advantage for Quimsby—masks. Don't panic, he reminded himself; you don't even know if Quimsby's going to be there.

As soon as he got back in his apartment, he made two calls. First, Jose.

"I'm going to a masquerade ball tomorrow night, partner."

Jose made his voice high and mincing. "And I just know you'll be the *queen* of the ball!" Then in a deeper voice, he asked, "Don't you have anything better to do? Tomorrow's only two days from Friday."

"It might be a lot closer than that, partner." And he explained to Jose what he'd learned about the ball. "Tomorrow may be it!"

"Sounds good," Jose replied. "Be great if tomorrow *was* it. Maybe it won't be. Remember, we got this far with some luck and a lot of hard work, a lot of questions, phone calls, doorbells, and all that. We gotta keep it up. It doesn't look like Quimsby's going nowhere, but we should be checking other names, too. Tomorrow has gotta be a lot more names checked and doorbells rung."

Terry knew Jose was slowing him down on purpose, but it was deflating anyway. He didn't see how it could *not* be Quimsby. Yet he knew Jose was right.

"Stop trying to cheer me up," he said, and Jose knew what he meant.

"Listen, my friend, if it's Quimsby, we haven't lost anything but a few phone calls. See you in the morning. Don't be discouraged. Things are looking better all the time. Don't forget, tomorrow we get the warrant."

"I'm not forgetting," Terry said. "How could I forget?"

Next call was to McDougal. Terry found him at his home.

"What are you doing tomorrow night?" Terry asked.

"Make me an offer," the columnist replied.

"Ever hear of the ARC Ball?"

"Shit yeah, two hundred fifty dollars a ticket, Waldorf, private ballroom, a chance for the jetters to compare the blue of their blood and the green of their money."

"Meet me there tomorrow night."

"What the hell are *you* doin' there, fireman? Trying to pull yourself up by your rubber bootstraps? Don't try to horseshit me."

"I'm not horseshitting you, McDougal. I'm handing you a Pulitzer prize."

"I'll be the judge of that."

"Just be there."

"I'll be there."

"It's a costume ball, McDougal."

"I'll come dressed as a Pulitzer prize winner. Don't make me look bad."

"Just be there."

Terry went to bed, but couldn't fall asleep, and when he finally did, he dreamed of running after someone, catching him, only to find his face a blank.

At three in the morning he awakened, feeling he had left something undone. The feeling was so strong he turned on the light and looked around the room. On his bedside table, under a copy of the *Times*, he saw the slim book Melissa's professor friend Landon had gotten for him, *The Day of Doom*, by Michael Wigglesworth. He'd been too busy or too tired to read it. He picked it up now, to look for sinful wights and cursed sprites, whatever they were.

An hour later, nearly finished with the poem, he was still looking. *The Day of Doom* was a stilted, gloomy poem: Terry could never see his old man putting down Joyce or Synge or Yeats in favor of Wigglesworth. But just a few pages from the end, there it was:

Ye sinful wights, and cursed sprites,
    that work Iniquity,
Depart together from me forever
    to endless Misery;
Your portion take in yonder lake
    where fire and brimstone flameth . . .

My God, Terry thought, here it is, in black and white—"Depart . . . forever . . . lake . . . fire." But could you offer a poem in evidence?

Wednesday

By nine, Terry and Jose were at their desks, making more phone calls, checking insurance beneficiaries. Terry tried to focus on the papers in front of him, but his mind was on the big wall clock. At 9:55 he couldn't hold off and dialed Mrs. Fields's number. He got her maid, pulled out all the stops: fire marshal, urgent, life-and-death, and of course a friend of Agel Reid. Something—he suspected it may have been the last—got Mrs. Fields to the phone. Terry got right to the point.

"Mrs. Fields, this is very important. Will Leland Quimsby be at the ARC Ball tonight?"

Obviously, she didn't have to consult her list for the answer. "He accepted," she replied, and Terry's heart jumped.

"But only last night he phoned and left a message that he would *not* be able to make it."

He slumped in his chair, asked softly, "Are you sure?"

"Yes, of course," she replied impatiently. "One

makes a point of knowing whether or not the editor of *D and D* will be at one's benefit. I *am* certain. *And* disappointed."

He wanted to say, "Don't be, lady." Instead he said only, "Thank you," and hung up.

He turned to Jose. "Shit, partner, shit!"

"What's the matter?"

"Quimsby is *not* going to be at the ball tonight."

"How do you know?"

"The lady in charge said he'd first accepted, then bowed out. Why the hell . . ."

"Easy, buddy. First you're *too* hipped on Quimsby, then you're too turned off. There are no easy answers in this business, only hard ones. It's not all or nothing."

"You mean I shouldn't turn in my powdered wig?"

"Hell, no! Maybe he just wants to set up his alibi. Maybe he'll change his mind. Maybe he *won't* be there, but you'll feel a lot better if you're there to look after your beautiful lady and her folks, won't you?"

"Yeah, I will." Terry shut up and pretended to be going through names, insurance figures; actually, he was barely able to concentrate. He welcomed the interruption from the chief fire marshal.

"I got to a judge in the criminal court," Burke said, "an old professor of mine. He said he'd consider the application, and if he issues the warrant, he'll hold the issuance report for twenty-four hours. That's it."

"That's something," Terry replied, and he brought Burke up-to-date on new developments. The chief whistled. "That sounds good, that sounds strong. I just hope Judge Morris agrees with me. You two had better come into my office so we can update the application."

An hour and a half later, Jose and Terry finished and went out for a quick, late lunch. They returned to some bad news. Burke's judge, Morris, would not be able to consider the application for the warrant until he was through sitting for the day and had cleaned up some other work, too. Not before five, probably more like six.

Terry felt as close to losing control as he ever had. "What is this, a damn conspiracy?" he shouted at Burke. "Lettington, Sirkin, the P.D., the courts, getting together to make the city safe for Quimsby and unsafe for fire marshals?"

"Now don't get paranoid, kid," Burke responded. "Things are tough all over. Morris is the best judge I got. You got a better judge, go to him. If not, let's all wait like gentlemen."

"Gentlemen?" Terry felt his face getting red. "Chief, let me explain something to you. People start arriving at seven for cocktails before this ball. If we get the warrant at six, how are we going to get to Quimsby's apartment, search it, and get to the Waldorf by seven? Did it occur to you, Chief, that if Quimsby wants to firebomb the place, he may decide *not* to be fashionably late about it?"

"Listen, kid," Burke replied. "Don't give me that 'fashionably late' shit. I don't know who you've been hangin' around with, but you're still a fireman talking to a superior officer, and don't forget it." Burke stared at him evenly. "Now, when you're calm, I got somethin' else to tell you. What you just heard, believe it or not, is the *good* news. Because, effective Friday at five o'clock, the Bureau of Fire Investigation is out of business, practically. The mayor signed the order today. The bomb squad gets it all, all investigations in every borough. We get cause and origin only, and we're being cut to less than half the staff."

Now Terry *was* calm. "What's the use of killing ourselves?" he said.

"You're supposed to be an idealist," Burke replied. "The use is to take a maniac off the streets. To go out in a blaze of glory, no pun intended."

Jose put a hand on Terry's arm. "Come on, partner,

here's how we do it: I stick around to get the warrant, rush right over to Quimsby's place to look for the stuff. You go home, dress for the ball, go and keep your eyes open. As soon as I get something, I meet you at the Waldorf. Go on home, get your costume on. Be beautiful. And you know what? You even get the keys to the car. But be in by eleven!" The two men grinned at each other.

○ ○ ○

Back home, Terry fished his dress uniform out of a closet and tried it on. Not just as a costume, he thought bitterly. Effective Monday, he'd be wearing it again. He wondered if he wanted to. Or could. The bell rang just as he was pinning his badge on the breast of his jacket.

"Oh, don't you look stunning!" Melisa said as he opened the door.

"Glad you like it. From now on it replaces my civilian clothes." And he told her about what had happened.

"What's wrong with this city?" Melissa asked.

What's wrong with it, he wanted to say, but didn't, is that *your* kind of people grab hold of it, and have no faith in *my* kind of people. They think we're dummies. And maybe they're right, he would have added. He didn't say any of it.

"Well, tonight," he said, echoing Burke's words, "maybe we can go out in a blaze of glory." Then, remembering Quimsby and the Sophia fire, he wished he hadn't said that, either.

"Cheer up," Melissa said, and kissed him on the mouth. "I have a couple of things which will make you stand out at any firehouse." And from a bag she pulled a white wig and a red mask.

He was just putting the wig on and beginning to grin at himself in the mirror at the silliness of it when his phone rang.

It was his mother, although he could barely recognize her voice for the sobs and the sounds of hysteria.

"Terry, Terry, your sister. . . . It's awful what's happened."

"Calm down, Mom. Tell me what you're talking about."

"She and your father have been fightin' every day, all week. You see, last weekend she went away again with that . . . guitar player. Your father was drunk when she got home Sunday night and they had a terrible battle. Since then it's been one fight after another. Today, she got home from work, your father was drunk again . . . and . . . and he started punchin' her! I've never seen anything like it! Your father's crazy! He blackened Maureen's eye, made her lip bleed, told her to get out. Then he stormed out of the house, said if she wasn't gone by the time he got back, he'd kill her! Maureen's locked herself in her room. She won't leave. You've got to come over right away, Terry! Right away! He'll kill her. I've never seen him like this!"

"Mom, take it easy, he's not going to . . ." Christ, Pop, he thought. Christ.

"Terry, you should see her face! You've got to come!"

He'd never heard her voice like this—and what a time for it to happen! "Mom, I'm working on a case where *lives* are in danger. . . ." What's *wrong* with you, Pop, he thought.

"More important than the life of your own sister!"

"You don't understand, Mom!" It *was* a goddamn conspiracy! Sirkin and Lettington were buying the old man booze, to get him off the case! Then he thought, maybe Burke is right, maybe I am paranoid.

"You've *got* to come, Terry!"

He looked at his watch: 5:25, the height of the rush hour. Forty minutes out there, maybe twenty-five back; that'd give him a half-hour of peacemaking. "Okay, Mom, I'll be out as soon as I can."

"How soon?"

"Forty minutes, I hope."

"You heard enough to know what's going on, sweetheart," he said to Melissa. "I'll meet you at the ball." And before she could answer, he grabbed the wig and mask and ran out the door. He thought he'd try the Brooklyn-Battery Tunnel, but knew there'd be traffic everywhere. And there was. Crawling along in the junk heap at ten miles an hour, he thought about fathers hitting their children and suddenly remembered something that had happened years ago.

He and his father had been to a basketball game at the old 50th Street Garden and they were returning to Brooklyn on the Seventh Avenue subway. It was late at night, and he was eight or nine years old. He was tired and leaned into his father, smelling the tobacco and beer through the wool of the old man's pea coat. They were in one of the last subway cars with cane seats stuffed with cotton and springs, and he put his feet up and placed his hands across the old man's extended stomach, much as he would hold a pillow. He curled up as close as he could against his father, felt his large powerful hand gently envelop his thigh, and closed his eyes to the rattle of the train and the rhythm of his father's breathing, feeling at one with him, dreaming of frankfurters and sodas and the security of his father's hand when they'd stood within the crush of towering strangers in the halls of Madison Square Garden.

At the 14th Street station a man got on with a boy about his own age. Terry opened his eyes, for the boy was crying. "Shut up," the man screamed at the boy. The boy started to cry so hard that he was losing his breath, and the man slapped him sharply across the face, grabbing him roughly and pushing him down onto a seat across from the Ahearns.

Terry remembered feeling his father's hand squeezing into his thigh and hearing his demanding, gravelly voice over the rattling of the subway. "You know, pal," his father said to the man sitting across the aisle, "there's never any good reason to hit a kid like that." Terry could still feel the tension in his father's voice.

"It's none of your business," the man across the aisle snarled.

"I'm makin' it my fuckin' business," the old man said, " 'cause that kid is a part of all of us, just like this kid here is a part of all of us."

And Terry remembered his father's hand moving from his thigh and up his body until it came to his shoulder, where it held him firmly, drawing him even closer to the old man's heartbeat.

He remembered, too, the old mán shaking his head as the man across the aisle took the boy in hand and moved through the heavy door to the adjoining car. "Sad," Petey Ahearn had said.

Inching his way through the traffic, Terry couldn't believe his father had hit Maureen. But when he got to the apartment, hugged his mother, and walked into Maureen's room, the evidence was in front of his eyes. Her right eye was blackened and swollen, the right side of her mouth bruised and puffy.

"Oh, Terry, I hate him! What have I done that's so bad? He still thinks I'm a twelve-year-old he can order around. I don't want to stay here any more. But where can I go? Take me with you, Terry!"

He spent some time talking with her, looking at his watch every few minutes. At 6:30 he said, "I've got to make a phone call," and dialed the office.

The chief fire marshal answered the phone himself. "Everyone else is gone," Burke said wearily. "It's like a funeral around here. But the judge did come through for us; Jose went down to the Tombs an hour ago to pick up the warrant. And there was a . . . let's see, I got it somewhere here . . . a phone call for you a couple of hours ago. Some character said he promised he'd call you. One of the guys took the number. Here it is."

The number meant nothing to Terry, but he dialed it.

"Leathersex. Our desire is your desire!"

Terry could feel his heartbeat pick up. "This is Fire Marshal Ahearn, Mr. Leathersex. Thanks for calling me. What do you know?"

"Hi, muscles. I know a lot. Your friend, the uptown faggot with the red eyes, was in today. His eyes weren't so red, but he was as bitchy as ever, and his tastes haven't changed. He bought another three bottles of Jac-me."

"What time?"

"Around lunchtime. I remember it because I was hoping he'd come in for something to eat. No such luck." Terry stifled a laugh.

"Did he say anything?"

"Besides asking for the Jac-me? Nothing. He looked *wild*. What a turn-on."

"Thanks. I appreciate this."

"Then why not drop in sometime, just for fun, muscles?"

"Thanks, I don't think so."

"Don't knock it if you haven't tried it."

"Yeah. Right. Hey, thanks."

Terry hung up and looked at his watch: 6:40. Guests might start arriving at the ball in twenty minutes, but he knew he had a little leeway. If Quimsby were making his move tonight, he'd wait till many people were there.

Especially till Agel Reid was there! Quickly he phoned Melissa; she was gone. Then he remembered: they were to have met the Reids for a drink at Peacock Alley first. He couldn't stop the Reids. That meant he had to get there and stop Quimsby.

"I gotta go," he said to his mother and sister, almost fiercely. His mother started to cry, Maureen began to wail.

"Don't leave me, Terry!"

Instantly, he decided. "I'm not leaving you. Come with me. You can stay at my apartment. You too, Mom."

His mother shook her head. "I've got to be here for your father."

Of course she did. He rushed his sister out the door without giving her a chance to take anything, pushed through moderate traffic, went for the Brooklyn-Battery Tunnel again, with good results. His mistake was to go up Sixth Avenue so he could drop Maureen near his apartment. He didn't get her there until 7:20.

"Sit in the car a minute," he ordered, dashed over to the nearest street phone. He called information and prayed that Quimsby was listed. He was.

If he's home, Terry told himself, I can relax, at least for a while. If no one's home, I got trouble.

The phone was picked up after five rings.

"Hello." The voice sounded fruity.

"Leland Quimsby?"

"Who's calling, please?"

Too fruity for Quimsby, Terry decided. Maybe it was a new friend and they were in the middle of something. Terry hoped so.

"This is Fire Marshal Ahearn."

The fruity voice said, "Want to come over for a quick one . . . Terry?"

"Jose, you do a lousy imitation of a fag, eh, homosexual."

"But I do a hell of an apartment search, partner. Let me tell you what I got. I got the Montini bottles, I got straw from the bottles, I got a lot of Jac-me bottles; I got an old diagram of how to make a Molotov cocktail from something called the *New York Review of Books*. I even got the Wigglesworth poetry book. And you know what's just inside the cover? A family tree. Do you know this crazy fuck Quimsby is related to Wigglesworth—a couple of great grandsons away?"

"Great!" Terry shouted. "Quimsby must be climbing the walls! Is he giving you a hard time?"

"Quimsby I ain't got, partner. He's not here. It wouldn't be so easy with him here."

"You've got a lot of fresh straw from the wine bottles, don't you? And three new-looking bottles of Jac-me, don't you?"

Jose got it. "He's going tonight, isn't he? He's gonna hit the costume ball."

"He bought three bottles of Jac-me from Leathersex this afternoon. Get over to the Waldorf as soon as you can."

"Where are you?" Jose asked.

"Thirteenth and Sixth, in traffic, but I'm going to use the light and the siren. See you."

O O O

Terry raced back to the car. It was 7:30. The Reids would damn well be arriving by now.

"What is this?" Maureen asked, her swollen face smiling. She held up the mask and the wig.

"No time now, honey," he said, handing her his key. "Get out of the car, quickly. Go to my apartment and relax, huh? See you later. Go on now, go on." He almost pushed her out of the car. Then he rolled down his window, groped for the red light, stuck it on the roof, held it with his left hand, switched on the siren with his right, and fought his way through traffic to the Waldorf in eight minutes. He double parked his car, grabbed his wig and mask, and ran into the hotel.

He put the wig under his firecap, the mask on his face, as he walked through the lobby. He could see people staring at the bewigged, red-masked New York City fireman.

Instead of waiting for the ballroom elevators, he took the stairs two at a time, approached the desk at the entrance. "Guest of Melissa Reid." A security guard looked at him curiously as the woman at the desk checked her list. "Very good, sir," she said, handing him a ticket. "And a *very* clever costume!"

"Thanks," he said. "It's part of my life. Can you tell me if Leland Quimsby has arrived yet?"

"Most of the guests arrive *with* their tickets and do not stop here, so I have no way of telling, sir. And of course, with masks, it's hard to recognize anyone! Cocktails being served in the room to your left as you enter, sir."

The room was dark and noisy and packed. At once he spotted a couple of fire exits. He also spotted miles and miles of red, white, and blue bunting which had been put up for the ball. He wondered if it was fire retardant, or if Lettington had fixed this one up, too. He wondered if Lettington would be here. Just his kind of party, Terry thought.

He didn't know who to look for first. His impulse was to find Melissa and her parents and get them out. Then he realized that he had no idea what the Reids were wearing, and though he'd seen Melissa's gown, there seemed to be so many like it, he couldn't even spot her. He pushed his way through a sea of court gowns and taffeta and knee breeches and lace and ruffles, all on guests rendered maddeningly anonymous by their masks. He also saw leather motorcycle jackets, sequined jumpsuits, even velvet jockey caps, incongruously juxtaposed with period costumes.

Frantically, he kept pushing his way through, staring, not knowing what he was looking for, realizing his best hope was for Melissa to spot him.

In a few moments, she did. "I'd give you the prize for best costume," a voice at his elbow said. He wheeled around. "Oh, sweetheart, am I glad to see you! Where are your parents?"

"Around here somewhere."

"Can you find them?"

"Can anyone find anyone in this madhouse?" She seemed elated by the costumes, the crowd, the disco music, which was another incongruity of this American Revolution celebration. Terry didn't want to frighten her. Nor did he want to do anything, make any announcement, that would trigger Quimsby.

"Would you find them and take them to the desk outside, as soon as you can? I have something very important to tell the three of you. Please?"

"Wait a minute," she said. "There's Rodney; maybe he's seen them."

"Rodney Lettington? The deputy mayor? Terry was clearly confused.

She laughed. "I just met him, and he even flirted, but I remembered what was said about him at Orpheus. I gave him the polite brush."

They glared at the deputy mayor who was dressed as Benjamin Franklin and holding a kite and a key. He felt like going up to him and saying, You son-of-a-bitch, you're as much responsible for the Sophia fire as Quimsby, you're a coconspirator, now help me find the maniac! He didn't say any of it. Instead, he turned to Melissa and asked, "Could you recognize Quimsby?"

She shook her head. "I don't even think I'd recognize him *without* a mask." Alarm came into her voice. "Is he going to be here?"

No point in scaring her. "I don't think so. I just want to make sure. Now will you find your parents and get them out?"

"Out? I thought you said meet you at the desk?"

"That's what I mean, sweetheart. I'm just a product of the parochial schools of Brooklyn. I don't express myself as well as a Brearley girl. Now, go on!"

She looked hurt. He had been a little sarcastic, but he was getting a little nervous, too. The party was in full swing, the room was overloaded. If Quimsby was here, Terry thought, now would be as good a time as any to throw a firebomb.

It was as he was turning away that he saw the man with the cape. He pushed his way through the crowd, angling so that he'd approach him from the rear. Grabbing the man's arm above the elbow, giving it just enough pressure to show he wasn't kidding, he said softly, "Mr. Quimsby."

"I beg your pardon!" The man turned as he spoke, and as Terry heard the voice was different. He could also see the build was different, heavier, the man's jowls below his mask much fuller.

"How could anyone confuse me with Leland Quimsby?"

"I beg *your* pardon. I thought he'd be wearing a cape. . . ." Terry said.

"And I imagine he will. But then so will at least a dozen others. Capes are *in*. Didn't you read *D and D* this morning?"

"No." Terry was surprised. "Why?"

"Leland Quimsby said it in his column, 'Leland Loves,' and if he *says* it's so, it *becomes* so. You'd better hurry before the shops are out of them. And while you're at it, junk the fireman's outfit. It is *funky*."

Terry let go of him and walked off. The clever bastard, he thought. He may be nuts, but he's not dumb. Now, *he'll* be here in a cape—and so will a dozen others. And I'll have to check them all, before he . . .

He kept pushing through the crowd, trying to work his way from the far end of the room toward the entrance so as not to miss anyone. He'd spotted and was approaching a second cape when he realized that if a man in a fireman's outfit walked up to the real Quimsby and spoke his name, Quimsby would just say, No, I'm not. And how would Terry tell? He could unmask him, but that would make a scene, which could be dangerous, and let Quimsby get away or maybe light the wick in a bottle of sand, soap powder, and Jac-me. He was right next to the second cape when he thought of the solution. "Sinful wights and cursed sprites!" he said, as if to no one in particular. No reaction. He said it again.

The man turned and said, "Were you talking to me?"

"As it turns out, I wasn't. Sorry." Terry moved on to a third cape, walked up and said brightly, "Sinful wights and cursed sprites!" This one replied, "Another drink might help."

Terry drew blanks with capes four, five, six, seven—people did read *D and D*, he had to admit—and was approaching the open space near the entrance when he saw Melissa, walking with her parents. The three stopped for a moment to talk with someone, and Terry silently urged them to keep going. He could see by the kite and the key that it was Lettington they were with. Without losing track of them, he moved through the fringe of the crowd, watching for capes, when he saw, near the entrance, one more cape, a man in a long, brown, curly wig. In number eight's right hand, Terry could see the glint of a cigarette lighter. He was walking slowly toward Melissa, her parents, and Lettington, and as he did, the three Reids started toward the entrance, where they were to meet Terry.

Terry saw number eight reach his left hand under his cape, and now, still ten yards away but moving fast, he shouted, at the top of his voice:

"Sinful wights and cursed sprites!"

Quimsby jumped as if he'd been shot. Then for an instant he froze. . . .

"He's a killer! Grab him, Lettington!" Terry screamed as he started forward, pushing past the few people between him and Quimsby.

But only for an instant did Quimsby freeze. Then his left hand reappeared, in it the Montini bottle with a cloth wick poking out of the mouth.

Lettington saw the bottle and the lighter, and he dropped to the ground in terror. Terry, racing for Quimsby but not yet close enough, watched Quimsby bring the lighter to the wick. If it lights on the first flick, we're all dead, he thought.

Quimsby flicked it. It missed.

Then Terry was on him, head down, his firecap aimed like a battering ram at the hand with the lighter. The impact knocked the lighter from Quimsby's hand, drove him back. Terry locked him in a bear hug, wrestled him to the ground, pressing close to keep the bottle from spilling.

"Don't move," Terry warned as he seized the wine bottle then, clutching it, got to his feet. "Don't move."

Standing over Quimsby, he announced to the crowd surrounding them in a tight circle, "I am a New York City fire marshal, and I am placing this man under arrest. Please stand back." He didn't want to call the police, and he wondered if he could get Quimsby out of there alone—the way to the entrance was the one open part of the circle. He wished Jose would show up!

"Get to your feet!" he ordered Quimsby. The man could give him trouble; he didn't want to have to pull his gun, with the crowd around. He wanted to cow Quimsby with a show of authority. He started talking to him quickly, forcefully, emphatically. "I must *tell* you, Mr. Quimsby," he began, "that you are being placed under *arrest* for starting the *fire* in the Sophia Club in the basement of the Astor Hotel, and that anything you say might be held *against* you, and that you have the right to remain silent and to consult a *lawyer* before you speak, but *really*, Mr. Quimsby, it doesn't matter what you do, because we know *what you did*, we know that you had hopes of making a business deal with Mrs. Lucy Hartfield, we know that it *fell* through, we know that you bought three bottles of *butyl nitrite* on Forty-second Street, we know that *Howard Bates* brought you a bottle of Arghilla Rosato wine, and that you ripped the straw from it, and that you filled it with butyl nitrite, and that you looked at a drawing of a *firebomb*, and that *you made a firebomb* and threw it down on innocent people and that forty-three of those innocent people died *horrible* suffering *deaths*, and that you lied to us about owning a *black cape*. We know that Michael Wigglesworth told you *what* to do. You read it in his book. There's not much more we need to know, Mr. Quimsby, not much more. We *have* you, Mr. Quimsby, you're ours now. *Your life is ours*." He took Quimsby by the arm. But just then he felt a hand on his other arm, and he wheeled around. It was Lettington.

"Fireman!"

Terry tried to shrug his arm off. "I can't talk to you now."

Lettington grew peremptory. "Fireman. This will take only a minute. You saved our lives. You . . . saved my life. We're grateful . . ."

"I don't have time now," Terry said sharply.

"I am Deputy Mayor Lettington, and you can be assured I'll see to it that this man . . ."

And as if cued, Quimsby wrenched his arm free and took off, screaming, "My life is *mine!*"

"Shit!" Terry said, and went after him. He had three steps on Terry and, moving fast down the long hall, made a wide right turn at the bank of elevators. Terry tried to close the gap by turning sharply around the corner and ran right into Jose, who had just gotten off the elevator and had turned to look at the running man. Terry and Jose were down; Terry rose quickly, looked at Jose, who'd fallen hard on his bad leg. His face was screwed up in pain, but he gasped, "Go man, go."

Quimsby had run into the first open elevator, which closed in Terry's face. What the hell could he do now? He pushed both buttons, kept an eye on the needle above Quimsby's elevator, and watched it sail straight up to the top floor.

He remembered Quimsby's words, "My life is mine," and he knew what the man was going to do. "Roof!" he shouted back at Jose.

The next elevator had one passenger. Shit, Terry cursed to himself as he pushed the man out. It was a gesture. The elevator stopped anyway on the twenty-third floor. Another twenty seconds gone. Shit. The doors closed and he rode to the top floor. Looking down the hall on the forty-second floor, he spotted the exit sign marking the stairwell, ran to it, and opened the door. The stairs led down, but he didn't think Quimsby would be taking those. Terry headed toward the roof, opened the door, and stepped out onto a large tar and asphalt roof with protruding shafts and vents and fans. It was enclosed by a straight parapet made of a series of stone walls with intervening wrought-iron fencing. In the gloom of small service lights, he began searching. Finally he saw Quimsby huddled in a dark corner of the roof, his cape over his knees, shivering, curled up like a child.

Terry's hand was on the pearl handle of his holstered pistol, but he relaxed now. Quimsby was in a corner. There was nowhere to go. "It's all right, Mr. Quimsby," he yelled. "It's all over now."

Quimsby jumped to his feet, turned, looked at his pursuer fleetingly, and then turned again, facing the United Nations Building, and brought his leg over the iron fencing connected to the weathered stone square at the corner of the roof. He was forty-three stories above the street.

Terry moved forward quickly. He was just ten feet from Quimsby when the man cried out, "Stop there! I'm going to jump."

Terry froze.

Quimsby looked at him, smiling agreeably. "So you know it," he yelled.

Stall, Terry said to himself. "What, Mr. Quimsby? What do I know?"

"Wigglesworth." Quimsby began to recite:

Oh happy Man, whose portion is above,
Where Floods, where Flames, where Foes cannot
    bereave him
Most wretched man, that fixed hath his love
Upon this World, that surely will deceive him.

Quimsby now sat his full weight upon the wrought-iron fence, and Terry heard the creak of the fencing bolts, bolts set in the Waldorf stone nearly fifty years before. "They deceived me," Quimsby whispered. "They all deceived me." The fence moved, just a little at first, but then the bolts tore from the stone and the fence swung out like a gate as Quimsby shifted his weight to the roof side, gasping. He sent a shriek through the cold city air. Frantically, his hands reached toward the roof's edge, but the fence swung entirely out from beneath his leg.

He began to fall.

God help this man, Terry thought, as he dove headlong toward the square cornerstone, never for an instant taking his eyes from the wobbling figure before him. His left shoulder hit hard on the stone as he wrapped his left arm around it, his fingers clawing for a grip, and his right arm shot out furiously over the roof's edge, searching passionately for a piece, any piece, of the toppling figure. God help him, Terry thought. Then he felt the cloth of Quimsby's jacket as it slipped through his grip, downward, until cloth ended and was replaced by the skin of the falling man's wrist. Terry tightened his grasp of the wrist with one hand and the stone corner with the other as Quimsby crashed against the side of the building, but the force of the falling weight was too great, and his fingers were wrenched from one side of the stone corner as his own weight shifted, his downstretched arm being pulled from his shoulder, his cap falling down toward the street. The fingers of his left hand slid across the rough stone, the skin scraping as if his fingers were on a grinding stone. Finally they came to the next edge of the square stone corner and stopped. The bloodied fingers shaped into a forty-five-degree angle around the edge of the cornerstone, and Terry braced himself there, the palm of his hand buttressing the cornerstone.

Quimsby became a flailing pendulum attached to his right arm, the weight more than Terry could endure. He knew his grip was weakening, the pain in his shoulder becoming unbearable; Terry realized he could not hold on much longer. The pain in his left hand, wrapping the cornerstone, was running through him like gunshots, and he himself was perilously close to the roof's edge.

"Help!" Terry screamed. But who'd hear? Where are you, Jose? It's time, Jose; you're letting me down. Christ. And I ruined your gimpy leg, so you couldn't make it when I needed you! "Help!" he yelled through the black air. "Jose!"

Terry held on, Quimsby's watchband now cutting deeply into his skin, the blood dripping, making the grip slippery. "Jose!" Terry yelled, his voice wavering across the rooftop in desperation, and in pain.

It was then that Jose arrived. Terry could hear him running, hopping toward the corner of the roof, yelling, "I'm here, man, I'm here." Somehow the gimpy son-of-a bitch had made it!

Terry felt his partner's body on top of his, lifting his uniform jacket, searching for his belt strap, getting a grip.

"I can't hold much longer," Terry yelled, his body slipping down over the roof's edge even as Jose wrapped his hand around the belt leather.

"Let him go," Jose yelled, as his weight began to shift toward the roof's edge with Terry's.

"No, it's my left hand, the grip's coming out. I can't hold."

"Let the mother go!" Jose yelled again.

Quimsby suddenly began to move in desperate kicks and turns.

"Christ," Terry yelled. "Hold me. Hold me, Jose, my fingers are coming off." The pain from his fingers and from his shoulder overwhelmed him, and he thought, God help us. I must hold him. I must.

Terry then saw in his mind the haze of smoke and death of the Sophia Club, clearly, in its black, unalterable, absolute violation. Forty-three charred, mangled bodies. He felt Jose's arm move around his waist fully, sinking into his own skin, pulling at him. How easy it would be to loosen his grip, to purge the pain in his shoulder and fingers!

He heard his father's voice for the second time that evening, powerful and brave, saying, "That kid is a part of all of us, just like this kid here is a part of all of us."

"Drop him!" Jose screamed.

Forty-three dead. *They* were part of us too, destroyed by *this* man. Christ, is *he* a part of us?

Terry felt his bloodied fingers slipping from the stone corner, his body sliding farther over the roof's edge, and the images began to race fleetingly through his mind: His father's big fist crashing into the fine, delicate skin of his sister's face; the half-moon rain roof of the Harlem warehouse caving in below the firemen; the sound of their cries; the mound of bodies, the fire-eaten flesh at the kitchen door in the Sophia Club, murdered by this weight below him that was pulling his arm out.

He felt his body slide again. Jesus, he thought, was my father right? Would they bring me home wrapped in wood? Should I drop him, this piece of shit? Him or me, now. Christ. No, goddamn it, hold on, pull. Pull. It's not for me to judge.

Terry became aware once more of Jose's strong arms enveloping his waist and pressing into his stomach. He held the grip, understanding that the pain would soon be over, that his strength had been taken from him, and the grasp was now secure only in a final, a spiritual desire to save another human being.

He was sliding.

He felt the pain in his stomach as Jose's arms pressed into him like vise grips. Still he was sliding. But suddenly he realized he was not sliding downward over the roof's edge, but *up*, onto the roof.

He and Quimsby rose little by little, until Quimsby's arm was over the roof's edge. "Hold him," Jose yelled, pulling Terry back and releasing him on the roof tar.

Quimsby clawed and pulled, and Jose gathered the back of his jacket, lifting him. The watchband moved deeper into the wound on Quimsby's wrist as Terry began to pull with both hands. Finally Quimsby's waist, his thighs, and his knees were supported by the flat of the roof. He was puffing, his body heaving. "Oh Lord," he moaned, "I shall serve in retribution. I shall be your boatman on the lake of flames."

In the car, Terry wrapped his handkerchief around Quimsby's wrist, and he wrapped Jose's handkerchief around his own fingertips.

Quimsby was crying, but as the car rolled away with the siren breaking the winter air, he suddenly turned toward Terry. "I was deceived," he said defiantly. "That is the unalterable fact. I cannot let my life be manipulated by lesser men. I am substantial, my family is substantial, and our blood has contributed to this country's history, molded it, made it."

O O O

In the 17th Precinct, Quimsby was sitting in a high-backed wooden chair, his hands stretched tight and bloodless like lion's paws over the ends of the chair arms. His left wrist was bandaged; his eyes, half-closed, were tearing. In his shirt pocket was a card with the *Miranda* rights. He had read them. He had made a statement, and he had signed it, writing the letters carefully and elegantly: *Michael Wigglesworth.* Now he sat staring out blankly under drooping eyelids, mumbling. He seemed to be making his own world. His wig, somehow still in place, lent the proper look of madness to the scene. His mumbling became clearer and louder now, and all eyes turned toward him as he recited:

> *For what is Beauty but a fading Flower?*
> *Or what is Pleasure, but the Devil's bait,*
> *Whereby he catcheth whom he would devour,*
> *And multitudes of Souls doth ruinate?*

239 O

Terry looked around; Jose was there, and perhaps half a dozen cops. Off to one side was Deputy Mayor Lettington, talking to the desk sergeant. Mike McDougal was walking toward Terry.

"Feeling any better than you look?"

"Worse." Terry managed a smile, although he felt as if every muscle in his arms and upper body had been pulled loose from its anchor. "You were late getting there."

"Yeah, but I made it in time, Ahearn. Thanks. I *got* my story. *You're* my story."

Terry shook his head. "No. I'm *everybody's* story. I'll be in everybody's paper tomorrow, on everybody's six-o'clock news. Your story has always been the other story, the one everyone else didn't get, about the *other* bad guys. Not a maniac, who we can't expect anything from, but a deputy mayor and his father-in-law and a police lieutenant—all the supposedly solid citizens of this town—who are in cahoots, along with God knows how many others, to line their pockets and build their careers. Who are willing to send the fire marshals down the drain to help themselves. That's your story."

"Kid," McDougal said, "I don't teach you how to catch firebugs, don't teach me how to write columns." He started to walk away.

Terry reached out and grabbed McDougal's shoulder, the stretch sending shooting pains down the length of his arm.

"Listen, Mike. I'll give you a real personal, exclusive story on me, if you want it. Stuff no one else has or can get, about me and my partner and this whole case. . . ."

"Now you're talking."

"But," Terry went on, "you've got to run the story on Lettington and Sirkin and Samuels—the other pricks—*tomorrow*, when it's hot, when people are paying attention to this case. Is it a deal?"

"Let me think about it. Maybe," McDougal said, and walked off.

As if he had been waiting for McDougal to leave, Lettington now walked over to Terry.

"I want to shake your hand, Ahearn," Lettington said. "I want to thank you, man to man, for saving my life." He extended his hand, Terry took it indifferently. Lettington saw the absence of enthusiasm. "If there's anything I can do—you know, I *can* do things down at the Hall—just name it."

Terry stared at him. "Do you mean that?"

"Of course," Lettington replied with a confident smile. "I can get things done."

"Okay, Mr. Deputy Mayor. My partner, Jose Gillespie, and I broke this case. We are fire marshals, not cops, and we were able to catch Quimsby because we're specialists in arson. But as of Friday, we're going to be plowed under. You know about that and you can stop it if you want to, Mr. Deputy Mayor. I was there to save you because I was a specialist in arson. So you can consider it paying a debt to me for saving your life, or other lives, or just a debt to the people of the city, who deserve our expertise. But *do* it!"

Lettington paused a moment. Then he said, "You've made me look at the situation in a new way, Ahearn. I'm going to give it some good hard serious thought. I really am." He reached for Terry's hand, pumped it up and down.

Maybe he actually meant it, Terry said to himself on his way home. He treated himself to a cab ride down to 13th Street and sat there feeling exhausted, in pain, but good. Maybe Lettington really meant it.

He walked gingerly up the steps of his building, being careful not to jar his shoulder. Melissa's door was not closed fully, and he pushed it open. The apartment was empty. He went to his door, started to unlock it, when someone inside opened it. Melissa was standing there.

241 o

"He came just a few minutes ago," she said. "He knocked on my door."

Terry looked over Melissa's shoulder and saw his father sitting on the couch. His sister, Maureen, thin and delicate, lay coiled up against him, her head pressed deep into his chest. She was crying, and the old man was rubbing his hand tenderly up and down her bare arm.

Petey Ahearn looked up at Terry. He held his daughter by the arms and nudged her gently back onto the couch. Then he stood up and walked to his son. A single tear ran down the side of his large nose, and it was reflected in the light as he walked. "Terry," he said clearly, and without the sludge of drunkenness, his hand moving tenuously toward his son, "there ain't a lot of things I've been sorry for in my life . . . but sometimes a man . . . a man can do things . . . sometimes he doesn't understand . . . Jesus, Terry."

The old man's hand reached for Terry's arm, and his son moved in closer to him. Petey Ahearn threw his arms around his son, and Terry hugged him, smelling the nicotine, the grime, the smells of the neighborhood bar, the smells he remembered from childhood.

Terry felt his face scratch against the old man's whiskers, and he closed his eyes. "It's all right, Pop," he said, "things happen sometimes."

Thursday

The story was big enough to rate a City Hall press conference, set for 10:30 the next morning because that was the most convenient time for the TV stations' camera crews. Terry and Jose stood behind the lectern, next to Chief Fire Marshal Burke and a half-dozen other officials, blinking in lights that had already been set up by the crews. The room was packed with press. Standing off to one side was Mike McDougal, as if he were one of them, yet special.

Cameras were still being set up. Terry stepped out of position and went up to McDougal, who had a copy of the *Daily Post* under his arm.

"Can I have a look?" he asked, reaching for the paper. McDougal stared at him quizzically, handed him the paper. "I can save you the trouble, though. As I said yesterday, I don't tell you how to catch firebugs."

Terry opened to McDougal's column. There was a picture of himself and a headline that read: THE KID FROM BROOKLYN. He gave the paper back to McDougal. "I handed you a Pulitzer prize and you threw it away."

McDougal just shrugged. "Maybe another time, fireman."

It must be, Terry figured, that when he spoke with McDougal, Lettington got nervous, because the deputy mayor was waiting to talk to him, just as he had been last night.

"Well, it's all set!" Lettington said enthusiastically.

Terry's eyes widened. "No kidding?"

"No kidding. Your job is safe."

"The order has been revoked?"

Lettington looked indignant. "Of course not! I found a way to get around the seniority rules for you, so you won't be dropped with the others."

Terry spoke from between clenched teeth. "You . . . listen, I was *not* out to . . . Not everybody devotes his life to saving his own ass, did you know that?" Terry was trying to keep his voice down and was finding it tough. "You've cut the balls off our department—the department that saved your life. I guess you know what you are. You're a . . ." But Terry couldn't find the words worthy of the man, so he walked back to his place behind the lectern.

Lieutenant Sirkin began the press conference. "Right after the tragic fire at the Sophia, the mayor set up a special task force under my command to find the cause and the perpetrator, and last night two and a half weeks of intensive investigation paid off with the apprehension of a suspect."

Sirkin went into a rambling and inaccurate account of the case, and not until he was finished did he add, "The men who played a key role in the investigation as part of the task-force team, and who made the actual arrest, are Fire Marshals Jose Gillespie and Terrence Ahearn, who are standing right behind me." He pointed to them. "Now I'll take any questions."

Terry waited and hoped. The fourth question gave him what he wanted. "Can I ask something of the man who made the actual arrest?"

Sirkin turned reluctantly. Terry was on his way to the mikes; he was scared as hell. He grabbed the lectern with his hands and squeezed to steady them.

"Yes." He hoped his voice sounded steadier than it felt.

The question came from a pudgy young man in the second row; he held pad and ball-point pen in hand as he asked, "What was the first clue as to the identity of the suspect, who discovered it, and how?"

"My partner and I discovered it. We sniffed it when we first entered the premises of the Sophia Club. It was butyl nitrite. We traced it and it gave us a lead to the suspect. . . ."

Hands were shooting up as he spoke, but he had to say more. He *had* to. He put a hand up for quiet. "One more thing. My partner and I are specialists. Fires are our specialty. We've investigated dozens and dozens of them. That's why we knew where to look, where to sniff. Other investigators don't, no matter how good they are. . . ." He stopped.

Shit, he said to himself, I haven't said it. But he waited and hoped someone would ask what he meant. Instead he got a barrage of questions about the butyl nitrite and other clues. He'd have to pick his spots.

Then: "How did the fire spread so rapidly?"

A woman reporter with a TV crew asked it. Thank God for you, miss, Terry said to himself.

"Because there was cloth draped over the ceiling. Because the sprinkler system had not been turned on. No C of O—certificate of occupancy—should have been issued. But it was." Again he wanted to say more; again he was tongue-tied. All he could do was pray. This time his prayer was answered at once, by the same woman.

"So then why was it issued?"

"That's a good question . . ." Terry steeled himself to go on, "but I can't answer it. I'd like to know the answer myself, in fact. I think when you're through with me you ought to ask it of Deputy Mayor Lettington, who's standing right over there." Terry looked straight at Lettington, who glared back, moved as if wanting to leave. But by then dozens of pairs of eyes were on him. He couldn't go anywhere.

Good, Terry thought to himself. Hands were popping up all over the room. He felt braver; he had more to say. "Another question I can't answer is why was the Sophia issued a variance to allow it only one alternate exit, through the kitchen—the one where the bodies were all piled. I think Deputy Mayor Lettington might be able to help with that one, too."

Out of the corner of his eye he could see Sirkin moving to stop him, and quickly he pointed to another raised hand.

"What did you think of, what went through your

head, while you were holding on to the suspect, Quimsby, on the roof?" an elderly reporter asked.

"It was a funny thing," Terry began, "because all the time we were chasing the suspect, I hated him, but when I was holding on, trying to save him, asking myself why I didn't let go, I suddenly realized I didn't hate him at all. Because he was probably nuts, and I felt sorry for him. And I realized who I really hated, who really killed those forty-three people: I hated the ones who let the Sophia have the variance when it should have had another exit. Who gave it the certificate of occupancy with no sprinkler system working and those draperies on the ceiling. And I was angry at politicians who value power over human lives, whose greedy politics are putting the fire marshals out of business. . . ."

Now Sirkin, big and bulky, was shouldering in next to him, reaching for a mike. "We got to stop now, ladies and gentlemen, we're . . ."

Terry held his ground and spoke into the mikes. "All right, one more question!" Hands were up all over the room, but Terry knew this one had to be about the fire marshals. And he knew only one person could ask it. He looked to the corner of the room and said silently, Come on, you son-of-a-bitch, do one thing for me. This one thing. He looked straight at McDougal.

McDougal stared back but did nothing.

For an instant they just stared, then Terry thought, Well, fuck it. "Mr. McDougal, you got a question." He didn't ask it, he said it.

McDougal returned a half smile. "Yeah," he said loudly. "I got a question. Did you say the fire marshals were going out of business? Why?"

"Yeah, that's what I said." As Terry spoke, he tightened his grip on the lectern, shoved back at Sirkin's hefty body, and leaned into the mikes. "As of Friday, the main part of our work is being taken away from us and being given to the police. Orders from the mayor's office. Why? Well, my old man used to say to me, 'As long as somethin' stinks, I'm gonna keep on sniffin'. And don't tell me I ain't polite.' The reason we're being cut to pieces is we've kept on sniffin'. I guess they think we're not polite."

Hands were waving, reporters shouting at him. He had just a little more to say. "That was the last question I'm being allowed. Why don't you ask Deputy Mayor Lettington why the fire marshals are being destroyed Friday? While you're asking him about those other things. Hey, and please don't be too polite."

"Mr. Lettington!" someone shouted. Then others took it up. Terry saw Lettington couldn't get away, so he walked away from the mikes, off the platform, down the side of the room, right past Lettington.

"You're a dead man!" the deputy mayor hissed at him, his face close to Terry's.

"You would have been a dead man last night," Terry replied. "Remember who saved you?" And he kept on going, to where McDougal was standing.

He rapped the columnist on the shoulder.

"Don't say I never done nothin' for you, fireman," McDougal said, and slapped him back.

Terry pushed his way out of the room, down the hall, through the high-ceilinged corridor, down the flat City Hall steps, turned right. He'd made it to Broadway and a block north before Jose caught him.

"You trying to finish off my bad leg, partner?"

"Nah, I figured you'd want *your* mike time."

Jose laughed. "Uh-uh, Lettington is getting *his* mike time. And he's not liking it."

"He told me I was a dead man," Terry said. "Do you suppose that means a firehouse in the South Bronx? Or Staten Island?"

"You feel bad?" Jose asked.

Terry stopped, and stared at the cracks in the

sidewalk concrete as he thought about an answer. People in the crowded street walked busily around the two fire marshals. The horn of a traffic-stalled truck began to blow relentlessly. Suddenly, Terry's face broke into a wide, carefree smile as he yelled above the traffic. "Hell, Jose," he said, "my old man'll be proud of me, of both of us. We did some good sniffin'."